LAURA RESNICK

POLTERHEIST

An Esther Diamond Novel

DAW BOOKS, INC.

DONALD A. WOLLHEIM, FOUNDER

375 Hudson Street, New York, NY 10014

ELIZABETH R. WOLLHEIM
SHEILA E. GILBERT
PUBLISHERS

www.dawbooks.com

First Printing, November 2012
1 2 3 4 5 6 7 8 9

DAW TRADEMARK REGISTERED
U.S. PAT. AND TM. OFF. AND FOREIGN COUNTRIES
—MARCA REGISTRADA
HECHO EN U.S.A.
      PRINTED IN THE U.S.A.

This book is dedicated to
the memory of my friend
Dick Spelman

1

I became convinced that something strange was going on at Fenster & Co. when a singing tree tried to strangle me.

Prior to that, I'd had my suspicions, of course. But my attention really got *focused* on the subject when the mechanical arm of a fake tree suddenly twined around me and squeezed like a determined python—while several of the thing's other limbs violently knocked away anyone who tried to interfere. The real clincher was when the tree's animated eyes glowed red with demonic fire while it growled in a low, gravelly voice, "Kill . . . *kill* . . . I want flesh! And *blood*."

Okay, *that* was more than just a mechanical malfunction, and no one was going to convince me otherwise—though NYPD's Detective Lopez, as was his wont, certainly tried.

My name is Esther Diamond, and how I came to be

dressed as an elf who never feels the cold, performing musical duets with an animated tree (much *too* animated) in retail hell, is a fairly standard tale of woe in my profession. I was in an Off-Broadway play that closed right before Thanksgiving, and although I'd had several auditions that autumn, I hadn't been cast in anything.

Meanwhile, Bella Stella, the notorious restaurant in Little Italy where I usually worked as a singing waitress when I was "resting," was temporarily overstaffed with musical theater students who were home from college for the holidays. So Stella, the owner (and bereaved mistress of Handsome Joey Gambello, who got whacked right there in the restaurant a few years ago), could only offer me a handful of shifts until they all went back to school. Although the wiseguys who ate at Stella's tipped well, the income from a few scattered shifts wasn't covering my rent. So when the opportunity arose to work at Fenster's through Christmas Eve (I use the word "opportunity" in its most abstract sense), I took the job.

Fenster & Co. was a well-known landmark in the competitive retail world of midtown Manhattan. Shopping at this upscale, family-owned department store had long been a tradition for New Yorkers and tourists, and Fenster's famously extravagant Christmas displays had made the place a mainstay of the season for decades. Generations of kids had visited Santa Claus at Fenster's. Indeed, generations of them seemed to be present on the day I was homicidally assaulted by a caroling tree.

I was hired late in the season, weeks after jobs like this were usually filled, because my predecessor had stopped coming to work. Actually, a *number* of seasonal staffers and benighted performers had stopped showing up for their shifts. By the end of *my* first shift at Fenster's, I found the employee exodus easy to understand. The dense crowds shoving and stepping on me, the discomfort of my skimpy costume as December winds whipped through the store via the busy entrances and exits, the long hours on my feet, the fascistic management policies and humorless floor managers, and the seasonal hysteria of holiday shoppers and their overtired children were enough to make *any* sane person stop showing up to work here. But I gritted my teeth and stuck it out because I needed the money. Pluck and dreams don't pay the rent—especially not in New York City.

On the day of my arboreal asphyxiation, I was industriously working my way through the various duties of my twelve-hour shift (the attrition rate among the seasonal staff ensured that I was able to sign up for quite a few overtime hours).

I started my shift by assisting Santa Claus, who spent every day enthroned on the fourth floor from opening until closing. With thousands of kids per day coming to see him (not all of the children hygienic or calm, and not all of the parents well-behaved), portraying Father Christmas was such a stressful job that we always had two Santas in the store, so they could swap out regularly with each other throughout the shift. Only one Santa at a time was allowed on the floor—out in the public area of the store where people could see him. The "relief" Santa relaxed in the break room while the "floor" Santa listened to Christmas wish lists and posed for photos. Elves kept things running smoothly by ensuring that the relief Santa was ready to start working the moment his counterpart stepped off the floor.

The two-Santa system was also designed to ensure we never had a day like *today*.

The store opened at ten o'clock in the morning, by which time I had donned my costume, left the ladies' locker room, and was pacing in front of Santa's empty throne, which was placed prudently near the fire exit and at the very back of Solsticeland—Fenster's immersive multi-cultural extravaganza, which was erected every year to celebrate (and profit from) the holiday season. It was a true test of stamina for parents to get all the way to this spot, since it involved wending their way, with kids in tow, through a marathon maze of elaborate exhibits and retail displays stocked with every conceivable toy, gadget, and trinket that money could buy. The delights of these items were demonstrated by elves whose job was to convince young children to go tell Santa, loudly and within their parents' hearing, that *this* was what they wanted for Christmas.

Sure, seeing Santa was free, but there was plenty of *cost* involved.

As usual, despite the considerable distance from Fenster's main-floor entrances to this section of the fourth floor, and notwithstanding the dense seasonal obstacle course which separated the store's escalators from the spot where I was standing, eager children and cranky parents descended on me like the Golden Horde only minutes after the store opened for business that day.

First in line was a wide-eyed, pink-cheeked, little blond boy who clung shyly to his mother's hand. At her nudging, he politely bade me good morning, then asked, "Where's Santa?"

Good question, I thought, glancing at the empty throne. Another reason we had a couple of Santas working every shift was so that *this* would never happen. With two dozen children already lining up at the throne within minutes of the store opening, we were currently Santaless.

I gave a meaningful look to Candycane, the other elf assigned here this morning. She nodded and went in search of a Santa.

Assuming that she would be back with one in tow within minutes, I smiled perkily and explained to the gathering throng, using suitably melodramatic tone and gestures, "There was a *big* snowstorm in the North Pole last night. Santa woke up to find his sleigh *buried* in snow! So he's going to be a little late getting here today. He said to tell everyone he's very sorry about this. But he's on his way here right now!"

As more parents and children piled into the area, a father said snappishly, "Santa's late? He's *late?* What do you *mean* by 'late'?"

Ignoring him (I had learned quickly that, whenever possible, this was the best strategy with irate parents at Fenster's), I asked the little blond boy who'd been the first to arrive, "What's your name?"

"Jonathan."

I gasped. *"You're* Jonathan? Really?" When he nodded, looking startled by my excited reaction, I said, "Oh, Santa especially wants to meet *you.* He told us so when he phoned in to say he'd be late."

"Santa has a phone?" a little girl asked with interest.

"A smart phone," I confirmed. "He just loves it." Then I bent over to tell Jonathan, "Santa said he'd heard you were coming today. He said, 'Tell everyone I'm sorry I'll be late—and, please, especially tell Jonathan not to leave before I get there. I really want to meet him!'"

Jonathan' pink cheeks went bright red with delight. Then, overcome with emotion, he buried his face against his mother's coat. She patted his back as she smiled at me and said that, in that case, they would certainly wait for Santa.

"How late?" the same irate father demanded. "Five minutes? *Ten?"*

"Look! There's Rudolfo!" I cried out. No, I had no

idea why *our* red-nosed reindeer was Italian. He just *was.* "And Twinkle is with him! Yay! We can have a song while we wait for Santa!"

Rudolfo, played by a pudgy middle-aged actor with roving hands, was sort of a giant, fuzzy-brown sock puppet with massive felt antlers. Twinkle, dressed in a traditional red and green elf costume, was an accordion-playing college kid who defied management policy by wearing his glasses when in costume on the floor. He insisted he couldn't see without them. Judging by their bottle-bottom thickness, I believed him.

My cry of delight had startled the pair as they were passing us on their way to their assigned post else-where in the fourth floor's seasonal wonderland.

"Please, Twinkle and Rudolfo," I called merrily. "Give us a song while we wait for Santa to arrive! Santa is *late* today due to a snowstorm in the North Pole."

"*How* late is he gonna be?" demanded the fuming father. "I don't have all day for this."

Rudolfo recognized my problem and shifted course to start working the crowd that was lined up at Santa's throne. He shook hands, patted cheeks, and posed for pictures while Twinkle, fiddling with his accordion, came over to join me beside the elaborate empty chair.

"Santa's not here?" Twinkle muttered, peering at me through his thick lenses. "He'll catch H-E-double-hockey-sticks for this. Whose shift is it, anyhow?"

"Moody Santa, I think," I said.

This being a short-term job, and all of us in costume

for it, we mostly knew each other by our floor names: Twinkle, Candycane, Rudolfo, and so on. To differentiate between the half-dozen Santas on staff, we used descriptive monikers: Moody Santa was a morose new graduate of the Yale School of Drama who hadn't expected *this* to be his first professional job as an actor; Wheezy Santa suffered from allergies; Diversity Santa was my friend (and, years earlier, had been my boyfriend), an African-American actor named Jeff Clark who'd been hired recently to replace Giggly Santa after he stopped coming to work.

"Who else is scheduled for this morning?" asked Twinkle. "Where's the back-up Santa?"

"I don't know."

With two Santas assigned to the shift, why wasn't one of them here? Why hadn't Candycane come back yet—either with a Santa or with an explanation? I figured Santa was at least ten minutes late now (this was a guess, since elves didn't wear wristwatches). Fenster's was inflexible about its punctuality rules for employees. And with a growing crowd of excited children and restless parents around me, I feared that Santa's tardiness could prove to be life-threatening for an innocent elf who was just trying to earn some honest overtime wages.

The bell on the end of Twinkle's red stocking cap jingled noisily as he said to me, while bobbing his head emphatically, "You *know* they'll dock Moody Santa's pay for this. He won't like that. Really needs the money.

Student loans, dontcha know. Yale Drama ain't cheap."
He snickered.

"Yeah, whereas you and I dress like elves for love alone," I said. "Come on, play something, Twinkle."

When he started playing Handel's "Messiah," I gave him a sharp enough nudge to unbalance him, which halted the music on an off-key wail of accordion chords.

"Something the kids can join in singing," I clarified. "How about 'Deck the Halls'?"

Twinkle rolled his eyes but complied. I started singing, and Rudolfo joined me in leading the children in several verses. Then we sang "Jingle Bells" (I accompanied the accordion by rhythmically shaking the bells on my festive boots), "Frosty the Snowman," and—of course—"Rudolph the Red-Nosed Reindeer." During this rendition of his signature tune, our fuzzy companion mimed and hammed it up shamelessly. It kept the kids entertained, so I was in favor of it—until Rudolfo used the song as an excuse to embrace me from behind, his reindeer-clad hands clasped over my breasts. Under the guise of doing a little two-step dance, I stomped hard on Rudolfo's hoof and kept on singing as he staggered away.

As soon as the song ended, I could hear a toddler crying, a child whining about wanting to see Santa *right now,* and a couple of mothers complaining about the wait.

"Where's Santa?" a child demanded.

"Yeah, where *is* Santa?"

"How about another song?" I said brightly.

"No! I want Santa!"

"Where's Santa?" a high-pitched voice shrieked somewhere at the back of the still-growing line. *"You said Santa was here!"*

Jonathan, still clinging to his mother's hand, piped up, "Santa is coming! He'll be here soon. He's coming to see *me*."

That kid deserved to get every single thing on his Christmas list this year.

"Jonathan is absolutely right," I assured the seething throng. "Santa will be here any minute. He's so excited about meeting all of you! Especially Jonathan, who Santa heard has been a very good—and very *patient*—boy this year."

"I've got shopping to do!"

"I want my money back!"

"*What* money?" said another parent. "This is free."

"And it damn well *should* be, since there's no Santa!"

"I want Santa!"

"Where is Santa?"

"I WANT SANTA!"

Under my costume, a drop of cold sweat trickled down my back. I recalled the advice imparted during my training: *Never let them sense fear. These Christmas crowds will descend like a pack of ravening wolves if you reveal any weakness.*

I took a steadying breath and glanced at Twinkle. His forehead was shiny with sweat now as he stared glassy-eyed at the restless masses Rudolfo was trying to humor and soothe. I nudged the elf, who flinched violently in startled reaction, making his pointy ears bobble.

"Another song," I urged.

"No, it'll never work," he said, his voice cracking with fear. "We've got to retreat. *Now.*"

"No!" I said. "We hold the line."

"But what if—"

"We hold the line," I repeated firmly. "Now play a jolly song, damn you!"

By the time we finished "Good King Wenceslas," it was clear we were on the verge of disaster. More children were crying and whining, parents were bickering shrilly, and even young Jonathan was starting to look unhappy.

Someone started a chant, which began spreading through the crowd: *"San-ta! San-ta! San-ta!"*

"It's not safe here," Twinkle said desperately. "We've *got* to fall back."

"No, we can't." I gestured to Rudolfo, who was at least thirty feet away from us, trying to cheer up weepy toddlers and angry parents. "We'd be leaving the reindeer alone and exposed out there."

"He knew the risks when he signed on for this job," Twinkle said ruthlessly.

"We can't just abandon him," I argued.

I was startled by an officious voice coming loudly from behind me. *"Where* is Santa?"

I whirled around and found myself facing Miles, the floor manager. As always, he was wearing a gray suit, a nametag, and a censorious scowl.

"Miles! Thank God you're here," I said with relief. "We don't know. Where *is* Santa?"

"Don't say 'God' on the floor," Miles snapped.

"Santa never showed up," Twinkle said, raising his voice to be heard above the dull roar of the restless crowd.

"And where is Candycane?" Miles demanded. "Isn't this her shift?"

"Candycane went to find a Santa and still hasn't came back," I said. "Something's wrong."

Twinkle said, "We've got to cut and run before it's too late!"

"You will stay right where you are," Mile ordered.

"But what if—"

Miles looked at his watch. "Santa is nearly *thirty minutes* late. I want an explanation!"

"I'm sure you do, Miles, but you're obviously not going to get one from me or Twinkle," I said reasonably. "We have no idea what's happened to Santa. Our pressing concern right now is, what do we do about all these people?"

"No, our pressing concern is," Miles said crisply, "where is Santa? I will go find out. You will keep these people entertained."

"*What?*" bleated my companion. "No! We've got to—"

"That's an order, Twinkle," Miles said coldly. "Play something. And *you* . . ." He looked at me. "Sing and dance. Be merry. Or we'll have to rethink whether you're really elf material, young woman."

"Now that was just *unkind*," I said as he walked away.

"What do we do now?" Twinkle asked with panic in his voice.

"Steady on, Twinkle. This the moment that every elf is destined to face." I clapped him on the back. "Today is the day you find out whether you're really made of sugarplums."

"What?"

"Let's do another song."

He sighed in resignation. "Which one?"

" 'Twelve Days of Christmas,' " I said decisively.

The song was interminable, so I figured Miles would have enough time to go out and kidnap a Santa from some *other* store before we finished performing it.

I started singing the first verse, trying to get the children to join in—and ignoring the groans, boos, and tears that greeted my efforts. Beside me, Twinkle trembled a little, which made him miss some notes.

The more experienced elves at Fenster's had warned me *never* to let the line for Santa's throne get too slow. And now it had been at a complete standstill for a half hour. We were dicing with death.

"Life is cheap in the throne room," battle-hardened Santa's helpers had advised me. "When the first kid breaks formation and rushes for that chair, you've had it. Just run for your life—and don't go back for stragglers. Once a six-year-old with blood in his eye leads the charge, it's every elf for himself."

While singing about turtledoves, golden rings, and swans a-swimming, my wary gaze roamed the crowd, trying to spot the loose cannon, the inevitable ring leader, the child whose patience would snap and lead to a stampede.

And then it happened.

The rumble of rebellion started at the very far end of the Christmas queue, among people who were so far from the throne that they were out of my sight line. But I could *hear* them. Oh, yes, I could hear . . . and I felt paralyzed with fear.

Rudolfo, who was still farther away from us than safety or sense dictated, heard it, too. He stopped his merry little dance and stood straight and stiff, gazing in the direction of the ominous shrieking and shouting.

Twinkle's hands froze on the accordion and the instrument went silent. "This is it," he croaked out. "Here they come."

"Rudolfo!" I cried. "Fall back! *Retreat!*"

We heard a long, piercing, horrified scream somewhere at the back of the seemingly endless line of visitors. It was picked up and passed along by others. Within moments, most of the crowd was screaming hysterically.

"You break right, I'll break left," shouted Twinkle,

abandoning his accordion lest it slow him down. "Good luck!"

"Wait a minute," I shouted back, even as Rudolfo fled the scene. "Listen to that."

"Go!" Twinkle gave me a shove.

The crowd broke at all once, everyone running in different directions, people screaming and shouting.

Little Jonathan ran straight past me, his face white with fear now. His startled mother lost sight of him, looking around in panic as she shouted, "Jonathan? Jonathan!"

"They're not attacking," I shouted in confusion, clinging to Twinkle's arm as he tried to escape. "They're *scared*—or startled."

"Who *cares?* Let go!"

Twinkle threw his whole body weight into trying to break my hold on his arm. I released him, and he flew straight backwards and then hit the floor in an ungainly sprawl. I winced as shrieking children trampled him without hesitation or mercy.

I leaped out of the path of the stampeding crowd and climbed onto Santa's throne for safety—which was when I realized that they weren't rushing it. Or me. They were fleeing from something that was coming in this direction.

"Twinkle! Get up!" I shouted.

"I'm . . . *trying!*"

While the elf fought his way out from beneath the squealing children who were scrambling over his prone form, I rose to my feet, stood on the throne, and peered over the heads of the chaotic crowd, trying to see what had incited the mob to this hysteria.

Whatever I had expected to see (a raging fire? armed robbers? a pack of wild hunting poodles?), I was unprepared for the alarming spectacle that met my gaze. "Good God!"

My friend Satsy (aka Saturated Fats, a cabaret performer), known at Fenster's as Drag Queen Santa, was racing toward this spot as if his life depended on it, arms outspread, screaming in terror, his Santa costume torn, singed, and smoking sinisterly. Although Satsy's ultra-long, glittery purple eyelashes were still in place, his usually glamorous eye makeup was smeared and running, making him look like some sort of goth monster—especially with his white Santa beard sticking out sideways from his head and flapping madly as he ran. Given that Satsy was a large man—tall and heavyset—his overall appearance was terrifying, at the moment, as was his screaming sprint straight in this direction.

No *wonder* kids at the back of the crowd had gone berserk and started the stampede. If I were six years old, I'd be fleeing in terror now, too.

I supposed the adults could also be forgiven their reaction, considering the stress already inflicted on them by the season of joy. The sudden screeching arrival of Lunatic Monster Santa had probably just been the tipping point for them.

I jumped up and down on the throne as I shouted, "Satsy! Satsy!"

Much of the shrieking crowd had vacated the area by the time my friend reached this spot. I saw that he was soaked with sweat, which probably explained why his makeup was running and his Santa beard had come unglued. He was panting so heavily he couldn't speak—but also, thank goodness, couldn't keep screaming. As I stood on the throne, staring at him in dumbfounded alarm, he sank to his knees before me, his head bowed as he wheezed and gulped in air.

"What's going on here?" Miles demanded, pushing his way past the last of the stampeding throng. "And why is Santa worshipping that elf?"

I glanced at Miles and realized he meant me.

Twinkle pulled himself together and started crawling toward me and Satsy, his glasses crazily askew, his pointed elf ears and stocking cap lying trampled on the floor behind him. "That was the second scariest experience of my life," he said in a shaky voice. "My entire life!"

I hopped off the throne and knelt beside Satsy, helping him turn around and slump into a sitting position with his back supported by the chair. I patted his smoking red costume, making sure no part of it was on fire. There were singed bits and scorch marks, but Satsy didn't seem to be burned. Meanwhile, Miles shrilly demanded explanations, which none of us were in any condition to provide. And Twinkle, babbling nervously in the aftermath of mortal terror, was recounting the *scariest* experience of his life, which seemed to involve a fantasy role-playing game and an angry alpaca farmer—but I wasn't really paying attention.

Satsy was still sweating and hyperventilating, Miles still demanding explanations, and Twinkle still babbling when Candycane joined us. She saw Satsy and gave a startled shriek, then realized he wasn't a grotesque monster, but just a very disheveled Drag Queen Santa.

"What the *fuck?*" said the dainty elf.

"*That* is a warning offense," Miles snapped, pointing an accusing finger at her. Profanity was strictly forbidden on the floor. "This is going on your record, Candycane."

Candycane looked worried, since this was her second warning. Official warnings could go on your record at Fenster's for a myriad of petty offenses, and store policy was that the third warning led to automatic termination of employment.

"Oh, lay off her, Miles," I said as I patted Satsy's back soothingly. Twinkle and Satsy were both still semi-hysterical, and we could hear terrified children wailing and parents shouting all over the fourth floor in the wake of the stampede. "These are exceptional circumstances."

"There are *no* circumstances under which an elf can use that kind of language with impunity!" Miles said shrilly.

"Oh, for God's sake," I muttered.

"You are dangerously close to receiving a warning yourself," he said.

"Hiring and training an elf takes at least two days, and Christmas Eve is only three days away, Miles," I pointed out. Our holiday employment would end when the store closed on the evening of December 24th. "So it's too late to replace any of us, and we're already so understaffed that most of us are working overtime. Do you really want to lose more elves *now*?"

"Hmph."

I turned to my traumatized friend and asked, "Satsy? Are you all right? What going on?"

"As for me, I *like* alpacas," Twinkle was saying. "I guess. I mean, I don't *dis*like them. Anyway, I meant no harm, and I tried to explain that . . . But you can't really reason with an enraged farmer who's waving around a cat-o'-nine-tails."

"Huh?" said Candycane.

"Jonathan? Jonathan!" a mother was calling—and I realized whose mother it must be. The frightened little boy had fled the scene well ahead of his parent, and she evidently hadn't found him yet.

"Oh, my *God*," panted Satsy. "Ohmigod, ohmigod, ohmigod!"

"What happened?" I prodded.

"I thought I would *die!*" Satsy wiped his sweating face with his sleeve—thus smearing his makeup even more and ruining his furry white cuff. "I thought I'd die in there!"

"*I* thought I'd lose an eye," said Twinkle. "Or a very valued appendage."

"Where?" I asked.

"The field where we were jousting on the alpacas we'd liberated," said Twinkle. "Well, *trying* to joust."

"You should stop talking," I told him. "Satsy, where did this happen? And *what* happened?"

"I was trapped in the freight elevator," Satsy panted. "Esther, there is something evil in there!"

"Evil?" I said alertly.

"*Evil*," he repeated significantly, his spookily smeared, long-lashed eyes meeting my gaze.

"I see . . ."

Satsy and I had a mutual friend who specialized in confronting Evil.

"Jonathan!" I heard a worried mother calling out again from elsewhere on this floor. "Jonathan, where *are* you?"

"Wait, why were you in the freight elevator?" Twinkle asked Satsy, finally distracted from his jousting-alpaca tale. "You're not *that* fat."

"Really," I said to him, "just stop talking."

"There was growling and laughing and *flames* . . ." Satsy shuddered and made a terrified sound. "I thought I'd die in there!"

Since he started hyperventilating again, I decided not to press him for clarifying details at that moment.

Miles looked at his watch. "We've got to get things back on track."

I looked away from Satsy long enough to realize that the manager was right. Despite what had just happened (and despite the fact that security guards *ought* to be flooding this floor now in response to the noise and chaos, but were nowhere in sight), I could already see many people lining up nearby to visit Santa—presumably not the exact same people who had just fled in panic.

Miles said in exasperation to Satsy, "And *you* obviously can't work until you've cleaned yourself up. Go to the break room and compose yourself."

It would clearly take more than a little composure to make Drag Queen Santa presentable again. He was a sweaty, smeared wreck, and his costume was badly damaged. But Satsy nodded and, with help from me and Candycane, rose shakily to his feet.

"Where is Santa?" Miles demanded of Candycane. "The *other* shift Santa, I mean."

The elf said, "He didn't show up for work."

"*What?*" Miles snapped.

"I couldn't find Moody Santa anywhere. Then I found out that he never clocked in," said Candycane. "He's not here."

"What?" Miles repeated.

"I gather he didn't call in sick?" I asked.

"No," the manager said darkly.

"Ah," I said.

This was by now a familiar problem. My old boyfriend, Jeff, and I had both been hired to replace AWOL employees, and more staffers had disappeared from our ranks since then.

"Oh, well," I said to Miles. "I had the impression that Moody Santa felt his role didn't really challenge him artistically. I guess this was bound to happen."

"We need a *Santa*, not levity! And we need one right now!" Miles gave Satsy a ruthless appraisal, then said sternly, "You've got exactly five minutes to get cleaned up and get seated on that throne, mister."

Satsy shook his head weakly. "I can't."

"That's an order!" Miles said.

I argued, "Can't you see he's in no condition to greet children and defend himself from crazy parents?"

"I *insist* you get to work in five minutes!"

"So fire me," Satsy croaked, looking far more like a Halloween ghoul than a Christmas tradition.

"You're being unreasonable," I said to Miles, putting my arm protectively around Satsy's bulk. "Post a sign and some elves to explain that Santa's been called away on a Christmas emergency. Maybe that will hold off a seasonal riot and give you time to find a fresh Father Christmas."

"Jonathan! Jonathan!" The boy's mother was starting to sound frantic. I realized that we should alert security that he needed to be located. If we could locate security, that was. Those guys were never around when you needed them. "Jonathan!"

Miles glared menacingly at Satsy for a long moment, then his shoulders slumped and he sighed. "Yes, all right, this Santa obviously can't work this morning. You and Candycane escort him to the break room, make sure he's all right, and get the costumer to do something about his outfit. I want him ready in time for the afternoon shift!"

"I don't think he should work today," I said, still wondering what had driven Drag Queen Santa into such a frightened frenzy.

"Nonsense!" said Miles. "The show must go on!"

"But—"

"It's all right, Esther," said Satsy, starting to regain control of himself. "I need a little time, but I'll be able to work later."

"Are you sure?"

Satsy nodded, his beard flopping askew against the side of his head. I reached up to remove it.

"I'll call Rick," said Miles, pulling a cell phone out of his pocket. "At least *he* can always be relied on."

Rick was a grad student in psychology, rather than an actor or cabaret artist. We called him Super Santa because he was amazingly good with crying kids, shrill parents, high-strung elves, and cranky managers. He was also punctual and always eager to work extra shifts; like me, he needed the overtime pay.

"You'll need a relief Santa for this shift, too," I said to Miles, thinking of someone else who needed the extra money. "Call Jeff Clark."

"Which one is he again?" Miles frowned. "It's been a revolving door of Santas this year."

"He's the black guy," said Twinkle.

"Diversity Santa," I added.

"Oh, right," said Miles with a nod. "I'll call him next."

"You really think he'll show up?" Twinkle asked me. "That guy *hates* this job."

"So do I, and *I* keep showing up," I said. "He'll come in, if he's available."

Miles was holding the phone to his ear, evidently waiting for Rick to answer his call, as he told me and Candycane, "I want you two back on the floor and working as soon as you get this Santa settled down. I don't want any more prob—"

"*Eeeeeeyaaaahhhh!*"

We all froze and looked in the same direction. I realized that the high-pitched, blood-curdling scream had come from a child at the same moment that I heard his mother shrieking frantically, "Jonathan! *Jonathan!*"

And my day was just beginning.

2

let go of Satsy and was already running in the direction of that eerie scream when I heard wailing and crying. It was coming from the North Pole—or, rather, the section of the fourth floor that was called "the North Pole" and decorated in traditional style. This was where the original Fenster's Christmas exhibit had been for decades.

The boy's mother again screamed, "*Jonathan!*"

"Jonathan!" I shouted, with Miles, Twinkle, Candycane, and Saturated Fats running right behind me.

As I reached Santa's Workshop—where little mechanical elves engaged in a very limited range of repetitive-motion activities twelve hours per day, every day, throughout the season—I was relieved to see the child and to find him apparently unharmed. He ran toward his mother as she sobbed his name with relief, having found him at last, and scooped him up into her arms.

Something had obviously terrified the kid, though. He was red-faced and sobbing loudly, his nose running and his face screwed up with emotion.

"What happened?" I asked, coming to a halt beside the pair.

"He got lost," said the mother, her voice breathless with relief as she clutched Jonathan in her arms and stroked his blond hair. She crooned to him, "It's all right, sweetie. Mama's here now. You're okay, you're okay."

The boy kept crying hysterically.

Behind me, Satsy asked with concern, "Is he going to be all right?"

The mother started to say something reassuring, but Jonathan opened his eyes at the sound of Satsy's voice—and when he saw Scary Face Santa, he started shrieking, "Santa tried to eat me! He tried to *eat* me!"

"Fuck me," said Candycane.

"That's *enough*," said Miles, glaring at her. But I'd evidently been right; he wasn't going to fire her for profanity three days before Christmas Eve, not when we were so understaffed. "Candycane, get back to work. *Now.*"

The elf turned and left with alacrity.

Twinkle said that he needed to find his abandoned accordion and then find Rudolfo, and he left, too.

While Jonathan's mother tried to soothe the boy (but he would *not* be soothed), Miles said censoriously to Satsy, "Now do you see the consequences of your actions? Do you *see* how your irresponsible behavior has upset this child?"

"Well, the freight elevator tried to eat *me*," said Satsy. "I was upset, too."

Miles, perhaps fearing that the mother was thinking about suing Fenster's for emotional trauma, grimaced alarmingly at the child (a moment later, I realized this was intended to be an ingratiating smile), gestured to Satsy, and said, "Santa is very sorry that he frightened you, young man. And he's going to apologize to you personally for that. All right?"

"No, no, no!" Jonathan shrieked. "I don't want to see Santa again! No!"

Now Satsy looked distraught. He was doing this nightmarish gig for the second year in a row primarily because he liked kids—and, indeed, he was good with them. *Frightening* a child was certainly not what he wanted to do, let alone ruin a little boy's faith in Santa Claus.

So Satsy approached the child tentatively, his scarily streaked face gentle and concerned as he said, "Jonathan, I'm so sorry I upset you. Especially since I was looking forward so much to meeting you! But I had a really scary experience when I was on my way here from the North—"

"Not you!" Jonathan said to him.

"—Pole today, and it made me—"

"Not *this* Santa!" Jonathan said tearfully to his mother.

"—made me . . . made me . . . Huh?" Satsy's long, purple lashes fluttered a couple of times as he gave the boy a puzzled look.

"It was the *other* Santa," Jonathan said, tears of fear still running down his face.

"The other Santa?" I repeated blankly.

"The *other* Santa tried to eat me," Jonathan said, exasperation creeping into his voice. "The other one! The scary one!"

"This isn't the scary Santa?" I asked in surprise, nodding toward Satsy.

"No, the *other* one tried to eat me! The one with big fangs and claws and glowing eyes!" Jonathan buried his face against his mother's shoulder and cried loudly again, overcome anew.

His mother's expression was appalled as she asked us, "Do you really have a Santa here with *fangs* and *claws* and—"

"No!" Miles said, while I shook my head and Satsy stared at the child with his jaw hanging open.

Jonathan's mother said indignantly to Miles, "Then I guess one of your Santas is going behind your back to pull nasty pranks on children who get separated from their parents!"

"I assure you," said Miles, "if that's the case, the employee will be dealt with very severely."

"*If* that's the case?" she repeated angrily, still trying to soothe her son. "What else could it be?"

"Well, your child had just been frightened by the,

uh, unfortunate event which occurred earlier . . ." Miles gestured again to Satsy. "An event he associated with Santa . . . He was separated from you and probably feeling scared and disoriented. He was wandering around this exhibit alone, where it's rather dark and perhaps very easy for a frightened and imaginative child who can't find his mother to think that things from his nightmares are actually coming to life and menacing him."

It was a reasonable suggestion. And the sobbing child's mother, though still very angry about her son being traumatized by his visit here, was obviously realizing that this could indeed be what had happened.

But Jonathan had been listening, and now he insisted tearfully, "I didn't make it up! I'm not lying!"

"Shhh, sweetie. No one's saying you lied," said his mother gently. "But this is a big scary place, and you were all alone, and maybe—"

"I *wasn't* alone! Santa was there—right *there!*" The boy pointed to the shadowy Enchanted Forest that lay beyond the North Pole; the forest was rather dark and creepy by the standards of childhood (and sometimes also by the standards of grown-up elves). "And he tried to *eat* me!"

The mother gasped as she realized what might really have happened to frighten her son—who may have interpreted a genuine threat to his safety in a way that made sense to his young imagination in these surroundings. She looked pointedly at Miles. "Do you think there could be someone lurking around here who . . . ? I mean, so many children come here, and some of them are bound to get separated from their parents . . ."

Miles said, "Never fear, ma'am. We maintain heavy security on this floor to prevent such a problem."

"We do?" I blurted. This was certainly the first I had heard of it. I'd been working here for two weeks and seldom even saw a security guard on this floor.

Miles' cold glance warned me to keep my mouth shut. He continued, "At this time of year, we also have extra security at all the exits from Fenster's." He neglected to mention that the guards at those doors were looking for shoplifters, not kidnappers. "But in case Jonathan did encounter someone who poses a threat—"

"I saw *Santa*," the boy insisted.

"—I'll have security scour this floor right now."

"If you can *find* security," I muttered.

Attempting to close the matter, Miles said loudly, "Now, if you and Jonathan are willing to accompany me to our Customer Relations office, Fenster & Co. would like to offer you a special holiday gift to express our heartfelt apologies for your trouble today. Right this way, please."

"Well . . ." The woman tightened her arms around her distraught son. "All right."

Miles gave me and Satsy a "get back to work" look before he escorted the pair out of the North Pole toward the escalators at the other end of the fourth floor, making sure to avoid going through the Enchanted Forest. We called our farewells to Jonathan as the threesome departed, leaving Satsy and me alone here.

As soon as we were alone, I turned to Satsy and said, "Now tell me. What happened to you?"

"Oh, *Esther* . . ." He wiped his forehead with his other white cuff, ruining that one, too. "It was a nightmare!"

"Go on."

"I'm the relief Santa for this shift—or I *was*. I got into my costume and clocked in on time, but it's usually at least forty minutes into the shift before we do the first swap. So I figured I had plenty of time to go down to the shipping and receiving docks for a friendly smoke."

I frowned. "Since when do you smoke?"

Satsy performed nightly as a drag queen at the Pony Expressive downtown, and he was sensibly protective of his voice, as far as I knew.

"Oh. Ah . . . not cigarettes," he said, looking a little sheepish, his long purple lashes fluttering. "The guys down at the docks have some *primo* weed. And I enjoy a few tokes now and then."

"Wait a *minute*," I said, outraged. "I can't even say 'God' when I'm on the floor, but they're smoking pot down in shipping and receiving? I totally signed up for the wrong job here!"

"But when I got into the—"

"And you guys were having a joint at *this* hour?" I said incredulously.

"I know, I know," said Satsy. "But I wanted something to soothe my nerves after I got here. Haven't you noticed how *tense* it is around here this year?"

"You mean it wasn't like this last year?"

"Not like *this*." Satsy waggled his hand. "Oh, sure, kids cry, families fight, couple breaks up. That's just what people *do* at Christmas."

"You gentiles really know how to celebrate," I said.

"But the atmosphere is different this year. I wouldn't have taken this job again if I'd known it would be like this. I wouldn't have helped *you* get this job if I'd realized in time that something was wrong here."

Satsy and I had bumped into each other a couple of weeks ago at Zadok's Rare and Used Books in the West Village. The occult bookstore was owned by our mutual friend, Max—the friend who specialized in confronting Evil. I spend a lot of time with Max, especially when I'm out of work, as I was then. He and I have formed a close friendship despite our age difference: Max is at least three-hundred-twenty years older than I am. Saturated Fats is a regular customer of the store, and he sometimes looks after the place for Max in exchange for free books on magic and mystical phenomena.

Upon hearing, during our reunion that day, that my only income until January would be from a few scattered shifts at Bella Stella, Satsy had told me about the attrition rate among Fenster's elves and suggested I come along to the department store with him to apply for a job, supported by his personal endorsement. I did so, and Fenster's hired me on the spot.

"I still can't decide whether I'm grateful to you for the overtime I'm earning here," I said to him now, "or if I blame you bitterly for getting me into this seasonal nightmare."

The hiring process took a full day. To become an elf, I'd had to fill out a mountain of paperwork, submit to drug testing, and be evaluated for psychological stability. The evaluation was done by a pale, pimple-faced guy so painfully shy that he trembled and seemed on the verge of tears every time I spoke to him. There was also an audition to test my performance skills. Then the training process took another couple of days. I was assigned an elf identity, fitted for my costume, and rotated through various floor assignments as a trainee under the supervision of Jingle, who was working his fourth Christmas season in a row here.

Although Jingle took this job more seriously than I really thought a grown man should, he certainly knew Fenster & Co. well. The veteran elf was a font of experience and information, and he'd helped me get into the swing of things pretty quickly.

"So you're down at the docks getting high with your new butch friends," I said to Satsy. "What happened next?"

"Oh! Speaking of which," he said, enthusiastically distracted from the subject, "there's a really cute guy down there—very butch, *indeed*. His name is Lou. *Much* more Jersey Shore than I usually go for, but I really like him. And you should see his arms! He keeps saying he wants to come see my show. I think that's code for something."

"Code for what?" I asked. "I'm on the down-low? Or: I want to experiment with my sexuality? Or: There's a hot girl I think I can get in the sack if I show her how cool I am by taking her to a downtown club where I know one of the queens?"

"I'm not sure," Satsy admitted. "I'll keep you posted."

"*Anyhow* . . ." I prodded.

"Anyhow . . . So the boys have some unloading to do, and I realize it's about time for me to go back upstairs, so I get on the elevator—"

"Oh, *that's* why you were on the freight elevator. Because you were coming from the docks."

He nodded. "It lets me off on the other side of the floor, of course. But I'm usually able to sneak behind the solstice mural and get into the break room without being seen."

"But something went wrong in the elevator today?"

"Uh-huh. It suddenly stopped right between the third and fourth floors. At first I thought it was an ordinary malfunction, and I was just worried about how I'd explain being in there instead of where I was supposed to be. I waited a minute to see if it would start moving again on its own, but it didn't. So I figured I had no choice, and I pressed the emergency button."

When he did so, the lights went off. The elevator was suddenly shrouded in complete darkness.

"I didn't think that was supposed to happen, but it's not as if I *know*," he said. "So I wasn't scared right away, just surprised."

Then he heard deep, heavy, excited breathing. Right there beside him. And since he knew he was alone in the elevator . . .

"*That's* when I got scared," said Satsy. "And then all hell broke loose."

His gasp of fear and the pounding of his heart seemed to set off a whole chain reaction of horrifying events. He heard ferocious growling in the darkness—

"Growling?" I repeated.

"Uh-huh."

—and felt hot, foul-smelling breath on his face. He screamed like a girl (he said), and this incited a long, loud burst of maniacal, menacing laughter. The elevator was shuddering and quaking, bobbing wildly up and down, as if threatening to fall four floors and crash into the ground. And then it burst into flames.

"Flames?" I said.

"Flames." Satsy nodded emphatically. "All around me. I was drenched in sweat, screaming in terror, and certain I'd die in there!"

"So . . ." I looked in the direction of the freight elevator. "Did it burn up? It is a charred wreck now?"

"No. It's perfectly fine. *I'm* not." He gestured to his

damaged costume. "But suddenly the whole crazy thing stopped cold. Just like that. As if it had never happened. The lights came back on, the elevator stopped rocking and shaking, and everything around me looked perfectly normal. Then the doors opened and I was ejected by an unseen force—one that was still laughing!"

I stared at my friend, dumbfounded. Now it was easy to understand why he had careened screaming with mad terror into Santa's throne room, looking like a demented nightmare and creating a stampede among the volatile visitors.

"*Satsy.*" I gave him a hug. "How horrible!"

"Esther, there's something here at Fenster & Co.," he said in a low voice. "Something that shouldn't be here. Something . . . *evil.*"

Realizing that Satsy had endured a mind-boggling shock, I decided I'd better get him off the floor and into quiet surroundings. I escorted him into the men's locker room, helped him remove his costume, got him dressed and then wrapped in a blanket that I found, and then gave him a cup of hot cocoa in the break room.

While I was handing the cocoa to him, the Russian elf came into the room. She was a sullen, dour woman about my age, with dark hair, a pretty face, and a strong foreign accent. All I knew about her was that she came from Moscow and seemed to hate everyone and everything. I had worked with her only once and couldn't remember her name. Holly? Ivy? Merry?

I gestured to the big garbage bag into which I had stuffed Satsy's Santa costume. "Hey, can you do us a favor and take this upstairs to the costume mistress? Tell her there's been an accident and it'll need to be repaired or replaced—preferably by this afternoon?"

She looked at the bag, then looked at me. "No. I am not your servant."

I blinked. "I didn't mean you were my servant. I just thought maybe you could . . ." I said to her back as she stalked out of the room. ". . . do us this favor?" I called after her, "Elves are Santa's *helpers*. Have you forgotten that?"

Twinkle, who passed the Russian elf as he came into the break room, said, "What—the bitch queen wouldn't help you with something? What a surprise."

"I guess you've worked with her?" I said.

"Oh, yeah." He gave a dramatic shudder, which made his bells tinkle.

"You're on break now?" When the bespectacled elf responded with a nod, I said, "Good. Can you stay here with Drag Queen Santa for a while? I need to take his costume upstairs."

"Sure," said Twinkle.

"Don't leave him alone," I said. "He's had a shock today."

"So have we all," said Twinkle.

Satsy asked the elf, "How did your alpaca story end? I think I missed that part."

"Ah! *Well* . . ."

"Okay," I said quickly, gathering up the garbage bag. "I'm out of here. Oh, and then I'll check out, um, that thing, Satsy."

"What thing?" he asked, his lashes fluttering.

"The place where you . . . had your shock."

"Oh! Right. Oh, my God. Be *careful*, Esther."

"Absolutely." I exited the break room. In the hallway that ran alongside it and the locker rooms, I bumped into Jeffrey Clark. "Hey, you got here fast!"

"I was on my way to the subway when Miles called my cell," Jeff said with a shrug. "I had just been wondering how to pay for a Christmas present for Puma, so it seemed like a good idea to cancel my plans and come here when Miles offered me the extra hours."

Puma Garland was Jeff's girlfriend, whom he'd been dating since summer. I had introduced them, in a sense, when dragging Jeff along with me to her voodoo shop one hot day while investigating some mystical mayhem in Harlem with my friend Max. A lady of strict ethics, Puma had asked for my blessing when romance developed between her and Jeff, since I'd previously been his girlfriend. *Way* previously, in fact. There had been a gap of four years between when I had broken up with Jeff (and, nope, no regrets) and when we'd unexpectedly reconnected this past summer. Puma was a fine woman and undoubtedly better than Jeff deserved, and I had granted the relationship my dubious blessing.

I asked Jeff, "Did Miles tell you we had some unexpected excitement this morning?"

He shook his head, which was now covered by a light fuzz of hair. He had been shaving his head regularly in recent months, for his previous job. Jeff was a handsome man, but I thought the cue ball look didn't suit him at all. I was glad to see he was abandoning it, now that he was no longer playing a gladiator at the Imperial Food Forum, a Roman-themed gourmet superstore that had recently gone bust.

Jeff said, "Miles only told me that Moody Santa's gone AWOL and they needed a replacement ASAP."

"Two replacements," I said.

He raised his eyebrows. "*No one* showed up for the shift? Man, people are dropping like flies around here."

"The guys in the break room can tell you about it. I need to go deal with this." I hefted the plastic bag over my shoulder.

"They're making us take out the garbage now?" Jeff said, outraged. "*God*, I hate this job."

"No, it's . . . never mind." As I moved past him, he asked me who the other shift Santa would be. I answered, "Rick, I think."

"Super Santa? Oh, great. I can't stand that guy."

"I know."

Most of the Santas resented Rick to some degree; he was so good at the job and so popular in the role, they felt inadequate by comparison. But I thought Jeff mostly disliked him for *enjoying* the job.

"Who are Santa's elves this morning?" Jeff asked. "Am I working with you?"

"I *was* assigned to Santa," I said. "But I've got to go deal with this costume and then—"

"Oh, *please* tell me I won't be working with that Russian chick again."

"Um, actually, she's on the clock now, so she might be your—"

"Shit." Jeff stomped off toward the men's locker room. "Why am *I* always the lucky one?"

I rolled my eyes and headed toward the staff elevator. Then, recalling Satsy's experience, I changed my mind and decided to take the stairs.

Jeff was not a negative person by nature. He was just unhappy these days. Four years ago, shortly after we broke up, he had left New York with high hopes for the original new show he was cast in, but it had died in Boston. (Since it was called *Idi Amin: The Musical*, I thought its fate seemed not entirely unpredictable. But Jeff was very disappointed.) For several years after that, he tried to launch a TV career in Los Angeles, but his efforts didn't lead to anything.

Now he was back in New York . . . and so far, since returning to the Big Apple earlier this year, he'd gotten work as a gladiator play-acting with a sword at an uptown store for rich food-fetishists and as Diversity Santa at Fenster & Co. (He blamed me for the latter, since I had introduced him to his job the way Satsy had introduced me to mine.) Jeff was a dedicated actor who increasingly felt his talent was going to waste (and, although I was rarely in the mood to tell him so, I agreed that he deserved much better opportunities than he was getting), and he thought the jobs he was reduced to working were unseemly for a man in his thirties.

I wasn't too crazy about some of the jobs I had to take, either—particularly this one. But my stint as Santa's helper notwithstanding, I'd certainly had a much better year than Jeff. I'd worked in the chorus of *Sorcerer!*, a short-lived Off-Broadway musical. I'd had a plum guest role on *The Dirty Thirty*, a cult hit cable TV series in the *Crime and Punishment* spin-off empire of award-winning police dramas. And I'd spent the autumn as a female lead in a sold-out Off-Broadway adaptation of Dr. John Polidori's influential nineteenth-century tale, *The Vampyre*. (Though, admittedly, it was only sold-out because hordes of feverish fans flocked to the show to see its leading man, Daemon Ravel, who claimed to *be* a vampire. And thereby hangs a tale . . .)

I also had a dedicated, hardworking agent who believed in my future (and who shared an additional bond with me, since we'd supported each other through a nasty vampire incident during the limited run of *The Vampyre*). Whereas Jeff's agent had dumped him last year—something that too many agents tend to do whenever a client's career requires them to do some actual *work*—and he'd so far been unable to get another. I had introduced him to mine, Thackeray Shackleton (not his real name), but Thack, though he liked Jeff's audition and suggested some other agents for him to contact, had declined to take him on as a client.

Thack had told Jeff candidly that he already had two African-American men of similar age, build, and type on his client list, and there just wasn't enough work available for black actors for him to serve a third such client well, too.

That had put Jeff in an understandably dark mood even before he lost his gladiator job and wound up, at my urging, applying to Fenster's about a week ago. He considered his role as Diversity Santa a real low point in his career, and that was *without* regularly overhearing parents asking the elves if there wasn't a *white* Santa available whom their children could visit instead.

So although a year of dating him, back in the day, had taught me the folly of putting up with Jeff's foibles and twitches in silence, I was mostly letting his ill-humor at Fenster's roll off my back. He had his reasons for being grumpy, and I understood them.

The costume room, where I was headed with Satsy's wrecked Santa outfit, shared the sixth floor with the store's various administrative offices. This floor was closed to the public and accessible only by climbing these stairs, taking the staff elevator, or using a special key (which wasn't issued to seasonal employees) in the public elevators.

I opened the door from the stairwell and started to enter the hallway. At that moment, I heard a man scream.

Startled, I staggered backward into the stairwell. As I did so, a chubby white man walked past me in the hall, moving so quickly that he didn't seem to notice me or the swinging door. I thought he looked slightly familiar, even though his face was hideously contorted by strong emotion as he stormed past me, screaming, *"Freddie!"*

3

I stood in the stairwell, blinking in surprise and confusion as the door swung shut, muffling the man's scream.

He hadn't looked like he needed help. He'd seemed enraged.

"Oh . . ."

I realized now why the man looked familiar. He was Preston Fenster, one of the company executives and private stockholders in this family-owned retail empire. I had seen him briefly twice before, both times when I'd been on this floor: once during the hiring process and once when being fitted for my costume. He had been noisily enraged on both of those occasions, too. It seemed to be his natural state.

Satsy was right about the tense atmosphere at Fenster's. But considering how virulently all the Fensters seemed to hate each other, based on staff gossip and what little I'd seen for myself, I found it difficult to believe that last year had been any better. (Though last year my friend had presumably not been attacked by a growling, laughing, flaming freight elevator.)

I opened the stairwell door again and stepped into the hall.

"So if you think for one goddamn minute that we're paying for all this crap, Freddie, *THINK AGAIN!*"

I winced at the volume as I glanced down the hall and saw Preston, red-faced with rage, standing just outside the office of (I assumed) his nephew, Frederick Fenster, Jr.

I hovered uncertainly where I was, wishing Preston would enter Freddie's office. If he remained in the hall, I'd have to pass right by him on my way to the costume shop, which was on the far side of this floor.

An overweight, doughy-featured, balding man in his early fifties, Preston was holding a pile of papers—bills, I supposed—in one hand. With his other hand, he was peeling pages off the stack, one at a time, and flinging them into Freddie's office while he continued shouting.

"This family is not made of money!" Fling. "This company is not your personal plaything!" Fling! "Entertaining Russian gangsters is *not* a deductible expense!" Fling, fling, fling! "And *this* will get you arrested and indicted if the police ever find out about it, never mind the IRS!" He threw the whole remaining pile into Freddie's office and stood there panting with rage. Then he added, "And for *God's sake*, Freddie, learn to lock your damn door when you've got—got—got *company* with you!" Preston pulled on the doorknob to slam the door shut with a resounding *wham!*, then he stormed down the hallway, moving in my direction.

Clutching my garbage bag, I hugged the wall, intending to stay well out of his way.

Preston saw me, came to an abrupt halt, and shouted, "My God, what are *you?* Another of Freddie's bright ideas?"

"No, sir," I said with dignity. "I'm an elf."

"No, you're not!" he bellowed. "Our elves wear red and green!"

Unlike Santa's other elves, I wore a costume of blue and white. Because of this color scheme, shoppers and store staff (and Fenster family members, I now gathered) didn't always recognize me as an elf, even though the cut of my costume was identical to that of the other female elves: a micro-velvet bodice with short sleeves and a neckline too low to be comfortable in the chilly department store, high-cut shorts with a pointy scalloped hem, striped tights, and dainty boots with bells on them. While wandering the floors of Fenster's in this outfit, I had so far been mistaken for a hooker, a cocktail waitress, and a store model for an absurdly expensive line of teen clothing featured on the third floor.

I thought my pointy elf ears, which were attached to my blue stocking cap, were a dead give-away. But experience had so far proved me wrong.

"I'm a Jewish elf," I explained, thinking that Preston looked overwrought enough to have a nasty medical episode right in front of me. "These are the colors of the Israeli flag. Blue and white. I'm called Dreidel. You know the spinning top that children play with at Hanukkah? It's got four sides, with a Hebrew letter on each side? That's a dreidel. And it's my elf name."

"A Jewish elf?" Preston shouted into my face.

"Yes."

"A JEWISH ELF? Since when are there *Jewish* elves?"

I looked around, hoping someone would come to my rescue. The hallway was completely empty. Of course. Everyone on this floor was probably waiting for Preston to disappear into his office—or maybe keel over dead from the heart attack he was so ardently courting.

I said, "You're perspiring, Mr. Fenster, and you look pretty red. Maybe you should get a glass of water and—"

"What the *hell* are we doing?" he shouted at me. "Whose idea was this? How much did that costume cost us? What are we paying you?"

"Not nearly enough," I said. "Er, my pay, I mean. I don't know what the costume—"

"You're fired!"

"What?" I said. "What did *I* do?"

"Oh, for God's sake, Preston," a woman said behind me. "Don't take out your frustrations on this girl."

I whirled around, grateful for this support by someone brave enough to face Preston Fenster's noisy wrath. My savior was his older sister, Helen Fenster-Thorpe. We'd never met, but I recognized her face from my employee manual. Helen obviously took excellent care of herself, and she seemed to have a talented plastic surgeon; the result was a triumph of will (and money) over nature, if a little eerily plastic.

I knew some of her personal history, thanks to Jingle's gossip during my training. Helen was currently on her fourth husband. Her first marriage, when she was nineteen, had lasted barely two weeks before her mother—Constance Fenster, the Iron Matriarch—had gotten it annulled. Even Jingle didn't know who that short-lived spouse had been. Helen's current (and not necessarily final) marriage was to a gorgeous "tennis pro" twenty years her junior; according to Jingle, although the guy looked hot in his sporting gear, no one had ever seen him play tennis, let alone engage in it professionally.

"Oh, so you finally deigned to show up, did you?" Preston roared at his sister. "It's almost time for the board meeting to start!"

"And I'm here in time for it," Helen said coolly. "So do try to calm down. The doctor warned you, after all . . ."

"Mind your own goddamned business!"

"The entire floor can hear you screaming, Preston," she chided. "In fact, I suspect that all of Manhattan can hear you!"

"Have you *seen* the bills for Freddie's latest escapade? Does he really think we can afford this shit now, on top of everything else? We're going to need cash flow to pay the lawyers if we have to fight another lawsuit from the—the—the . . ." Preston turned red again. "You know. From those *bastards*."

"They wouldn't dare. They were beaten for good last time," Helen said, though she sounded hopeful rather than confident. "These new threats of a lawsuit now that Mother's dead are just so much saber rattling."

Clearly unconvinced by this assertion, Preston continued, "And we've got the hijackings to deal with, too! Do you know how much merchandise we've lost this season? So this is no time for Freddie to pull one of his expensive stunts!"

Helen Fenster-Thorpe sighed in disgust. "What has that little wretch done now?"

Seeing my chance, I tried to slip away unobtrusively. I failed.

"Never mind that! Who's responsible for *this?*" Preston blocked my path and barked, "A Jewish elf! Are you *kidding* me? First it was solstice! Then Kwanzaa! And now *this!* What next? Should we get an imam in here for the holidays, so that *everyone* can feel included?"

"That's not a bad idea," said his sister. "We live in a multicultural society, Preston. Fenster's must keep moving with the times." Over her shoulder, she said, "Tell him, Arthur."

"Um . . . well, er . . . ah . . ." A timid voice floated out of the open office door behind Helen.

A man of about fifty, Arthur was the fourth and final child of the late Constance Fenster. Helen, who was Constance's only daughter, was the Iron Matriarch's eldest surviving offspring. Constance's first child, Frederick Senior, had died in a liquor-soaked car accident twenty years ago, though the stripper riding with him that night had survived (and promptly sold her story to the tabloids). According to Jingle, Frederick Senior's merry widow rarely made an appearance at Fenster's, though she owned a chunk of the stock. She usually let her son, Freddie Junior, vote for her at Fenster board meetings.

"Oh, come out of there," Helen snapped over her shoulder at Arthur. "And speak up, for God's sake."

Arthur partially complied, creeping up to the doorway and hovering there. Although the youngest of the three siblings, he looked the oldest, his face heavily lined with stress, his hair completely gray. A thin, soft-spoken man who wore wire-rimmed glasses and always dressed formally (even at company picnics, Jingle said), Arthur had never married, nor did he date. Some of the staff thought he was in the closet; others thought he'd been psychologically castrated by his notoriously ruthless mother, who'd died only a few months ago.

"Well, er, actually, yes," Arthur said, looking around anxiously as he tried to avoid eye contact with his siblings. I must have looked innocuous (Santa's elves weren't supposed to be threatening, after all), because his gaze zeroed in on me, and he began speaking directly to me, as if I had asked for this information. "Demographic statistics show that ethnic and religious minorities by now form a substantial portion of the city's residents and also its visitors, particularly if we consider these disparate groups as one combined whole in comparison to the population we would describe as white and Christian."

He looked so anxious for my approval that I couldn't help giving him an encouraging little nod, which made the bell on my stocking cap jingle as I said, "Ah! Yes, I see your point."

He smiled, bashfully pleased by my response. "In fact, actuarial studies suggest that—"

"I don't give a damn about actuarial statistics!" Preston roared, the veins at his temples bulging so alarmingly that I thought he was on the verge of *becoming* an actuarial statistic. "Fuck your demographics!"

"You are such a vulgar ass," his sister said with open revulsion.

"This is not an actuarial demographic," Preston shouted. "This is Christmas! *Christmas.* Do you know what Christmas *means?*"

If I had expected him to deliver a speech about what the Christian savior's birth meant to Catholics and Protestants around the world, or to reflect on the central theme of this season as a time of love and joy, I would have been sorely disappointed. However, I had by now seen enough of the Fenster family not to expect anything of the sort.

"Profits!" he said. "December should be our most profitable month of the year. And instead, it's *breaking* us. Do you know *why?*"

"Because our merchandise keeps getting hijacked en route," his sister said tersely.

"What?" I blurted. "Seriously?"

"Oh, yes," Arthur said with a nod. "Three trucks have been seized at gunpoint in the past ten days. The trucks have been found afterward, but not until after the culprits and all the goods are long gone."

"Has anyone been hurt?"

"No," said Helen.

"Not yet," Arthur added anxiously.

"Wow, I had no idea." There was a lot of staff gossip about shoplifting, which was an obsession with Fenster managers and security guards, but I didn't think I'd heard anything about hijackings. Which made sense, I supposed. If the trucks were being hijacked out on the road, the heists wouldn't involve store premises or affect anyone whom the seasonal staff knew. I wondered if the guys down on the docks had mentioned the hijackings to Satsy, since they might know some of the truckers affected by it.

"Don't you follow the news?" Helen said, looking at me critically. "This has been all over the media."

"*All* over," Arthur added, looking distressed.

"I haven't had time for the news lately. I'm always *here*," I said. "Armed robberies? That's scary."

"Also expensive." Helen gave Preston a pointed look. "Of course, we *could* put a stop to it."

"You could?" I asked, puzzled.

"The *police* will put a stop to it," her brother said brusquely.

Helen said, "All we'd have to do—"

"*No*," said Preston. "Fenster's is *through* dealing with criminals and giving in to extortion!"

Helen persisted, "This mess is turning order fulfillment into a catastrophe and costing—"

"The police will take care of this," Preston snapped.

His sister shook her head. "My God, you're naïve. Doesn't it even *occur* to you that the police might be in their pockets?"

"Whose pockets?" I asked.

"Anyhow, I wasn't talking about that when I referred to our losses," Preston said impatiently. "I was talking about your goddamn Solsticeland! It's draining us dry!"

"Really?" I said in surprise. "I thought the whole idea was that it brings a lot of people into the store. And it sure seems to work. I'm always amazed at how crowded this place is." Since Arthur was nodding at me with approval, I continued, "Just like your ad slogan always says, 'At Christmas, *everyone* comes to Fenster's.' And they come to see the holiday displays. You have the most elaborate ones in the city, after all."

Looking bemused, Preston asked me, "Who *are* you?"

"I'm Dreidel," I reminded him. "I sing Hanukkah songs and teach Santa's visitors Hebrew words like *shalom* and . . . um . . . No, just *shalom.*"

Sure, I had been sent to Hebrew school as a child. But I was such an inattentive student that our nice rabbi—who was unusually progressive even for the Reform movement in Judaism—eventually agreed to let me focus my studies on Yiddish theater, a unique legacy of the Jewish diaspora, for my bat mitzvah. Which is not to say that I know Yiddish any better than I know Hebrew; just that I knew, even as a child, that theater would be my lifelong vocation.

"This elf is right, Preston," said Helen. "Solsticeland brings in the crowds. People who could go to half a dozen other flagship stores in Midtown come *here* instead, because we've got the biggest, best, most extravagant holiday exhibits you can find anywhere. We aren't *a* place to shop at Christmas, we are *the* place. And it's because of Solsticeland!"

"First of all," Preston said loudly, "I don't take business advice from an elf. Not even a Jewish one. Secondly, do you two have any *idea* what it costs us to run Solsticeland? No matter how many people it might be bringing in—and you've shown me no proof that it makes the difference you say it does—it's bleeding money!"

"Proof?" Helen shouted back. "You want *proof?* Look at our holiday revenues!"

"They're not impressive compared to our holiday expenses!"

Arthur broke in timidly, "It's also our mother's legacy. Solsticeland was her vision. She saw the future and—"

"Oh, my God, do not drag *her* into this again." Preston looked suddenly queasy. I wondered if mentioning his mother always had that effect on him. "Look, when Holidayland was a popular Christmas display that took up a modest portion of the fourth floor, it was cost effective. When Mother and Frederick Senior doubled its size and turned it into an 'immersive experience,' we still broke even on it. But ten years ago, when Mother blew that good idea all out of proportion to create a multicultural theme park covering the whole goddamn fourth floor for six weeks every year, she fucked us over. And she's still fucking us over from the grave with this thing."

Arthur looked upset at hearing an obscenity used in relation to their mother.

Helen said in exasperation, "Are you *completely* dense? Are you so stupid you're incapable of understanding that the sort of holiday attraction that brought in crowds way back when Frederick Senior was alive and still occasionally sober is so uncompetitive in today's retail world that dogs wouldn't even bother coming to Fenster's to piss on it?"

"*Enough.*" Preston held up a chubby a hand. "I don't

intend to waste any more time arguing with you two—
or with your elf."

"I'm not *their* elf. I'm *an* elf."

"I've made my decision," Preston declared. "Mother
is gone and no longer controls this company. So this is
Solsticeland's final year."

Helen sneered. She did that well, I noticed. "You say
that as if it were up to you."

"Money talks, and it's speaking in my favor," he replied. "So I can persuade the rest of the family to vote
with me, even if you and Arthur refuse to see reason."

"Oh?" Helen said with disdain. (She was good at
that, too.) "After the scene you just threw with Freddie,
do you really imagine he'll vote with *you* on anything?"

"If there's one thing that Freddie and his idiot
mother both love, it's money. When I explain to them
how much more of it there will be for them if we're not
flushing it annually down the drain called Solsticeland,
they'll vote my way," Preston said confidently.

Looking amused rather than convinced, Helen said,
"And I suppose you think Elspeth will vote with you,
too?"

"She's my daughter," Preston replied, obviously expecting filial loyalty to weigh in his favor. "And since
the twins are too young to have a say in the matter . . ."

Helen glared at him but didn't argue. I recalled that
she'd had her twins, a boy and girl, with her third husband, an oil baron named Thorpe. She still kept his
name attached to hers with a hyphen, perhaps because

Thorpe was her kids' surname. She'd conceived the twins, her only children, late in life (and thanks to the help of expensive fertility treatments, it was said), and they were now still minors. According to Jingle, the twins were spending the holidays this year skiing in Switzerland with their father. Sure, that sounded enviable; but at the moment, I was inclined to think they'd probably prefer scrubbing floors in Poughkeepsie to spending Christmas in the collective bosom of the Fenster family.

Preston said triumphantly, "The vote will be four against two. Solsticeland will be discontinued."

After a long, tense moment, the three siblings all looked at me, as if awaiting my judgment on the matter. I said, "I think something might be wrong with the freight elevator. Maybe maintenance should look into it?"

Well, that was what was on *my* mind, after all. I hated this job and never intended to come back here after my temporary employment ended in three more days, so I didn't care what happened to Solsticeland. I cared even less about how the Fensters used or spent their inherited fortune. As far I was concerned, they could all take their silver spoons and shove them up their—

"Ah! I see nearly everyone's here and ready for the board meeting," said Freddie Junior as he opened his door and exited his office. He came down the hallway toward us while making sloppy work of tucking his shirt into his trousers. His brown hair was tousled, and a faint sheen of sweat covered his face.

"Hello, Freddie," Helen Fenster-Thorpe said in a tone of chilly resignation.

"Aunt Helen, you look younger than ever! That's so *weird*." Freddie turned to me, looked at my neckline, and said to my breasts, "Hello! I don't think we've met."

"This is Dreidel, Santa's Jewish elf," Preston said tersely. "Was this your idea?"

Freddie studied me for a moment, then shrugged. "I really can't remember."

"I replaced someone else who was playing the Jewish elf," I said. "Mr. Fenster and I haven't met before."

"Call me Freddie." He tried to put his arm around me.

I shifted quickly, so that my garbage bag slid off my shoulder and thumped against him. "Oops."

Freddie, who did not seem to be the most sure-footed of men, staggered a little. Eyeing my bulging bag, he asked, "We're making elves take out the garbage now?"

"No, this is . . ." I said, "Never mind."

Freddie was about thirty years old and moderately good-looking, in a dissipated sort of way. He was only a couple of inches taller than my 5'6", and the effects of his notoriously heavy drinking were starting to show in his physique.

Although we'd never met, other employees had

pointed him out to me a few times in the store. A favorite subject of scandal mongers and society gossip columnists, Freddie liked booze, sex, gambling, high-living, and expensive toys. He was said to be undisciplined, unprincipled, and uncontrollable. On the other hand, it was also generally agreed that, unlike most Fensters, he was an easygoing guy who didn't hold grudges.

"Freddie, what are *they* doing on this floor?" asked his Aunt Helen, looking over his shoulder.

I followed her gaze and saw Naughty and Nice emerging from Freddie' office. Which no doubt explained why he'd looked a little sweaty and disheveled when emerging from that room a moment ago.

Freddie glanced over his shoulder and grinned. "We were conferring on business strategies." As he gave the elves a little finger-wave, he said, "Those girls are my best idea yet, Aunt Helen!"

"The bar was set very low," Preston muttered.

Naughty and Nice were a couple of bombshells whose special elf costumes, conceived by Freddie, made them look more like strippers than like Santa's helpers. The girls were each about 5'10", buxom, wasp-waisted, long-legged, and tan. Their wet-lipped smiles revealed shiny white teeth too perfect for nature, and they both spent a lot of time in front of the mirror in the ladies' locker room to achieve the carelessly waving appearance of their long blonde hair. Their skimpy red-and-green outfits were almost as revealing as bikinis, with little bells positioned to draw attention to their breasts every time they moved. Or inhaled. Or did nothing at all. Their black, thigh-high boots completed the look of two women better suited to solicit business in a red-light district than to escort children to Santa's throne.

In fact, Naughty and Nice were only seen in the North Pole when management wanted them to soothe the tempers of irate fathers who were complaining about the long wait to see Santa. The rest of the time, these two elves were usually working in menswear or sporting goods, encouraging male shoppers to spend money . . . or else they spent their time tending to Freddie's needs.

Since Naughty and Nice were adjusting their clothing (so to speak) when they came out of Freddie's office, I gathered they'd been tending to him just now. No wonder his enraged uncle had slammed that door shut a few minutes ago.

The girls finger-waved at Freddie and giggled.

Then Naughty noticed me and said, "Oh, look, it's *Dreidel*. Hello, Dreidel."

She was one of those women who could make "hello" sound like a snide insult.

"*Shalom*," I said.

Looking right at me, Nice whispered something into Naughty's ear, and the two of them burst out laughing.

"Freddie, since your playthings are presumably on the clock right now," Preston said through gritted teeth, "isn't there something they could be doing that at least vaguely resembles work?"

"Of course, Uncle Pres," said Freddie, making it

sound like he was granting the older man a special favor. He instructed his bimbos, "Run along, girls. I have to attend the Fenster family board meeting. Very important stuff!"

Giggling and whispering, the two blondes went halfway down the hall, pressed the button for the staff elevator, and then boarded it.

As the doors swished shut behind them, Preston said to me, "Did you say there's something wrong with the elevator?"

"The freight elevator," I clarified.

"Oh. Too bad."

"Hey, those girls are the best weapon in our marketing arsenal," Freddie chided. "If you run the numbers, I bet you'll find they've increased sales in menswear by twenty percent."

"You're talking through your hat, Freddie," said his aunt. "I'd believe those two witless sluts could sell Viagra, but not much else."

Freddie said to me, "Great ideas are rarely recognized in their own time."

"Uh-huh."

Arthur surprised us all by speaking up. "They don't seem like very . . . *nice* girls."

"Y'think?" I muttered.

"Oh, you'd like them if you got to know them better, Uncle Arthur." Freddie wiggled his brows suggestively at his uncle, who fell silent again as his face took on an expression of pained embarrassment.

The staff elevator beeped at us, and the door swished open. I had an unhappy moment of thinking that Naughty and Nice had returned to this floor for some reason (or maybe they just didn't understand how to operate an elevator). But instead of the mostly-naked elves, a newcomer stepped out of the elevator—and I flinched when I saw her.

4

I gave an embarrassed little shrug a moment later when Helen Fenster-Thorpe gave me a peculiar look for overreacting to the goth girl's arrival on the sixth floor.

I recognized the girl, having noticed her in Solsticeland a couple of times. I'd had a slight phobia about goths ever since appearing in *The Vampyre* this past autumn, where our audiences had an unfortunate tendency to burst into hysterical rioting. And she was particularly noticeable in Solsticeland, where chalk-white foundation accompanied by basic-black everything (dyed hair, clothing, accessories, lipstick, nail polish) wasn't the usual look for staff or visitors. I had realized from Miles' subservient behavior to her that she was someone he deemed important, but it hadn't occurred to me that she was a Fenster. I had vaguely assumed that Preston's Vassar-educated daughter, mentioned in his bio in my employee handbook, would be a well-groomed debutante, not a slouching rebel in combat boots and scary eye makeup.

"Elspeth!" Preston checked his watch as he greeted his daughter. "You're five minutes late."

"So sue me," she said sullenly, clumping toward us in her heavy boots, her various silver chains jangling as she walked. "I bumped into your revolting bimbos when I got on the elevator, Freddie. *God*, those girls are disgusting."

I started to like Elspeth.

As she came to a halt beside her cousin, she added, "And *you're* even more disgusting, Freddie. Is that really what you want in a woman? Fake boobs displayed like—"

"They're real," Freddie protested. "You can take my word for it."

"What*ever*." Elspeth looked at me and said, "I think I've seen you before. Downstairs somewhere. You're the Hanukkah elf, right?"

"Did everyone know about this but me?" Preston said irritably. "Why did we need a Hanukkah elf, for God's sake? We have a storage room *full* of Christmas costumes that no one's using! Any number of those costumes would have fit this girl just fine. Why did we waste money *making* another costume for someone we only employ for six weeks?"

"Jesus, Dad," said Elspeth. "Would you *chill*? You're totally harshing my vibe."

"Whenever you open your mouth," said her father, "I realize that the money I spent on Vassar was wasted, too."

I decided I had enjoyed enough of the Fenster family's company for one day—and, indeed, for the rest of my life. "Well, you people have a board meeting to attend," I said, starting to back away from them. "And I need to go do something about this damaged costume and then get back out on the floor. We're understaffed, you know, so—"

"Wait a minute." Elspeth grabbed my arm, studying me with a peculiar look. "I know you, don't I?"

"I don't think so." Although it was a little hard to tell for sure under her dyed black hair and heavy goth makeup, she didn't seem at all familiar to me, apart from my having seen her around the store a couple of times. And it's not as if I habitually meet so many heiresses that I might forget one. "Now if you'll excuse me—"

"No, I *know* you. I'm sure I do. Your voice." She eyed me analytically and added, "Your face . . . your cheekbones . . ."

I'm of average height and weight, with fair skin, brown eyes, and shoulder-length brown hair. I fit a lot of "types" and can be cast in a variety of stage roles, from romantic leads to character parts. My cheekbones are my best feature, though they don't elevate my face to Hollywood-pretty. My looks are okay, but they're not my meal ticket.

"Elspeth," said Helen impatiently, "the elf has already said—"

"What's your name?" Elspeth asked me.

"Dreidel."

"No, your real name."

I hesitated, feeling reluctant to give it to these people. It seemed as if that would make our acquaintance real, which didn't strike me as an appealing prospect.

"Dreidel," Freddie mused. "I like that. It's sexy."

"Shut up, Freddie," said his aunt.

"Elspeth," said Preston, "release the elf. We have a meeting—"

"What's your name?" she repeated.

On the other hand, I was just a seasonal employee, one whom they'd all forget (except possibly the outraged Preston) as soon as I left the sixth floor. So I said, "Esther Diamond."

"Esther Dia . . . *Oh, my God!*"

I flinched and dropped my garbage bag when Elspeth grabbed my shoulders and squeezed with excitement.

"It's you! Oh, my God! It's *you!*" she cried.

"Who the hell is she?" Preston asked.

"Yes, who am I?" I asked, as baffled as the girl's father.

"Jane! You're *Jane!*" Her sulky face was illuminated by sudden enthusiasm as she said to her bemused family, "This is Jane Aubrey!"

Oh, *no.*

I felt paralyzed with panic.

"No, I'm pretty sure that's Dreidel," Freddie said with a puzzled frown.

"Elspeth, this elf just said she's Esther Diamond." Helen added, "Pay attention, Freddie."

"Then who's Jane Aubrey?" her nephew wondered.

"You're one of *them*," I said, my well-trained voice barely a croak. I stared in dry-mouthed horror at Elspeth, who was practically jumping up and down in her excitement. "The vamparazzi!"

"The who?" said Freddie.

During the limited run of *The Vampyre,* I had been threatened, mobbed, tackled, harassed, punched, pummeled, and nearly suffocated by the crowds of crazed vampire fanatics and paparazzi who hung around the theater every night. I had also nearly been murdered by a vampire. And if asked whether I felt more haunted by my memories of that homicidal vampire or of the vamparazzi, I'd need to think long and hard about my answer.

Therefore, learning that one of the vamparazzi was here at Fenster's—indeed, was *a* Fenster . . . Oh, it was too infamous for words! I gaped at Elspeth in appalled shock, keenly aware of her fingers still digging into my shoulders.

"Yes, who *is* Jane Aubrey?" Preston asked.

"I can't believe you're *here!*" Elspeth cried again, the fanaticism in her face frightening me. She told her puzzled family, "Jane Aubrey is the woman Lord Ruthven loves!"

I blinked. *Oh*, please. *That does it.*

I tried to pull out of her grip; she tightened it.

Preston asked, "Who the hell is Lord Ruthven?"

"I think I met him . . ." Freddie said.

I regained full control of my motor skills and gave Elspeth such a hard shove that she let go of me and staggered backward into the timid Arthur.

"Stop right there!" I said sharply, pointing a warning finger at the goth girl. "I am *not* Jane Aubrey. I *played* Jane Aubrey in *The Vampyre*. And Lord Ruthven didn't *love* her, he *murdered* her."

Freddie said, "Hey, love hurts, baby."

"Shut up, Freddie," I snapped.

"You *played* . . ." Preston's expression cleared as he realized what I was saying. "Oh, you're an actress?"

"Yes."

Helen reminded him, "Quite a few of the seasonal employees are actors."

"Wait a minute," said Preston. "*The Vampyre?* Oh, good God, Elspeth! Wasn't that the stupid thing downtown that you were at night after night for weeks before Thanksgiving?"

"It wasn't stupid," she said sulkily. "It was brilliant! But you wouldn't understand." She returned her attention to me and asked, with exactly the sort of feverish obsession that had nearly led to my demise once or twice during the run of that play, "What's it like to be held in *Daemon Ravel's* arms?"

"Who's he?" Freddie asked me.

"The actor who played Lord Ruthven, the vampyre."
I said to Elspeth, "I have no idea what it's like to be
held by Daemon Ravel. I only know what it's like to be
held by Lord Ruthven, who embraced me eight shows
per week while I was playing Jane."

"Well, what was *that* like?" she demanded impatiently.

"Yes, tell us," Freddie said with interest.

"It was chilly," I said tersely. "That theater was
drafty and my neckline was practically down to my
navel."

"Oh, I wish I'd seen *that*," said Freddie.

I concluded, "Daemon Ravel and I were short-term
colleagues who barely knew each other, and we've had
no contact since the show ended."

And because life was intrinsically unfair, Daemon
was now prepping for his upcoming lead role in a
cable-TV movie, while I was working as an elf at Fenster's.

Elspeth said sulkily, "Fine. Whate*ver*." Evidently
thinking she was delivering a stinging insult, she
added, "You're really *not* Jane, are you? You're *nothing*
like her."

"Nope."

"Is Jane still coming, though?" Freddie asked in confusion. "We could order in some food or something."

"Jesus, Freddie," said his cousin, clearly in a sour
temper now. "Sometimes I'm amazed you can find
your own dick with both hands."

"Luckily," he replied, "I don't often need to find it by myself."

"That's enough, children," said Helen.

They *were* like children, I realized. Both of them. Freddie was older and Elspeth was younger, but they were each within a few years of my age. Yet they both seemed like teens to me—*immature* teens, struggling with too much privilege, too little responsibility, and no real guidance.

What a family.

"Just out of curiosity," Preston said to me, "not that I care . . . But if you were in a sold-out Off-Broadway play last month, where tickets were going for astronomical prices on the street—which I have good reason to know, since my daughter burned through a small fortune to see that play as many times as she could . . . What the hell are you doing here, playing an elf?"

Now that *did* sting. "I'm out of work."

"Bummer," said Freddie.

"That's life upon the wicked stage," I said. "Sometimes you're up, sometimes you're down. And, up or down, I have to pay my rent, after all."

"Hey! You see that? Right there?" Preston pointed at me while speaking to his daughter. "*That's* a work ethic. Why can't you be more like this elf?"

"Because she's an *elf*, Dad," Elspeth said with disdain. "Is that really what you want for me?"

That stung, too. I decided it was time to resurrect my plan to get away from these people.

"I've really enjoyed meeting you all," I lied, "but now I have to take Drag Queen Santa's costume to the shop for repairs. Or maybe for burial at sea."

"We have a *drag queen* in Solsticeland?" shouted Preston, his ire renewed. "What the *hell* is going on down there? That's *it*, I tell you, Helen. That's it! This is Solsticeland's final year!"

"Oh?" said Freddie. "Are you sure? I mean, doesn't it sort of depend how *I* vote when the time comes?"

"Yes, Freddie, it does," said Helen, turning on a dime and warming up to her loathed nephew with a lightning-quick change of attitude. "You're absolutely right, dear. But I suggest that we discuss the future of Solsticeland—"

"It has no future!" Preston insisted.

"—in the board room rather than continue to scream about it here in the hallway."

"Oh. Yes. Let's do that."

To my relief, the Fensters all moved off in the opposite direction from where I was headed. Preston, who was muttering angrily, paused long enough to bark at his brother, "Come *on*, Arthur! You can't attend the meeting from the doorway of your office!"

Looking small in comparison to his relations, Arthur trotted down the hall after them. I picked up my garbage bag, then turned and went in the other direction, heading for the costume shop. The voices of the bickering Fensters floated down the hallway to me until after I turned the corner and started following that corridor to the other side of the building.

The exact distribution of Fenster stock was kept private, but it was known that Freddie Junior had inherited shares from his father, of which he'd gained control when he'd turned eighteen, and that he had inherited more stock from his grandmother, Constance, upon her recent death. His mother tended to leave him in charge of her shares in the company, too, as well as her voting rights. So now that the Iron Matriarch was dead, Freddie—feckless, reckless, and not exactly the brightest bulb in the chandelier—reputedly had more control of Fenster & Co. than anyone else in the family. This undoubtedly drove the rest of them *nuts*.

I assumed it was also why no one got rid of Naughty and Nice, though the whole family obviously disapproved of having Freddie's bimbo elves on the payroll. Realistically, Freddie Junior was in a position to do almost anything he wanted, regardless of how his uncle screamed and raged at him.

All things considered, I suddenly wondered if Fenster's itself had much of a future, never mind Solsticeland.

On the way to the costume shop, I passed what always struck me as the strangest thing in the whole building: the holding cell. Fenster's had its very own jail cell, where it locked up shoplifters until NYPD came to get them. I found it weird—and a little unnerving—that I worked for a company that had its own private prison.

The cell was empty and no one was around. Security guards only got posted here if there was a prisoner.

When I got to the costume shop and pulled Satsy's ruined Santa outfit out of the bag, the costumer was appalled by the extent of the damage. After a few minutes of muttering and head shaking, she stuffed it back in the plastic bag and dumped it in the garbage can.

"He'll need another costume for the rest of the season." She snorted and added, "All three and a half days of it."

She took me down the hall to another room. When we entered it, I realized this was the storage area that Preston had mentioned, full of Christmas costumes that weren't being used. It was a large room containing half-a-dozen racks of garments (mostly red and green), boots, bells, caps, beards, antlers, and wings. ("We tried sugarplum fairies one year," the costumer told me, "but the wings were so fragile they needed constant repairs.")

We sifted through a rack of Santa costumes and soon found one that looked the right size for Saturated Fats.

"It's a few years old," said the costume mistress. "A little different than the style we use now. See how broad the cuffs and collar are? But Santa's look is always pretty much your basic red suit with white trim, so this will work." She tugged and twitched the fabric, checking for stains or weak seams. "If this were the start of the season, I'd have him come upstairs for a proper fitting. But since he only needs to get through a few shifts, it'll have to do."

"I think it'll be fine," I said, hefting the suit in my arms.

She asked, "What the hell happened, anyhow?"

"He had an accident," I said vaguely. "I'm fuzzy on the details."

After we exited the storage room, I realized there was something else I needed to do before returning to the floor. I asked, "Where's the nearest bathroom?"

She pointed further down the hall, past her workshop. Then she leaned forward and whispered, "It was Mr. Powell's private bathroom."

I didn't immediately understand the significance of this. "Who was Mr . . . Oh! *That* Mr. Pow—"

"Shh! We don't say the name out loud around here."

I nodded. This was one of the unwritten but well-known rules of Fenster & Co. It had slipped my mind, having no real relevance to my sojourn at the store, but Jingle had taught me the rule and explained its origin.

For decades, this company had been known as Fenster & Powell. When Constance, a pretty society debutante, had married into the Fenster family some sixty years ago, the profits and the power were shared equally by the company's two founders, one of whom was Constance's father-in-law. Mr. Fenster died a few years later, and Constance's husband took over his family's half of the business. A few years after that, he died, too—in a hotel room in Atlantic City. There was quite a whiff of scandal about it, but the family managed to ensure that very few facts were ever known.

Then Constance, a widow in her thirties with four young children, surprised everyone by taking her husband's place in the family business. She also disappointed the dismissive predictions that she'd soon wind up either selling out to the Powells or else bankrupting the company. Constance proved to be a dedicated, talented, and ruthless businesswoman. The founding Powell's immediate successor butted heads with her for about a decade before selling his shares to his nephew and leaving the company. Several more Powell men took his place over the years, but Constance increasingly became the captain of the ship and the driving force behind the retail empire's expanding success.

As I headed to the bathroom, I recalled that Helen's second husband had been a Powell. "And the less said about *that*, the better," Jingle had told me—before proceeding to say quite a bit about it. The Fenster-Powell marriage, which had been encouraged (or, rather, engineered) by Constance, soon spiraled into notorious public quarrels, private mutual loathing, and blatant infidelities.

It was through that hellacious marriage, followed by the divorce settlement a few years later, that Constance changed the balance of power by acquiring company stock that had always belonged to the Powells. That gave her the foothold she needed to start gradually squeezing them out of the business. Her strategy included taking their name off the company, which she reorganized as Fenster & Co. It took years of additional maneuvering to achieve her goal; but finally, the Iron

Matriarch, who was by then in her seventies, ejected the Powells completely from the retail company which their family had co-founded and helped build into a business empire.

Ever since then, according to Jingle, "Around here, it's not a good idea to say a word that even *rhymes* with Powell."

Predictably, Constance's coup led to years of legal battles between the two families. But the Iron Matriarch fought the Powells so shrewdly that all their efforts eventually floundered. In the final years of her life, Jingle said, Constance seemed to have beaten them.

However, the Powells may have been biding their time rather than accepting defeat. They were reputedly planning a new legal assault on the Fensters, now that the Iron Matriarch was safely in her grave and the company was in the hands of her bickering heirs, none of whom had inherited her cool-headed business acumen (though I thought some of them had probably inherited her highly flexible morality). I suddenly realized, based on something he had said earlier, that Preston considered a new lawsuit a serious possibility.

But I wondered why the Powells would bother? It had all occurred years ago, and the woman behind those events was dead now. Why not just let the past go and move on? What could the Powells hope to gain from yet another legal battle after all this time?

Money and power, said a killer's voice in my head. *It's* always *about money and power.*

That was probably an accurate assessment of the bitter Powell-Fenster feud in all its permutations; but I recognized that voice and didn't like hearing it in my imagination. So I gave myself a hard mental shake and tried to think of something else. Nothing else came to mind, though.

Months after she had tried to kill me on a storm-swept promontory in Harlem, that *awful* woman was still haunting me, I realized. She had murdered three men, and she came far too close to killing the man I . . . Well, she came far too close to killing him, too. Because of me.

"Be honest with yourself, Esther," she said. *"Would he be lying in agonized paralysis awaiting his death now if not for you?"*

"He's still alive, and you're not," I muttered aloud to my private demon. "So get out of my head already, would you?"

Feeling a little shaky, I splashed cold water on my face in what had once been the private Powell bathroom. I supposed the stress of this weird day was getting to me, and the result was that *she* crept into my head again. Or maybe I'd opened the door to her by thinking about Constance Fenster, who was a similarly merciless woman (though presumably not a similarly homicidal one).

As I washed my hands in what had been the private bathroom of the last Powell who'd been a partner of the Fensters, I reflected that I wasn't sorry that the Iron Matriarch had died a few months before I ever came to work here. Jingle said she succumbed to pneumonia, a complication that arose after she'd undergone surgery to remove a cancerous tumor. I suspected that, although very ill and in her eighties by then, she had been a formidably ruthless employer, enemy, and mother right up until her dying breath.

5

I took Satsy's new costume back down to the men's
locker room on the fourth floor, where I tapped on
the door and called hello before letting myself in. Life
in the performing arts forces you to shed conventional
physical modesty pretty quickly, so I didn't think any
of the guys would be upset if I caught them in their
briefs; but I wanted to give anyone who was naked a
chance to cover up.

"I'm the only one here, and I'm perfectly decent,"
was the friendly reply to my warning. I recognized Super Santa's voice.

"Hi, Rick." I pushed open the door, entered the
room, and went to hang up Satsy's replacement costume in his locker. Rick had evidently just arrived,
since he was still in his street clothes. I said, "I see Miles
tracked you down."

"Hi, Esther." He hung up his winter jacket in his locker. "It sounds like you guys had quite a morning."

"You heard what happened?"

"I was just in the break room. Twinkle and Satsy told me about it." He paused. "Their story was a little confusing. I'm still not really sure what happened."

"I feel the same way, and I was *there*."

Rick smiled at that. He had a solid, amiable face; nothing handsome or remarkable, but pleasant. Though still in his twenties, his hairline was receding, and it was easy to guess what he'd look like in middle age. He was a few inches under six feet tall, with a square, stocky build. What people mostly noticed about Rick, though, was his calm, reassuring manner.

"Actually," I said, "I told Satsy I'd check out the freight elevator. His story is so disturbing that . . . Well, it really seems like someone should take a look. And experience suggests we can't rely on Fenster's to do it."

Rick looked at his watch. "Jeff hasn't been on the floor that long, and I haven't clocked in yet—so, officially, I'm not even here. Why don't I come with you?"

"I was kind of hoping you'd offer," I admitted. The experience Satsy had described made me anxious about investigating the elevator on my own.

"Then let's go take a look," Rick said. "You're right about both things: Someone needs to do this, and Fenster's won't bother until someone actually gets hurt."

The store was keen on profits, obsessed with shoplifters, rigid about rules and punctuality . . . and very slack about safety.

I said, "Yeah, I'll bet you that despite Miles' promise to Jonathan's mother to have security 'scour' this floor, they never even showed up."

"Who's Jonathan?"

"Oh. I guess Satsy didn't tell you that part of the story? Come on, I'll tell you on the way to the elevator."

Following the route which Satsy had mentioned to me earlier, we cut behind the solstice mural and then proceeded across the fourth floor, finally going through the "Employees Only" doors at the other end of Solsticeland and coming to a halt at the freight elevator. I pressed the button to call it—and saw from the numbers that lit up on the panel that it was currently down on the same level as the docks. So it had evidently been used since Satsy's scary experience. I wondered if anyone else had been terrorized inside its confines.

When the elevator car got to our floor and the doors swished open, we looked inside.

After a moment, I noted, "Well, Satsy did say it looked perfectly normal when he left."

And it looked perfectly normal now. Just an ordinary elevator car, big enough to carry large freight, with a scuffed floor and fluorescent lights.

"Let's make sure," Rick said, entering the car. "Why don't we take a ride?"

"What?" I blurted, hanging back.

Seeing my anxious expression, he said, "You wait here. That way if anything goes wrong—"

"No, I'll come, too," I said, shamed into accompanying him. I entered the car and pressed the button for the bottom floor. "Let's be thorough."

Rick said, "And whatever happens, let's keep our heads and not start another stampede of Santa's visitors, okay?"

I nodded. I wouldn't have done this alone, not after what Satsy had told me; but Rick's calm manner was easing my tension as the elevator descended. When we reached the bottom floor and the doors opened, I pressed the button to go back up to the fourth floor. A few moments later, we arrived there without incident. We exited the elevator, then turned around to look at it in bemusement.

"I suppose a more valid test would be to ride it alone, when no one knows you're there, the way Satsy did," I mused.

"I do have a theory." Rick said hesitantly, "Uh, do you know why Satsy went down to the docks?"

"I know it wasn't just because he likes a guy named Lou," I hedged.

"Right. Well, he's an imaginative person, a performance artiste, a creative . . . and he was under the influence of some pretty potent weed." Rick smiled and admitted, "I've visited the docks a few times myself, Esther, and that is some really good shit they're sharing down there."

"Did everyone know about this but me?" I wondered.

"I think that maybe the elevator stopped or malfunctioned—maybe even because, without being aware of it, Satsy leaned against a bunch of buttons at once, which screwed with the electrical system."

"And then he imagined all the rest?" I shook my head. "You didn't seen the condition his costume was in. There were scorch marks and places where it had been singed. It was a mess—even apart from all the smeared makeup."

Rick shrugged, unconvinced. "He was smoking on the docks. Maybe he got careless and burned a few holes in his costume."

"This was more than a couple of little spots from being careless while—"

"Maybe he still had the joint with him when he freaked out in the elevator, and he set his own costume on fire by accident, without realizing what he'd done." Rick added, "I've studied drug use in my psych courses, Esther, and there are instances of marijuana really messing with perceptions of reality. Also, it's possible there was something added to that joint which Satsy didn't know about—or that he knows about and hasn't mentioned."

"Hmmm."

Satsy *was* imaginative. And his interest in the occult ensured that, in an overstimulated state, his brain could certainly cook up the images and sensations he had described to me. So I recognized that Rick's theory was plausible.

On the other hand, I certainly knew by now not to dismiss a tale like Satsy's just because it sounded supernatural. My friendship with Max—Dr. Maximillian Zadok, a mage born in the seventeenth century and unquestionably the most unusual person I've ever met—has taught me that reality is much stranger than I ever imagined and that there are more things in it, Horatio, than were dreamt of in my philosophy.

"But that's just my theory. What's yours?" Rick prodded invitingly, "What do you think happened?"

"I have no idea," I said shaking my head. "But I do know that I'm not getting on that freight elevator alone any time soon."

He smiled again. "Actually, I don't think I will, either."

"And it bothers me that on the same morning that Satsy was terrified by a weird experience, this kid Jonathan was, too."

"Well, the boy's episode is pretty easy to explain, don't you think?" Rick's take on that was very similar to what Miles had suggested: a frightened young child, lost in a setting that strongly suggested certain things to his imagination. Rick added some background about child psychology and how a very young brain interpreted sensory information, and it sounded convincing.

"Yeah, maybe there really was only one weird incident here this morning," I said. "The one Satsy had." And since *that* experience had involved smoking some really good shit . . . I shrugged. Perhaps the bizarre events of the morning were indeed due to imaginative minds misinterpreting conventional experiences under the influence of stress or a psychoactive substance.

Even so, I decided to be thorough. Mostly because of how terrified that nice little boy had been. "I think I'm going to check out the area, though, and see if I can figure out exactly what scared the kid. I'll feel better if I know. And if it's something that might frighten another child, maybe I can get it removed from the floor." Miles might be persuadable; he wouldn't want another incident like Jonathan's.

Rick glanced at his watch. "I've probably got some more time before Jeff gets hot under the fuzzy collar and wants to swap out. I'll help you look around for a few minutes."

I smiled. "You really are Super Santa."

He made a wry face, as he usually did when someone used that name. "Well, we Santas have a big rep to live up to, you know."

"Of course." I was glad he wanted to help. With his knowledge of child psychology, I thought he'd be more likely than me to spot something that had turned into a terrifying threat in the little boy's mind. I led the way through the door that took us out of the delivery area and back into Solsticeland. "It happened way back near the North Pole."

"Let's go this way," Rick said, gesturing toward the path on our left. "It'll be less crowded."

Three main paths meandered through Solsticeland—which was overall an immense, winding labyrinth of side paths, loops, and dead ends where I still got lost at times. Getting lost was often part of the fun of visiting this place, of course—and not just for kids. Later in the day, our visitors would include groups of teens, couples on dates, and adults nostalgically revisiting their youth.

The path we were on passed by a giant hologram of floating ecofairies (I had no idea what an "ecofairy" was, but this was their official name), some little gingerbread condos that looked a bit like festively edible Anasazi ruins, and an elaborate manger scene. There was also a huge Saturnalia tree. I thought it looked exactly like the Christmas trees all over the store; but Jingle had told me emphatically that it was a *Saturnalia* tree, in honor of the winter solstice and in memory of the ancient Roman holiday which became Christmas after the empire converted to Christianity and needed to find a politically correct new frame for its popular pagan festival.

Many current Christmas traditions originated in the Romans' pagan Saturnalia, such as decorating the house with lights to ward off the encroaching darkness and with greenery to celebrate the imminent arrival of spring, as promised by the gradual return of the sun when the days start growing longer after the winter solstice.

Most of the rest of contemporary Christmas customs come from Dickens and Disney, Jeff had told me. And who was I to disagree?

Since night is longer than day during the winter solstice, and since the real North Pole is dark all season, the entire fourth floor of Fenster's was shrouded in nocturnal gloom to harmonize with those themes. Working for long hours beneath a dark, star-studded sky tended to make me sleepy during my shifts here. And it didn't strike me as a stroke of genius to have a vast immersive exhibit for children that was dark and shadowy; I thought Jonathan's experience here was starting to seem inevitable, if a little extreme.

In keeping with the multicultural concept of Solsticeland, scattered exhibits throughout the enchanted maze incorporated Hanukkah, Diwali, and Kwanzaa themes. As Preston Fenster had noted, Islam was not (yet) represented here, but speaking as one of the Chosen People, I envied Muslims for that; Solsticeland's Hanukkah exhibit was a collection of props that were simultaneously so garish and so stereotypical that they looked like leftovers from a Las Vegas casino production of *Fiddler On the Roof*. I was often assigned to work in the Hanukkah exhibit—where the predictable soundtrack, piped in through the speaker system, was always the sentimental squeal of klezmer music.

A marketing station was set up near the Hanukkah display for one of the season's hottest new products, a toy that Fenster's was promoting aggressively: Chérie the Chef. Since I worked this area a lot, I often got stuck demonstrating Chérie's selling points and urging people to buy her. As Miles had noted on a number of occasions by now, I didn't do it well or with sincere enthusiasm.

Chérie, a doll that was about twelve inches tall, made Naughty and Nice seem like flat-chested, fully clothed intellectuals who used admirable restraint with their cosmetics. She wore a tiny little apron—one that was better suited to a porn star than a child's toy—and not much else. She came with her own upscale kitchen, fully stocked with little plastic gourmet tools and food, so that she could whip up a five-course meal for her hungry man when he came home.

"I hate, loathe, and despise that toy," I told Rick as we walked past it. It pained me to see children and parents gathering around Chérie now, as they so often did, and expressing wonder and delight at her domestic attributes.

"Yeah, I think *all* the female elves hate her," Rick said. "And the male elves want to date her. Well, the straight ones, I mean."

"That's not exactly a big crowd." I guessed, "Maybe two?"

"I'm betting on three," he said. "Twinkle, Eggnog, and Thistle."

"Thistle, I agree. Eggnog, maybe. I haven't really worked with him." All I knew about Eggnog was that he had an MA in literature from Princeton, which is what *everyone* knew about him. You couldn't spend five minutes around Eggnog without him bringing up the subject, always with the shrieking subtext that elfdom was beneath an individual of his intellect and education. Frankly, I felt elfdom was beneath me, too; but I didn't cite credentials to prove it every time I opened my mouth.

"But Twinkle?" I said doubtfully. "Would a straight man really go along with being called *Twinkle?*"

We didn't necessarily get to choose our elf names, but we could object to an assigned name and suggest an alternative. I had objected to the attempt to name me Tannenbaum, the handle used by my predecessor in this role; she was a gentile who'd evidently been unaware it wasn't a Jewish name, but rather the German word for a Christmas tree.

"I think that Twinkle assumes we enjoy the witty irony of the name, given his obvious heterosexual masculinity." When I gave Rick a peculiar look, he added, "I'm telling you what I think *he* thinks."

"Oh." I thought it over. "Well, maybe."

As we continued our trek through Solsticeland, we enjoyed a jaw-wagging gossip session about our co-workers.

Princess Crystal had been caught smoking on the job again yesterday and received her second warning. Similar to me in age, size, and physical type, Crystal was also an actress. I assumed that her throaty voice was the result of her two-pack-a-day habit. She spent her breaks puffing away on the fire escape overlooking the outdoor ventilation shaft, regardless of the weather and despite the logistical difficulty of squeezing into that small and dirty area in her voluminous, sparkling white ball gown. She also often sneaked a cigarette while on the job, hiding in various spots around the store and puffing away . . . as if she believed no one would notice the smoke. I was a little surprised that management had only caught her twice so far.

Princess Crystal's primary workstation was Solstice Castle. The castle and its snowy grounds bordered one side of the Enchanted Forest, while the North Pole bordered the other. The North Pole was very popular with children, of course; it was also a favorite with adults who recalled their own childhood visits to Fenster's Holidayland, as it had been known back in the day. But the most-visited attractions on the fourth floor (except for Santa himself) were Solstice Castle and the Enchanted Forest. Neither of these immersive exhibits were holiday-themed (nor did they strike me as noticeably relating to solstice), but visitors loved them.

The castle was a pseudo-medieval fairytale structure, bigger than my apartment, built all in sparkly white-and-silver, with little pepper-pot towers, battlements, and a glittering moat. Children could venture through the various rooms of the pint-size castle and climb spiral steps ascending the mini-towers.

Princess Crystal spent much of her time on the castle's ramparts, gazing across the Enchanted Forest in hopes of seeing Prince Midnight coming to beg for her hand in marriage (which he did several times per day; it was a popular performance). The prince was played by Rafe, a model who never buttoned his flowing white shirt, no matter how chilly the store got.

"That guy just doesn't seem to feel the cold," Rick noted.

"Neither do Naughty and Nice," I grumbled.

When not proposing to Princess Crystal, Rafe could usually be found posing for pictures with gushing female shoppers, many of whom asked for his autograph. I didn't have the impression that Rafe's feverish networking with visitors was getting him that big break he kept talking about, but rumor had it that he was getting laid by enthusiastic Fenster customers every night after he clocked out.

"I don't have Rafe's abs," Rick said, "but sometimes I wish I could switch costumes with him, anyhow. My Santa suit gets pretty hot after half a shift under those lights in the throne room, with wailing toddlers being shoved onto my lap, one after another, while bickering parents take photos."

Elfdom was tough, but being Santa was certainly no picnic.

"I just wish I didn't jingle every time I move. It gets irritating after the first four or five hours of a shift," I said. I was sometimes tempted to sabotage my costume by removing the little bells from my cap and my boots. "And these ears chafe by the end of a twelve-hour day."

"But if you took off the pointy ears," Rick reminded me, "even *more* guys might mistake you for a hooker or a cocktail waitress when you're working on the other floors."

"True."

Although I experienced occasional problems due to my blue and white costume not always being recognized as ethnic elfwear, there were seasonal employees whose outfits were even less easily identified with the holiday season. An Asian-American dancer had been performing daily in Solsticeland's Diwali display, playing Ganesh the Remover of Obstacles, the Hindu deity who looked like an elephant; he was among the staff who had stopped coming to work lately. A blond bodybuilder had been cast as Thor, the Norse god of thunder. He was usually stationed in a display with a Yule log and the solstice mural, which portrayed pre-Christian festivities in some vaguely Northern European setting. When things were slow, Thor liked to keep busy by bench-pressing the Yule log.

Ever since my first day of wandering the thematically mixed and physically confusing maze, I wasn't at all surprised that kids tended to emerge from Solsticeland with their worldviews challenged and their religious teachings in disarray.

When we reached the North Pole, currently full of visitors milling around, I studied the setting, trying to figure out if something here could be interpreted as menacing by a small child. Once the centerpiece of Fenster's Holidayland, the North Pole was now just a portion of Solsticeland. It had a comfortingly old-fashioned atmosphere, and I thought Constance Fenster had been shrewd not to alter this sentimental favorite when expanding the seasonal concept to create Solsticeland.

A cluster of elves' cottages surrounded Santa's large, gift-laden sleigh, their tiny yards decorated with candy canes, Christmas lights, and gingerbread men. Their roofs were covered with thick snow, as was a nearby little hill where elf mannequins, forever frozen in time, were sledding and playing. A painted mural behind them portrayed more elves skating on an icy pond. Santa's house was near the toy workshop, and a mannequin of Mrs. Claus was inside, eternally paused in the act of cooking a hearty meal for Santa to eat before setting off on his worldwide journey on Christmas Eve. She wore spectacles, a gray bun, and a long skirt; I usually found her appearance soothing after spending time with Chérie the Chef.

"Did the boy indicate where he saw his scary Santa?" Rick asked me, speaking in a low voice so that the visitors around us wouldn't overhear this.

"He pointed toward the Enchanted Forest." Now *that* was a place where a lost and frightened child might very well have felt threatened. At twenty-seven, I had at least two decades on Jonathan, and even I found the Enchanted Forest a little spooky. "But this is where the Santa images are, in the North Pole. Not over there."

"Maybe when he saw something scary there, he

imagined it to be Santa, because he's afraid of St. Nick," said Rick. "He might have left the North Pole to escape the Santa images here—which is how he wound up in the scariest part of Solsticeland, poor kid."

"Let's check it out."

The Enchanted Forest was a large, shadowy, area illuminated by the moon and silvery stars in Solsticeland's sky, as well as by little glowing lanterns posted every few yards. Being dark and rather eerie, the forest was very popular with couples, teens, and older kids. It wasn't aimed at small children—and that was the whole idea, Jingle had told me. In creating Solsticeland, the Iron Matriarch had established an overall holiday attraction that New Yorkers and tourists would make a point of coming to Fenster's to visit even if they didn't have little kids in tow.

Narrow paths in the Enchanted Forest wound between large trees with expressive faces, creepily twisted branches, and artistically twining roots (which people were always tripping over). Some of the trees' faces were animated and programmed to speak, startling visitors by greeting them, warning them to leave the dark forest, or asking if anyone had seen Princess Crystal lately. The princess sometimes roamed the forest, looking for Prince Midnight and asking visitors if they'd seen him; at other times, he roamed the forest, looking for her.

I often encountered Crystal and Midnight there, since the Enchanted Forest was one of my regular posts. One of these trees was programmed to exchange some scripted verbal patter and sing Christmas duets with an elf. The performance lasted about twenty minutes and was scheduled to run during peak visiting periods. I usually did it at least once a day, sometimes twice.

As Rick and I wandered the Enchanted Forest, I thought that many things in this part of Solsticeland might have frightened Jonathan, but I didn't see anything that might suggest Santa to him. Nor did I understand why that jolly image would become a menace in the boy's mind.

"Why do you think he might be afraid of Santa images?" I asked Rick. "I mean, I talked to the kid, and he was really eager to see Santa."

"Plenty of kids who like the *idea* of Santa are frightened by various physical manifestations of him," Rick said. "Santa mythology is colorful and safe, and it leads to very attractive tangible rewards for kids: presents under the tree. All kids enjoy that."

"No, Christian kids enjoy that," I corrected.

"Ah! Right," he said with a nod. "As a Jewish child, what did Santa symbolize to you? Your outsider status as a religious minority, excluded from the normative customs of your wider sociocultural matrix?"

"That was it *exactly*," I said. "I was four years old the first time I told my parents that I felt excluded from the normative matrix because there were no presents under the Christmas tree that we didn't have."

Rick laughed. "So even though it wasn't part of your family's heritage, you still saw the appeal of the Santa mythology as a child?"

"Sure. Who wouldn't?"

"Right. But encountering Santa in person can be very different from enjoying the Santa mythology. It can be a negative experience with unsettling ramifications, just the way that encountering the real-world version of *any* idealized fantasy can turn out to be disappointing or even disturbing."

I thought of Elspeth Fenster's recent disappointment upon encountering *The Vampyre*'s Jane Aubrey in reality. "I see your point."

"Since these are children, who process information differently than adults do, it can even be frightening and disorienting. Sure, many kids make the transition from their fantasy of Santa to the 'real' thing very comfortably. But for others, visiting Santa is traumatic," he said, as we continued poking around the Enchanted Forest with no real idea what we were looking for. "After all, the child is expected to speak with, get physically close to, and share wishes and secrets with a grown man he doesn't know, one whose features are largely concealed by a theatrical beard and a wig. An event that was anticipated with excitement—meeting Santa—turns out to be emotionally uncomfortable or even intimidating, and the child becomes upset."

I nodded as I thought this over. Never having visited Santa, I had no such memories to draw on from my own childhood. But while working as Santa's helper during the past couple of weeks, I had seen any number of children become tongue-tied with shyness upon meeting Santa. And there were a few kids each day who started crying in panic or confusion when their parents put them on Santa's lap. I had also witnessed children get cold feet at the last minute and leave without meeting Santa, after having waited in line for a half hour to see him.

I thought I also understood now why Drag Queen Santa had fewer such incidents than the other Santas. Satsy's absurdly long, glittery, purple eyelashes (accompanied by the rest of his elaborate eye makeup and his favorite lipstick) were so unexpected, they altered the focus of the encounter. Some children were fascinated and impressed by his lashes, others were puzzled or bemused; either way, this distracted them and defused their anxiety. Above all, many children laughed about the lashes, especially if Satsy batted them playfully; and their own amusement put them at ease, so that the visit with Santa was buoyant and fun.

Thinking of Satsy also made me realize that his terrifying entrance this morning may well have created the equation in Jonathan's mind between Santa and a scary creature. After that, although the boy hadn't been scared of Satsy, he had been terrified of whatever he saw—or thought he saw.

"Esther?" Rick called softly to me as he peered around a trio of trees clustered at the edge of the forest, close to the cloth-covered west wall and the maintenance area beyond it. "I think we may have a winner."

I trotted over to him and peered around the trees, too. "Hey," I said in surprise. "I didn't even know that was there."

Tucked into a hollow at the back of this trio of thick tree trunks, huddling in his little cave-like shelter, was a chubby gnome, dressed in red micro-velvet with white trim. I thought the gnome was cute, but also startling, hidden from plain view as he was. It was easy to see how a young child might find him frightening. His spiky teeth were bared in a grimace (or possibly a gnomish smile), and his eyes glinted in the lantern light.

It wasn't a portrayal of fangs and glowing eyes, but it certainly could have seemed so to a scared little boy who couldn't find his mother. I supposed even the gnome's little hands could seem like claws to a child on the verge of hysterics.

"So Jonathan bumped into this and mistook it for a monster Santa?" I said with a sigh.

"I think it's the most likely explanation," said Rick.

"Well, I can understand why it scared him, but I'm not going to suggest to Miles that it be taken off the floor. A child that young wouldn't normally be in here without a parent, and anyone older than Jonathan probably likes this little guy."

"*I* do," said Rick. "He's so ugly, he's cute."

I was about to agree with this when we were startled by someone brusquely barking, "Hey! You!"

We both turned around. The Russian elf stood looking at us. I noticed how well this dark, eerie setting suited her dour demeanor.

She gestured in the direction of the North Pole. "Black Santa wants break. Me, too. You both come now," she said imperiously. Then she turned her back on us without waiting for a reply and stalked off.

"I am not your servant," I muttered.

Rick started to call after her, then paused and asked me, "Do you remember her name. Is it Merry?"

"Now that *would* be witty irony," I said. "I think she might be Holly. But I'm really not sure."

"Well, either way, I guess we should hop to," Rick said. "Considering what she's normally like, I don't want to find out what she's like when she's pissed off."

"Agreed."

Rick went to clock in and don his costume, then relieved Jeff—whom I instructed to spend his break keeping an eye on Satsy. (Jeff protested that I'd lost the right to boss him around when we stopped dating four years ago, but I overruled him.) I helped Candycane herd Super Santa's visitors for a while, until Miles came along and ordered me to go promote Chérie the Chef to the afternoon crowds. (I protested that I found the doll a blatant symbol of oppression and objectification, but Miles overruled me.)

I was starving by the time I got my meal break late

that afternoon. While I was finishing the microwaved supper that I had brought to work with me, Satsy came into the break room, wearing his replacement outfit and fresh makeup. He looked ready to make children smile and laugh.

"That costume's not a bad fit, is it?" I said.

"Yes, it works—though I really don't care for these broad cuffs," he replied. "They're so last season. But it'll do. I've only got a couple of more shifts, after all."

"Do you feel ready to go back to work?" I asked.

He nodded. "I'll take over for Rick or Jeff. Whichever one of them needs to leave first."

I looked at the clock. "I've got to get back out on the floor. I'm supposed to do the next scheduled set with the singing tree." The program was due to start running in a few minutes. I put on my hat-and-ears, left the staff area, and headed over to the Enchanted Forest.

We were approaching the peak hours for business, and Solsticeland was packed with people. I had to squeeze through a seething throng of families in the North Pole and then elbow my way through the multitudes of meandering teens and adults in the spooky forest of fake trees. When I reached my destination, I felt a little disheveled, so I straightened my outfit while waiting for the program to start.

Right on time, the tree spoke to me, bidding me good evening. I expressed surprise, with suitably melodramatic gestures, at being addressed by a plant. The tree's lumpy face contorted in various animated expressions while it explained to me that I was in the Enchanted Forest, where *anything* was possible. Some visitors who were passing this spot paused and stopped to watch the performance. Others joined them as the tree and I progressed through a short scripted routine about Santa's reindeer, mixing up their various names and inviting the children in the crowd to correct us.

After a few minutes of this, the tree suggested we have a merry song, and it launched into a duet with me, accompanied by the music coming through its sound system. We sang "It's Beginning To Look A Lot Like Christmas," after which we exchanged a little more patter. Then we sang "Jingle Bells," "It Came Upon A Midnight Clear," and "Here Comes Santa Claus."

At the end of that song, I asked for a show of hands. "Who's been to visit Santa already?" Then: "And who's on their way to visit Santa now?" I gave brief instructions for joining the line to see Santa, and then I talked about the other exciting attractions here in Solsticeland, urging all my new friends not to go home without seeing these wonders.

While chattering away, I saw Twinkle trying to make his way through the crowd, somewhat hampered by his accordion. Glancing in the other direction, I noticed a couple of security guards hovering just beyond the gathered crowd. They were speaking with an authoritative-looking woman who seemed to be all business. The guards were an unusual sight on this floor, in my experience, so I wondered if Jonathan's mother had filed a complaint about this morning.

Coming to the end of my spiel about the multicultural exhibits here in Solsticeland, I turned back to my arboreal companion and suggested we give these nice people one last song.

The tree did not respond. It sat there, silent and inert. I wondered if I had unwittingly rushed through my speech and finished too early. I ad-libbed a little, to fill the silence. Still no response from the tree.

"Oh, dear," I said to the crowd. "My friend may have fallen asleep while I was talking!"

Some of them chuckled at that. I was wondering by now if the tree's complex mechanism had broken down. If the thing had stopped working, I'd have to wrap up the performance without it. I glanced around and saw that Twinkle was still within sight, the density of the crowd ensuring that his progress remained slow.

I gave the tree an admonishing poke as I said loudly, "If you won't sing another song with me, then I'll just ask my friend Twinkle to play something for me!"

And that was when all hell broke loose.

The tree came to sudden, menacing life. Its eyes glowed red, its knobbly face contorted into a snarl, and it *growled* at me. Startled, I gasped and fell back a step. I heard some of the crowd laughing, assuming that this was part of the show. The Enchanted Forest was, after all, a deliberately spooky setting where, as the tree had already said, *anything* could happen.

And that certainly seemed to be true as the tree's glowing eyes focused on me while it whispered in a harsh croak, "Kill . . . kill . . . *kill you.*"

6

I choked out a scream and staggered backward. We were *way* off script now.

A big, solid tree branch hit me hard from behind, knocking the wind out of me and sending me sprawling forward into the tree's face. The branch was one of the mechanical arms which were programmed to wave and bounce in time to the Christmas carols that the tree sang. It swiftly wrapped around me and held me pressed up against the horrifyingly animated trunk, which snickered at me as I was shoved against it.

The blow had stunned me, but I was so frightened that adrenaline flooded my system, working wonders. I quickly regained my senses, took a noisy gulp of air, and started screaming my head off.

This set off a chain reaction of gasping and shrieking among the gathered crowd, who by now realized something was wrong.

The tree's mouth, already stretched in a vicious snarl, sprouted long yellow fangs. I didn't want to find out if they were as sharp as they looked, so I struggled with all my might against the dense synthetic branch that was trying to force me closer to that mouth.

"*No, no, noooo!*" I was screaming.

"Dreidel!" Twinkle shouted. "*Dreidel!*"

I heard the mad, musical screech of his accordion as he wrestled his way through the crowd, hollering frantically for maintenance, for help, for security, for *someone!*

With my arms trapped by the encircling branch, I lifted my feet and braced them against the tree trunk, fighting the mechanical branch's effort to drag me closer to the snarling, fanged mouth. I was panting hard with fear and exertion, struggling for air as the thick, twining branch tightened around me like a python, bruising my arms and squeezing breath from my body.

Some shoppers grabbed frantically at the branch and tugged on it, trying to release me. Another animated branch swooped down and knocked them away, throwing them into the crowd with industrial strength and power. I heard more screaming and, out of the corner of my eye, could see people falling and tumbling.

"*Nooo!*" My voice was thin and shrill. I was starting to feel lightheaded.

More people approached the tree, trying to help me. Through the blur of my misting vision, as I fought my

terrifying captor and gasped for air, I could see elf outfits, reindeer antlers, the bright red of a Santa suit . . .
two Santa suits . . .

"*Esther!*" Jeff shouted, bounding toward me.

Pow! A long tree branch whipped through the air
like a catapult, knocking Jeff off his feet. He flew backward into Satsy, and the two of them tumbled out of
my fading vision.

"Cut the power!" a man shouted.

I heard the ear-piercing squeal of children screaming
and the heavy thunder of feet stampeding.

"*Cut the power!*" the same voice repeated.

A huge man in a parka hurled himself at the tree,
screaming, "*Yaaaagggh!*"

Two snakishly animated branches scooped him up,
working in unison, and tossed him aside like a rag doll.

The tree's menacing mouth started drooling, and I
recoiled from the foul odor that started to pour out that
orifice.

"Help!" I croaked, dizzy and weak by now. My bells
jangled as I kicked ineffectually at the trunk with my
dainty boots.

"Dreidel! I'll save you!" Twinkle cried.

I kept kicking weakly as the encircling branch that
was squeezing the life out of me forced me closer to
that foul-smelling, drooling, snarling mouth.

"What are you *doing?*" a man shouted. It was the
man who wanted the power cut—as if *electricity* were
the problem here.

"I'm saving her!" Twinkle cried.

Through my swimming vision, I saw the elf wave an ax near my head, and I found the breath to shriek, "No!"

"Give me that!" the same man shouted, his voice starting to sound familiar through the haze of my suffocation and terror . . .

The tree's animated eyes glowed red while it growled softly to me, "Kill . . . *kill* . . . I want flesh! And *blood.*"

I hoped I would faint before this thing took a bite out of me. I didn't want to be conscious for that.

There was a sudden, powerful reek of sulfur. Black smoke clouded the glowing red eyes; one of the orbs cracked, and pieces of plastic fell to the floor. The drool pouring from the fangs seemed to freeze in mid-motion. The whole tree went rigidly still. Sensing my opportunity, I tried again to free myself. But I was weak, and the python-like branch, though motionless now, wouldn't release me. It was frozen in position, as if it had mechanically seized-up.

Then I heard a loud *whack!* nearby, like an ax hitting wood—and the oppressive branch dropped me like a hot rock. Startled, I staggered away dizzily, tripped over the synthetic tree roots, and hit the floor with a thud.

As I lay there on my back, panting and staring up at the star-studded solstice sky, I heard footsteps. Then that familiar voice said: *"Esther?"*

I didn't answer. Just lay there. Breathing hard and savoring the feel of air in my lungs.

"Esther." Holding a big wood-handled ax, Detective Connor Lopez of the New York Police Department stood looking down at me. He was breathing fast. "Of course. I should have guessed. I mean, who else *could* it be?"

"Lopez?" I croaked, looking up at him in bewildered surprise.

"Are you all right?" he asked. "Do you need a medic?"

"Why are you holding an ax over my head?"

He looked at the ax as if surprised to see it in his hands. "Oh. I used it to sever the power cable to that . . . that *thing*. What *is* that thing?"

Still, breathing hard, I gaped at him in amazement. "Wow. The slogan is true. At Christmas, *everyone* comes to Fenster's."

"Actually—"

"Dreidel!" Twinkle was at my side, his accordion still strapped to his torso. It groaned noisily as he sank to his knees. "Are you all right?"

"I thought you were going to behead me," I panted, recalling the sight of Twinkle waving the ax near me.

"No, I was saving you! I was attacking the tree!"

"I didn't mean," I panted, "that I thought you'd behead me on *purpose*."

"I didn't think so, either," said Lopez, shifting the ax to one hand. "Either way, though, it seemed like a good idea to take it away from him."

"Fuck *me*," said Candycane. "Twinkle, you could have killed her with that thing!"

Still lying flat, my heart racing in reaction to the attack, I glanced around and saw numerous anxious elf and reindeer faces looking down at me.

"I think *that* thing could have killed her." Prancer pointed to the tree. (Or maybe it was Dancer. Or Comet. A big, fuzzy, brown sock-puppet with antlers, anyhow.) "What the hell happened?"

"I'd say it was the mother of all mechanical malfunctions," Lopez said in disgust. "Don't they do maintenance around here? Safety checks?"

"No," said several employees in unison.

"For chrissake." Lopez shook his head. "What do they *think* will happen if they neglect proper maintenance on a thing like that—that . . . What *is* that thing, anyhow?"

Jingle's face hovered directly above me. He must have clocked in recently, since I hadn't seen him before.

"Dreidel! Are you okay?" Without waiting for my reply, he turned around and made the general announcement, in a loud voice, "Dreidel is all right!"

I heard a faint—very faint—cheer sweep through the Enchanted Forest in response to this news.

"You're sure you're okay?" Twinkle asked me.

"I'll live." I was profoundly grateful to be able to say those words.

"That was scary," said Jingle. "We nearly lost a good trainee!"

Lopez said, "Okay, everyone please take a step back and give Esther—uh, Dreidel—some room to breathe. Come on—*back,* everyone."

My co-workers complied. People often complied when Lopez gave orders. Not me, really, but lots of other people.

Born to a Cuban-immigrant father and Irish-American mother, Lopez was in his early thirties, slightly under six feet tall, with a slim, athletic build. He had straight black hair, dark golden-olive skin, and long-lashed blue eyes. The strength in his attractive face kept it from being pretty, despite his full, lush mouth. And although patience was one of his virtues, he wasn't someone you'd want to mess with.

"Where'd that *ax* come from?" Candycane asked. "We have *axes* here?"

Jingle said, "There's an emergency station next to the North Pole. This was covered in your training, Candycane. Fire extinguisher, first aid kit, ax, and so on. And getting that ax was good thinking, Twinkle!"

"Actually, I took it from a kid who'd gotten it," Twinkle admitted. "He could barely lift it, but he had the right idea."

"No, stupid idea," the Russian elf said brusquely. She added to Lopez, with grudging approval, "But you were cool-headed. Using ax to cut power. Much more intelligent than whacking tree."

"He's supposed to be cool-headed in a crisis," I said, still breathing hard. "He's a cop."

"A cop?" Twinkle bleated. "A *cop?*"

"Yeah, I'm a cop. But we're cool about the ax, so calm down." Lopez asked me again, "Esther, are you sure you're all right?" He knelt beside me and put his hand on my wrist. I thought this was an affectionate gesture until I realized he was checking my pulse.

"Yeah, I think I'm okay," I said, pulling away from his hand. *I* knew my heart was still racing. I didn't see that it would help matters for him to know it, too. "Just really shaken. And . . . ouch." I shifted uncomfortably. "Bruised."

Well aware, it seemed, of why I had rejected his touch, Lopez firmly put his hand on my wrist again, kneeling beside me in silence while he checked my heart rate. I noticed he was wearing a dark wool coat over a navy blue suit. The formality of his attire made me suspect he was at Fenster's as a detective, not a shopper.

He let go of my wrist, then slipped his hand into mine. Now that *was* an affectionate gesture. I felt the suddenly intent gazes of Santa's helpers on us as he said, "I want an EMT to look at you. They should be here any minute."

"When did you have time to phone in an emergency?" I asked.

"Someone else has done it by now." Confirming the suspicion that was forming in my mind, he said, "There are other cops here."

"Because of Jonathan?" I blurted. That kid's mom must have been really *mad*.

"Who's Jonathan?" he asked.

"A little boy who had a bad scare here this morning."

"Oh. Well, that's not hard to believe." Lopez glanced up at the tree. "But, no, that's not why we're here."

No, of course not, I realized. Lopez was a detective in the Organized Crime Control Bureau. I didn't think anyone was worried that Jonathan had encountered loan sharks or witnessed a professional hit in Solsticeland.

"Cops? There are *cops* in the building?" bleated Twinkle. *"Why?"*

Lopez said to him, "When the EMTs get here, ask them to come see Est . . . Dreidel. Go to the entrance of this place and wait for them. Go *now*."

Twinkle rose to his feet—assisted by two reindeer, since his accordion made the process awkward. "I won't fail you!"

"Good to know."

As Twinkle departed, I said to Lopez, "I really don't think I need an EMT."

"And I hope you're right. But humor me, okay?" he said as he set down his ax.

"Don't put down that ax!" I shrieked.

The elves and reindeer collectively fell back another step.

Lopez blinked. "Okay. I won't. Stay calm." He picked up the ax again. "I've got it. See?"

"I just mean . . ." I took a long, deep breath, trying to calm myself. "I mean, don't leave the ax lying around."

I had no doubt that what had just happened was a mystical incident, not a mundane one. And whatever force was animating that tree had dissolved *before* I heard the ax hit the floor and cut off the electrical power. The overloaded mechanics of the paralyzed tree had relaxed and released me when it was severed from Fenster's system; but it had already been abandoned by whatever Evil had caused it to act with such menacing violence.

I didn't know what had incited the tree to attack, or why it had stopped attacking. And I didn't know whether—or when—it might attack *again*. So I was emphatically against leaving a deadly weapon lying around within reach of its long branches.

Jingle said, "That's a good safety tip, Dreidel. I'll go put this ax away in a safe place. You can hand it over to me, officer."

Lopez looked at me to check my reaction to this.

I nodded my assent, adding to Jingle, "Stay away from that tree."

"It can't hurt anyone now," Jingle said soothingly.

"Oh, yes, it can," I said grimly.

Putting this incident together with what Satsy had told me about the freight elevator, I realized that the drag queen was right: There was something at Fenster & Co. that didn't belong here; something evil.

As I started to get up off the floor, I had a feeling I knew what I would see when I looked at the tree.

"Esther," Lopez said, trying gently to prevent me from rising, "I want you to wait until an EMT has had a chance to—"

"I'm fine," I said. "Help me up."

"I really think that . . ." He blew out his breath on a resigned sigh as I placed a hand on his shoulder to steady myself and rose to my feet. ". . . you should just ignore whatever I say and act as if absolutely nothing dangerous has just happened to you."

I took a few more deep breaths to steady myself, then cautiously approached the tree. As I had expected—as had been the case with the freight elevator—it looked normal now. It was completely dormant, severed from its power source, and one of its eyes was still ruined. But there was otherwise no sign at all of what had just happened. No fangs, no remnants of drool, no odor. Nothing.

I turned around and said to my colleagues, who were all watching me examine the tree, "Did anyone else hear the voice?"

"The voice?" asked the Russian.

"What voice?" asked Lopez, who was also examining the tree now.

"There was a voice saying it would kill me," I said.

"I heard a voice, but I didn't hear *that*," said Eggnog, the prince of Princeton, giving me a peculiar look.

"What did you hear?" I pounced.

"Well, to be honest, I wasn't paying that much attention to what it said. I was mostly, you know, trying not to get clobbered by a branch," he said. "But I thought it was reciting reindeer names."

"*That's* eerie," said one of the reindeer.

"No," said Candycane, "that's just part of its programmed patter."

"Did *anyone* hear it saying it wanted to kill? That it wanted flesh and blood?" I asked impatiently.

The elves and reindeer all looked at each other in perplexity and shook their heads.

"I only heard screaming," said the Russian.

"There was a *lot* of screaming," a reindeer agreed. "It's all I could hear, too. Well, that and the *smack!* of branches hitting people."

"I did hear Twinkle shouting that he'd rescue you while he waved that ax around. It was like his dungeons-and-dopes game had finally come to life for him." Candycane pointed to Lopez. "And I heard *this* guy shouting to cut the power, but I don't know where the power switch is."

Eggnog said, "I don't think that was covered in our training."

I supposed I shouldn't be surprised. The screaming had indeed been loud (especially my own, until I couldn't breathe anymore), and the tree's voice had been soft—intended only for me, the victim, I thought.

"Did anyone see the fangs or the drool?" I asked, ignoring the way Lopez was looking at me now.

"Fangs?" Candycane shook her head.

"Drool?" The Russian made a face. "Who drooled?"

I felt frustrated, but I knew this happened all the time on *Crime and Punishment* and *The Dirty Thirty*. Police and prosecutors on *C&P* shows were always questioning witnesses who all gave them different accounts of an event, none of which tallied with each other or with the physical evidence.

I looked again at the tree and realized that, trapped as I was by a large branch trying to feed me to that drooling, toothy mouth, I had probably masked the tree's face from view for most people. Add in the screaming, the confusion, and the fear, combined with people getting hit by flailing branches . . .

Lopez put a hand on my arm. "Esther, you're still shaken up. Maybe you should—"

"Did you notice the odor?" I asked him. "A really foul stench."

He sniffed the air. "There's no odor now. And I think it would be a good idea for you to—"

"Did *anyone* notice the odor?" I asked my colleagues, raising my voice.

Jingle returned from his errand in time to hear this, and he piped up, "Oh, yeah, that *smell*. Somebody messed his pants, for sure."

"No, that wasn't the smell," I said. "It was more like . . ."

"Like what?" Lopez asked.

"I don't know. Indescribable. Like nothing I ever smelled before." And I hoped never to smell anything that revolting again. "There was also sulfur, I thought. Did anyone else smell that?"

Eggnog said, "I thought I smelled something burning, maybe. But I wouldn't say *sulfur.*"

"You probably did smell something burning," Lopez said with a glance at the tree. "It's lucky that thing didn't start an electrical fire."

"No one else smelled anything?" I prodded.

"We were a little preoccupied," Candycane pointed out. "Oh! But now that you mention it, I did smell something foul."

"Yes?" I prodded eagerly.

She nodded. "Like, um . . . mothballs."

"Mothballs?" I repeated, feeling deflated.

"Mothballs," she said with conviction.

"Oh! I think that was me," said Prancer (or whoever). "My costume I mean." He held out one fuzzy arm for Candycane to sniff.

She did so and made a face. "Oh. It *was* you."

Oh, well. I sighed in resignation. My friend Max had told me any number of times that when confronted with mystical phenomena, most people interpreted the events in terms that made sense to them—such as a massive mechanical malfunction—and ignored that which they could *not* make sense of within conventional boundaries. And I had by now seen him proved right quite a few times about that.

"Well, I think we've all learned a valuable lesson here," Jingle reflected.

"Oh? And what would *that* be?" Eggnog asked.

"Training pays off," said Jingle. "The outcome of this incident might have been very different without our training. And I'm sure Dreidel agrees!" He concluded, "Very glad you're okay, Dreidel. Now I've got to get back to my station. Those toy army tanks won't just sell themselves, you know!"

As Jingle trotted off, I looked after him in bemusement, unable to see any way in which my elf training had helped me survive this brush with arboreal asphyxiation.

7

The other elves and reindeer decided to follow Jingle's example and get back to their posts. They traipsed off in different directions, chatting in amazement to each other about what had just happened and condemning the careless safety standards of Fenster & Co.

Avoiding Lopez's questioning gaze, I looked around the Enchanted Forest. A number of security guards were hovering in the area. They didn't seem to be *doing* anything, which certainly fit with my expectations of Fenster's security by now; but they were there. I noticed a woman talking into a police radio and realized she was the same woman I'd seen conferring with a couple of guards right before the attack began. I supposed she was a colleague of Lopez's.

A uniformed police officer was talking with the big man who had been thrown across the room after trying to rescue me. I was relieved to see he didn't look hurt. Most of the shoppers had already left the area—either when people fled in panic, or after being encouraged to vacate the area once the emergency was under control. I saw an unfamiliar man in a suit encouraging stragglers to depart, and I had a feeling he was another cop.

Lopez asked me, "What exactly happened here? I got off the elevator at this floor—an elevator, by the way, that's *also* malfunctioning. And—"

"What happened with the elevator?" I could see from his expression that my overreaction concerned him, given what I'd just been through and the strange things I was saying. Before he could suggest that I let an EMT give me a tranquilizer, I took another calming breath and asked more rationally, "What happened with the elevator?"

Eyeing me warily, he said, "It just sat on the sixth floor, the doors opening and closing, opening and closing. It wouldn't go anywhere for about five minutes."

I wondered if something had been deliberately trying to prevent Lopez from getting here, or whether he had merely experienced an actual mechanical malfunction.

Then I realized what else he had said.

"You were just on the sixth floor? Were you meeting with the Fensters?" I remembered what the family had said about the armed robberies. *"Oh.* The hijackings?"

"Is that guess due to staff gossip, or have you been watching the news?"

"The Fensters told me about it."

"Are you close to them?" he asked in surprise.

"*God*, no."

That made him grin.

"The information kind of slipped out when I was . . . Oh, never mind." I waved away that subject and asked, "So the elevator didn't do anything else that was . . . strange?"

Lopez glanced at the tree. "You mean, attack people? No. Nothing like this." After a moment, he said, "Anyhow, I got off on this floor and started walking in this direction—and suddenly I heard all this screaming from in here."

While he was speaking, I looked over his shoulder and was relieved to see Jeff and Satsy approaching us. Satsy looked unharmed. Jeff had a few bright red drops of blood on his Santa beard—from his lower lip, I guessed, which looked swollen and bruised. And he was limping a little. I recalled seeing the tree swat him away like a tennis ball.

"I broke into a run and followed the noise," Lopez said, "but I had trouble finding the source. Is there a straight line anywhere in this whole damn place? It's all dead ends and circles and . . . Anyhow, I finally find this spot. And I see *that* thing waving its arms convulsively, knocking people around, and almost electrocuting a girl in a clown costume."

"I'm not a clown," I said. "I'm Santa's Jewish elf."

"That was going to be my second guess." He looked at the tree again. "What exactly *is* that thing, anyhow?"

Coming up beside him, Jeff said, "It's an enchanted tree. It does stage patter and musical duets with—"

"Agh!" Lopez let out what could only be described as a little shriek and fell back a step when he saw Jeff.

Jeff gave him a peculiar look. "We've met before, detective. I'm . . . Oh! Sorry." Jeff took off his cap and pulled down his white beard. "Jeff Clark. Remember? We met this summer at the Livingston Foundation, when you were investigating there."

Lopez said a little breathlessly, "Right. Of course. Sorry, Jeff. Yeah."

"Jeff, are you all right?" I asked.

"Yeah," he replied. "A little battered and bruised, but nothing that a couple of cold beers can't cure. How about you?"

"I'm fine." Noticing how pale Lopez looked now, I asked him, "Are *you* all right?"

"Fine."

"You look a little—"

"I'm fine."

Right behind them, Satsy asked anxiously, "Are you sure you're okay, Esther? That was so scary!"

Lopez looked over his shoulder at Satsy, flinched, and blurted, "Jesus!"

"Are you *sure* you're all right?" I asked him.

"You shouldn't sneak up on people like that," Lopez said to Satsy.

"We've met before, too, detec . . ." Satsy blinked his

purple eyelashes a few times, then said, "Ohhh . . ." He pulled down his Santa beard and said, "Sorry, Detective Lopez. I didn't realize."

"Realize what?" I asked.

"Oh!" Jeff said, his eyes widening as he looked at Lopez. "Seriously?"

"Seriously, what?" I said.

"Nothing," said Lopez.

Satsy asked him, "Is this really a good place for you to be? I mean . . ."

"Esther! Are you all right?" Rick came trotting in from the North Pole. "I was in the break room. I just heard what happened!"

Lopez drew in a sharp breath through his nostrils when he saw Super Santa. A muscle in his jaw worked tensely.

"I'm fine," I said. "Actually, Jeff got hurt more than I did."

While Rick took a look at Jeff and asked him some medical-sounding questions, I said quietly to Lopez, "Are your teeth clenched?"

"How many more of them are there?" he asked in a low voice.

"Them?" I repeated, not understanding.

Looking uncomfortable, he stepped closer to me and muttered, "Santas. Just so I know. How many more of them are lurking around here?"

My eyes flew wide open as I realized the problem.

"Oh! You have a San . . . Um." Not wanting to embarrass him, I leaned close and whispered, "You have a Santa phobia?"

"It's not a phobia," he whispered back tersely. "It's just a—a—a *thing*. I find them . . . startling." He glared at the three Santas and added, "Especially when they creep up on me from behind."

"Oh, my gosh," I said, looking at him in wonder. "That must be so inconvenient at this time of year. How do you manage—"

"I just don't like it when they sneak up on me, okay? I'm fine otherwise." He glared at the Santas. "Do there have to be so *many* of them?"

"Probably you should stay out of the North Pole while you're here," I said.

"Where's that?"

I pointed. "It used to be Holidayland. But maybe you didn't go there as a child. Given your problem—"

"It's not a problem. It's just a . . . a *thing*."

"—I'm guessing your parents didn't bring you here?"

"Just the once," he said darkly.

"Why are all three of my Santas on the floor at the same time?" Miles demanded, approaching us from the direction of Solstice Castle. "And in here? *This* isn't Santa's station."

"Chill, Miles," said Jeff. "We're checking on Esther. Thanks to the shoddy maintenance practices around here, you were almost minus one more elf today. In a big way."

"But as you can see, Dreidel is fine," said Miles. "*Aren't* you, Dreidel?"

"Well, I—"

"Good."

I added, "But Jeff's been hurt—"

"We've closed off the Enchanted Forest for the rest of the evening," Miles said. "We're placing security barriers at the entrances to this area. The rest of Solstice-land will remain open. So let's all get back to work and let maintenance do their jobs."

"It's *very* lucky that no one sustained serious injuries here today," Lopez said to Miles. "When I come back tomorrow, I'm going to want to see proof that this incident is being investigated thoroughly and steps are being taken to prevent another event like it."

"There's *already* been another event like it," Satsy blurted. Ignoring my (admittedly unclear) signals to drop the subject, he continued, "This morning, the freight elevator went *crazy* while I was inside it! The lights went off, the thing started shuddering, and then it was bobbing up and down like a yo-yo. There were flames! Laughing and growling, too. I was terrified!"

We all looked at him for a long moment.

Then Lopez said to Miles, "Come to think of it, the elevator I was on a little while ago was malfunctioning. You people really need to overhaul this place."

Miles lifted his chin. "And who are *you?*"

Lopez pulled out his gold shield and showed it to

Miles. "Detective Lopez, NYPD. I'm investigating the hijackings."

"Oh, yes, the guys down on the docks have been talking about that," said Satsy.

"*You* hang out on the docks?" Jeff asked in surprise. "With those . . . Jersey Shore guys?"

I said to him, "I'll explain later."

"I'm here because of the hijackings," Lopez said to Miles, "but if Dreidel, Jeff, or anyone else had been badly hurt here today, I'd also be investigating criminal negligence and a pile of other charges I can think of off the top of my head."

"I *like* this guy," Jeff said to me.

"Of course, detective," Miles said, altering his attitude with the ease of long practice. "The matter is being given highest priority. Solsticeland is a seasonal destination, not a danger zone—and we intend to keep it that way."

"See that you do," Lopez said. "I don't want to hear about any more elves, Santas, or visitors being hurt or endangered by your props and displays."

"Absolutely understood, detective. And I *will* see to it."

"Good."

"Dreidel, do you feel ready to return to work?" Miles asked me.

"Oh, that's probably not a good idea, Miles," Rick said in protest, shaking his head. "Esther's had a shock. I don't think she should go back on the floor tonight."

Actually, now that I had calmed down, I pretty much felt fine; I'm seldom as sensitive as the men whom I know think I should be. But I started to agree with Rick's comment, because I wanted to get out of the store immediately and go confer with Max about what was going on here.

However, Lopez said, "Actually, I need to speak with Dreidel. After which, I think she should go home and get some rest."

"Speak with her? Has Dreidel done something that we at Fenster's should be aware of?" Miles asked.

Jeff said, "Yeah, you should be *aware* that she's just been mauled by one of your overblown props."

"Dreidel's not in any trouble. I just need to interview her." Lopez added, "I'll be talking to a number of employees in the next few days."

Miles looked offended. "I can assure you that employees in *my* department have nothing to do with the hijackings!"

"Ah. Right." Jeff nodded. "The hijackings."

"What's this about hijackings, anyhow?" Rick asked. "What exactly are you talking about?"

"You don't know?" Jeff said. "It's been all over the news lately."

"*All* over," Lopez agreed wearily.

"I don't have much time for news," Rick said. "I'm always *here*."

"Exactly." I nodded.

"Armed robbers have twice seized a Fenster truck

on the road and made off with boatloads of merchandise," said Jeff.

"Twice?" I said. "I thought three trucks had been hit by now?"

"I've only read about two." Jeff looked at Lopez for confirmation or correction, but the detective said nothing. So he continued, "And the local media's been putting a lot of public pressure on the Police Commissioner to crack down on organized crime this Christmas season."

"Oh." I looked at Lopez, too. "And the Commissioner has been putting pressure on OCCB?"

He nodded. Rick asked what OCCB was. Lopez replied, "The Organized Crime Control Bureau."

"Oh?" Rick said with interest. "So the police think this is a Mafia matter?"

"The media certainly think so," said Lopez. "But my job is to investigate the crime, not leap to conclusions just to boost ratings and ad revenues."

"Still," Rick said, "since OCCB is here, I guess that means there's some truth to it?"

"It means that we're public servants who respond to public safety concerns," said Detective Lopez, who was obviously disinclined to speculate about the perpetrators while chatting with Fenster employees. "And one thing the media have actually got right is that the hijackings are well organized."

"Well, it sounds like we *all* have a job to do here," said Miles. "So let's . . . Dreidel, where are you ears?"

"Oh." I put my hand on my hair. "I guess my hat fell off when—"

"There it is," said Rick, going over to retrieve it from the spot where it had fallen during the attack.

"Don't get too close to that tree!" I was still anxious about it.

He scooped my blue stocking cap off the floor and brought it over to me with a reassuring smile. "I'm okay. See?"

"Thanks." I accepted the hat from him and put it back on, feeling a little self-conscious as Lopez watched me don my pointy ears.

Miles said, "You know, I think Rick is right, Dreidel. You do look a little worse for wear. I suggest you go home and get some rest after Detective Lopez finishes interviewing you."

"Okay." Well, that had been easy, at least.

"Meanwhile, Santas, time to get back to work." Miles gave a little clap of his hands. "Chop-chop! And *I* will go check on Solstice Castle to make sure Prince Midnight's next marriage proposal will occur on schedule. We've got to keep the ship running smoothly after a mishap like this!" And off he went.

Rick said to Jeff, "You look like you need a cold compress on that lip and a hot shower for the rest of you. Why don't you go home, and I'll finish out the night with Drag Queen Santa."

Jeff nodded in agreement with this suggestion and

went to go clock out. "So long, everyone. See you to-morrow."

"Drag Queen . . ." Lopez was looking at Satsy with dawning recognition. "Oh, *that's* where we've met. You're one of Esther's friends from the Pony Expres-sive, right?"

Several other performers from the club knew both me and Max, who had helped them recover a friend who'd gone mystically missing. That was how we'd all met, actually. It was how I'd met Lopez, too. That had been a strange and annoying case for him, and I could see that he was ambivalent about encountering some-one again who was involved in those odd events.

Satsy, however, was pleased to be remembered. He patted Lopez's hand and said, "I understand com-pletely why you didn't recognize me, detective. This costume upset you."

"It just startled me," Lopez said uncomfortably.

"Oh?" Rick looked puzzled for a moment, then un-derstanding dawned. "*Oh.* I see. Hmm. You know, de-tective, a Santa phobia is nothing to be embarrassed about."

Lopez scowled. "It's not a phobia. I just—"

"It's far more common than you might realize."

That made Lopez pause in his denial. "Really?"

"Well, very common among young children," Rick amended. "Unusual in a grown man—very unusual, in fact—but not entirely unknown."

"It's not a phobia," Lopez repeated. "And I think

your boss made a good suggestion about getting back to work."

Eager to help ease psychological suffering, Rick said, "I don't have a license to practice, of course. I'm still just a grad student. But if you'd like to talk about your problem with someone, detective, I'm a good listener."

"It's not a problem," Lopez insisted.

"Or, if you prefer, I could refer you to a good psychiatrist," said Rick. "There's been some pioneering work in the past decade or so in the field of—"

"I'm going to interview Dreidel now. Go back to work, Santa. Little kids are probably waiting on line even as we speak, eager to meet you." Lopez turned to me. "Where can we talk without being interrupted?"

"Hang on, detective," said Satsy. "I need a few minutes with Esther. It's important."

Lopez nodded in acceptance of this. Rick departed to work another shift on Santa's throne. I led Satsy about twenty feet away, seeking privacy from the sharp ears of the NYPD, as well as the Fenster's maintenance and security people who were milling around the Enchanted Forest now.

"That wasn't just a massive electrical meltdown, was it?" Satsy said to me. "Something happened, didn't it? Something *evil*."

"Yes," I confirmed. I quickly explained my experience. I was disappointed to discover that, like the others, Satsy hadn't witnessed any of the phenomena that I was describing. "Not the smell? Or the fangs? Nothing?"

"We were coming from over there." Satsy pointed toward the North Pole, and I realized that from their angle, he and Jeff wouldn't have seen the tree's face. "And Jeff was in front of me, so all I really saw were some branches waving around and people fighting and ducking and screaming . . . Then *splat!* Jeff hit me like a giant bowling ball, and we both flew into that old display of penguins and baby reindeer playing in a snow bank . . . I think I blacked out for a few seconds. Anyhow, by the time we could inhale without coughing up fake snow and managed to stagger to our feet, the whole thing was over and Jingle was shouting that you were all right. So I staunched the bleeding on Jeff's lip before we did anything else."

"Hmm." I thought it over. "Well, maybe it's just as well that no one saw—or, at least, no one really recognized and processed—what *I* saw. It might be hard for Max to look into this if there were too much other scrutiny being applied to it now. As it is, what with the NYPD prowling around in search of hijackers, and maintenance looking for electrical problems—"

"Oh, I don't think we need to worry much about Fenster's maintenance," Satsy said darkly. "They'll probably just make sure the tree won't burn down the store, and not bother doing much else. They're not going to repair it with only three days left in the season."

I realized he was right. Slack safety measures seemed to be standard operating procedure around here. Moreover, with Preston Fenster determined to shut down

Solsticeland for good after this season ended, and with the rest of the family seemingly less organized than a random street riot, I suspected the homicidal tree might never get properly examined or repaired.

Satsy said, "So you *are* going to talk to Dr. Zadok about this situation? Good. That's such a relief!"

"Yes, I'll go over to his place after Detective Lopez is done interviewing me."

"Oh, the detective is looking *very* hot, isn't he?" Satsy said, enthusiastically distracted. "I think navy blue is really his color, don't you? It brings out those blue, blue eyes with those thick black lashes . . . He doesn't even use mascara, does he?"

I snorted involuntarily at the mental image this gave me. "No, I don't think so."

"But the poor man! A phobia can be *so* traumatizing."

"He says it's not a phobia." But I was skeptical that anything less serious than that could make a brave man as jumpy as Lopez was around Father Christmas.

"He's in denial," Satsy said. "That's understandable. People can be very judgmental, you know."

Looking at my three hundred pound, purple-lashed friend who usually dressed as a woman when he was working, I assumed he was speaking from experience. "I know, Satsy. And although Lopez didn't show it, I'm sure he appreciated that you were sensitive to his problem."

"Maybe you should encourage him to talk to Rick,

even though he was resistant to that idea," Satsy suggested. "Rick *is* a good listener, and his training gives him insight into people's little foibles. It might be a non-threatening way for Detective Lopez to start confronting his fear of Santa Claus."

"We'll see," I said vaguely. "Meanwhile, do you want—"

"And, girlfriend, there are *obviously* still sparks between you and the detective!" Satsy gave a little shiver of delight. "I mean, zing, zing, zing!"

"Satsy—"

"I really think you should go for it, Esther! Just grab that man by the—"

"Focus, Satsy," I instructed. "The subject on the table right now is the Evil at Fenster's, not my shipwreck of a love life. Do you want to come with me to Max's to tell him about what happened to you this morning? I could wait for your shift to end."

"Oh, I can't," he said. "You'll tell him for me, won't you? I have to go straight to the club to get ready for my first show as soon as I get off work here."

"That's a *long* day, Satsy."

"The show must go on." He added, "But I do think this is my final year here. It's not as much fun this year. And now it's dangerous, too!"

"Actually, I think it could be *everyone's* last year of doing this." I told him about the Fenster family quarrel over Solsticeland. "I wouldn't want to bet on how it'll be settled. Freddie Junior has got the deciding vote, for all practical purposes, but Preston's probably got more determination than the rest of the family put together. I think that may be the quality he inherited from his mother, more so than the other Fensters, even if he's not nearly as shrewd as she was, and probably not as ruthless."

"Oh, I met that woman, sugar, and I don't think there's a person in this whole city as ruthless as she was." Satsy shuddered a little. "But she did keep Fenster's running smoothly. If she were still alive, you can bet we wouldn't be short-staffed and having equipment problems, or having hijackings and the police prowling around here."

I suspected they also wouldn't be sharing weed down on the docks if Constance were still alive; but I didn't spoil Satsy's nostalgia by mentioning this.

"And you know what else? Evil wouldn't have *dared* move in here while Mrs. Fenster was still alive and in charge," my friend said. "It would have been too scared of her! Whatever is here now, Esther, I really think it waited for her to die first."

In which case, I supposed I was sorry, after all, that the Iron Matriarch was dead.

8

After Satsy returned to the break room, prepared to swap out with Super Santa at a moment's notice, I told Lopez, who was talking with a uniformed cop, that I was ready for our interview.

He nodded at me, but he was looking over my shoulder; something behind me had caught his attention. "Hang on a second, Esther. It's that guy with the accordion. Finally! What the hell took him so long?"

"Don't say 'hell' on the floor, detective," I admonished.

"Huh?"

"Never mind."

Having passed through the security barrier that was keeping people out of the Enchanted Forest now, Twinkle came trotting over to us, looking a little tired— possibly because he was still lugging around his instrument. He was alone.

"Still no EMTs?" Lopez asked with a frown.

I said, "I really *don't* need—"

"Oh, they're here," said Twinkle. "But right after they arrived on this floor, they got an emergency call to go up to the sixth floor instead, since there were no serious injuries down here."

"Why were they needed on the sixth floor?" Lopez asked.

"Mr. Fenster had a heart attack!"

"Whoa!" I said. "Just now?"

"Preston Fenster?" When Twinkle nodded in response, Lopez asked, "Did they say what happened?"

"Ms. Fenster-Thorpe said that when they heard about what had just happened down here—the tree going haywire and attacking people—Mr. Fenster went red as a beet and started screaming at the top of his lungs about how that was *it*, he was going to close down Solsticeland *now,* he wasn't even going to *wait* until the end of the season . . . And then he started breathing heavily, clutched his chest, and keeled over."

"Is he alive?" Lopez asked.

"Oh, yeah. Alive and kicking. They're going to take him to the hospital, but he's still upstairs right now," said Twinkle. "Actually, I thought he looked pretty good by the time I left to come back down here."

"You went to the sixth floor with the EMTs?"

"Yeah. I thought you'd want a full report, officer."

"Oh. Thank you."

"No problem. I was kind of curious. I've heard all

these stories about the Fensters from Jingle, you know, and I've seen them around the store—Oh! There's one now, in fact." He pointed across the forest. "But I never met any of them before."

I looked in the direction Twinkle had pointed—and I flinched when I saw her.

"What's wrong?" asked Lopez.

"That's Elspeth Fenster," I said anxiously. "Preston's daughter."

"Yeah? What's she doing down here?" Lopez wondered. "You'd think she'd want to be with her father right now."

"Oh, I don't think they're very close," I said.

"They're not," Twinkle confirmed. "I saw her upstairs, too. It would be exaggerating to say she seemed *glad* to see her father lying on a stretcher . . . Well, no, maybe not exaggerating."

What a family.

"But, actually, none of the family members seem that worried," Twinkle continued. "Not even Mr. Fenster himself. I gather this happens kind of a lot. Him having chest pains and keeling over, I mean."

"Even so," Lopez muttered, "you'd think he'd realize that one of these days will be the *last* time, and maybe make an effort to change his ways before then."

I nodded, keeping a cautious eye on the goth girl as I said, "Preston Fenster really does seem like a mortality statistic looking for a place to settle down and build a tombstone."

Elspeth looked this way and spotted me. I gasped and edged a closer to Lopez. He was armed; that might come in handy.

"It sounds like her dad might have reason to be a little tense around her," he said to me, "but why does she make *you* nervous?"

Elspeth started clumping gracelessly in this direction. I said urgently to Lopez, "She's one of the vamparazzi."

He frowned. "Are you sure? I know she looks the part, but—"

"Yes, I'm sure! We've already had a confrontation. I don't want another one." Losing my nerve, I slipped behind Lopez, standing on my toes to look over his shoulder at Elspeth.

"Okay, I'll handle this," he said soothingly, well aware of what I'd endured at the hands (and fists and feet) of the vamparazzi only a month or two ago. "Stay where you are. I'll deal with her."

Joining us, Elspeth peered at me over Lopez's shoulder, jerked a thumb at Twinkle, and asked, "Did this guy get it right? Are you the one who got mauled by the tree?"

I nodded, watching her warily.

"He thought you could've died," she said. "Is that right?"

"I guess so."

"So what was *that* like?" she asked with interest— and with a peculiar absence of any sort of sympathy or empathy. "Were you scared shitless? Oh, *did* you shit yourself? Elf boy says there was a foul odor that—"

"Miss Fenster," said Lopez, "don't you think your father needs—"

"Twinkle!" I blurted. "You smelled it, too?"

"I never implied it was Dreidel!" Twinkle said indignantly to Elspeth. "But, uh, I think *somebody* must have . . . You know."

"So tell me what it was like," said Elspeth. "Thinking you might die."

I stared at her with dislike, unwilling to answer. She had the right idea about Naughty and Nice, but she otherwise struck me as a repellant person. Her whole family was horrible, and her father seemed like a real bastard; but while that explained Elspeth's behavior to some extent, it didn't excuse it.

To be fair, I had met some very nice vampire fans during my sojourn as Lord Ruthven's hapless victim in *The Vampyre*. I had also encountered many perfectly harmless people among the vamparazzi.

I didn't know if Elspeth was the sort of vamp fan who physically attacked me, started violent altercations with other fans, stormed police barricades, broke into the theater, and/or rampaged backstage (the run of that show was one rough ride, let me tell you). Maybe, maybe not. I suspected she probably *was* one of the legions of fans who chatted on the internet about wanting to die in Lord Ruthven's (and/or Daemon Ravel's) toothy embrace; but this was only a guess.

But even if she was just a harmless vampire groupie with a healthy awareness of the difference between fantasy and reality . . . I found something really distasteful about the murky light of clinical and slightly malicious interest in her black-rimmed eyes now as she questioned me about the frightening and dangerous incident I had just been through.

Lopez evidently shared my opinion. He said, "Miss Fenster, I suggest you return to your father's side. He needs his family around him right now."

Elspeth snorted with amusement. "You don't know the family, do you?"

Lopez tried another angle. "If he's going to the hospital, he'll need an immediate family member present to assist with—"

"We have staff for that," Elspeth said dismissively.

"All the same, miss . . ."

Her gaze, which had mostly focused on me so far, now shifted to Lopez. She looked a little annoyed. "Oh . . . I'll bet you're one of the cops who was upstairs before, meeting with my father and my aunt."

When he confirmed this, Elspeth's gaze drifted down his body, then back up to his face. I could tell by the change in her expression that, now that she had bothered to look at him, she was recognizing what an attractive man he was. As the saying goes, he was a guy you definitely wouldn't kick out of bed for eating crackers there. Her attitude underwent another peculiar shift. Not friendly to him, exactly, but interested in him now. No longer dismissive. "What's your name?"

"I'm Detective Lopez."

"No, your *name*," she said.

"Detective Lopez," he repeated firmly.

That made her scowl. "What*ever*."

She looked away, avoiding his gaze after that, reverting to being dismissive of him.

"And since we still don't know whether this area is safe," Lopez told her, "this isn't a good place for you to be right now, miss."

"The little elf hiding behind you is the one who nearly got killed here," Elspeth said. "Not me."

"We're leaving this area in a minute, too," said Lopez.

In another swift change of attitude, Elspeth let her breath out in an exasperated gush, crossed her arms defensively over her chest, and looked around like someone waiting for a bus—which was something I suspected she had never actually done. "Is Rick around? I want to talk to him."

"Super Santa?" said Twinkle. "Yeah, I think he's still on the clock."

She rolled her eyes. "That *stupid* name."

"He's on the floor right now," I said. "He won't be able to talk for a while." It seemed very fitting to me, though, that Elspeth was seeking out someone with training in psychology.

"I'm heading for the throne room," said Twinkle. "Can I give him a message for you?"

Elspeth didn't even reply. Without bothering to take her leave of us, she turned around and walked away.

Twinkle called after her, "Oh, Miss Fenster? Do you think your aunt maybe liked my idea? I mean, I could go and talk to the guys in tech and give them—"

"She hated it," Elspeth said, without bothering to turn her head and look back at the elf. "It was stupid."

Seeing that Twinkle looked crestfallen, I asked, "What was your idea?"

"While I was upstairs keeping Ms. Fenster-Thorpe company, I told her I thought we could do a really cool display in the Solsticeland sky on Christmas Eve," he said.

"A bright star shining in the East?" Lopez said. "I think it's been done."

Twinkle shifted the weight of his accordion and stretched out his hands overhead, looking up at the starlit sky. "I want to stage a lunar eclipse," he said grandly.

"On Christmas Eve?" Lopez asked.

"Yes!"

"Why?" I asked.

"Because we're gonna have one on Christmas Eve!" Twinkle added, "I'm treasurer of the Astronomy Club at college."

"Of course you are," I said, unsurprised by this.

"A lunar eclipse on Christmas Eve!" Twinkle repeated. "Do you know what that means?"

"It'll be dark?" Lopez guessed.

"Uh-huh." Twinkle nodded enthusiastically. "Right!"

"This is solstice," I said. "It's dark all the time, anyhow." Or, at least, it sure *felt* like all the time, since I was always stuck inside Fenster & Co.

"No, *really* dark," said Twinkle. "The darkest season, the longest nights of the year . . . made even more profound on that holy night by a lunar eclipse!"

"Okay," I said. "Lunar eclipse. Dark. I get it."

"You *don't* get it." Twinkle's eyes gleamed behind his bottle-bottom lenses. "This is the first lunar eclipse on Christmas Eve in over four hundred years!"

"Four hundred years?" I repeated in surprise. "Wow. That's since before M . . ."

"Hmm?" said Lopez.

"That's a really long time," I amended.

I had started to say "since before Max was born;" but Max's age was a secret, for obvious reasons. He didn't want to get committed to a psychiatric ward. (Neither did I.) He also didn't want to become a science experiment, which was a fate he had already endured, albeit in other centuries.

Max had unwittingly drunk an age-retarding elixir prepared by the absent-minded mage whose apprentice he had been back in, oh, the 1680s. Decades later, he finally noticed—since *nothing* slips by Max!—that he was aging unusually slowly and still had the appearance of a young man despite being nearly sixty.

His colleagues in the Magnum Collegium—an obscure but important worldwide organization dedicated to confronting Evil in this dimension (apart from politics, which the Collegium shunned entirely, Max said)—soon became *very* interested in this phenomenon, and they insisted that Max submit periodically to various examinations, tests, and experiments. They wanted to find the formula which had altered his aging process. After a century or so of going along with this, though, Max decided to cease wasting any more of his long life in trying to find out *why* it was so long.

The other reason I'd stopped myself in mid-sentence was that I usually tried not to mention Max around Lopez if it wasn't strictly necessary. Lopez's "thing" about Santa Claus was nothing compared to how bad-tempered he could be about Max, whom he considered a well-intentioned but dangerous madman—and *that* was Lopez's opinion of Max on the days when he was feeling kind-hearted and generous toward him.

"A lunar eclipse on Christmas Eve is that rare?" Lopez asked, looking up at the Solsticeland sky. "And we'll get to see one this year? That's pretty cool."

I looked up at the fake solstice sky overhead and felt Twinkle's enthusiasm infecting me, too. I was impressed that, three nights from now, we'd witness a lunar event which had last occurred well before Max's birth.

I looked forward to telling my friend about it when I saw him later tonight. Although he probably knew, I realized. The movements of the celestial bodies seemed like the sort of thing Max would follow.

"I think reproducing the event on Christmas Eve in Solsticeland is a nice idea, Twinkle," I said. "Do you think Elspeth was right about her aunt hating it? Or was Goth Girl just being snide?"

"Well . . . I didn't really have the impression the idea went over well upstairs. Maybe my timing wasn't so good," he admitted, "pitching it to Ms. Fenster-Thorpe when her brother had just had a heart attack, medics and cops were all over the place, and—"

"Twinkle!" Candycane called irritably from somewhere in the North Pole. "TWINKLE!"

"Oops. I'd better get to work. Later, Dreidel. Bye, officer." The elf trotted off in the direction of Candycane's summons.

I turned to ask Lopez if he was serious about interviewing me on an official basis, but he was gazing across the landscape of Solsticeland with a frown on his face.

"I think we *are* having an electrical fire, after all," he said in alarm. "Is that smoke?"

"Where?"

"Stay here." Moving swiftly, he went through the forest toward the west wall.

I followed him. (Other people comply when Lopez gives orders. Me, not so much.)

He approached the same trio of thick tree trunks where Rick and I had located the grimacing gnome earlier today. And I realized he was right: There was smoke. I could see it in the dim light of Solsticeland now that I knew where he was looking.

But based on the way it was rising in a thin coil from behind the three trunks, then lazily dispersing itself through the surrounding air, I didn't think it was the start of an electrical fire.

"Oh, for God's sake!" Lopez said a moment later, and I knew for sure what the source of that smoke was. "Are you *kidding* me?"

I came to his side. He was so exasperated with our quarry that he forgot to be annoyed that I had followed him rather than staying where I was.

Her face and torso mostly hidden by the bunched-up folds of her voluminous white ball gown, Princess Crystal sat huddled in the hollow next to the grinning gnome, puffing away on a cigarette.

"What are you doing?" Lopez demanded.

I said, "She's having a cigarette."

"I can see that," he said with forced patience. "I mean, why here?"

Cigarette dangling from her lips, Princess Crystal said in her throaty voice, "I can't get out to the fire escape when it's not my break."

"What?" Lopez snapped.

"The fire escape is the only place she's allowed to smoke," I explained, "and only when she's on break. If she tried to go out there now, she'd be noticed."

Crystal took a long drag, then said, while smoke

poured from her nostrils and mouth, "God, it is *inhuman* to expect me to go so long without a cigarette!"

"But she can usually disappear for five minutes without Miles noticing, so she has some favorite spots around the store where she goes for a smoke." I added, "I didn't know this was one of them. Crystal, did you know this whole area is pretty much off-limits for the rest of the night?"

"Yeah, no visitors. So I figured I wouldn't be seen."

Looking as if he suspected she suffered from brain damage, Lopez pointed out, "There's been an accident here, and there are police, security guards, and maintenance workers roaming around this area."

"But no Miles!" she said triumphantly. "*Perfect* spot."

"You can't stay here," Lopez said firmly. "Come on, get out of there."

"Says who?" Princess Crystal challenged.

"NYPD."

"Shit!" She stubbed out her cigarette in the gnome's ear. "NYPD? Are you serious? I can't *believe* how strict Fenster's is about this!"

"Come on," Lopez said. "Let's go."

I stepped back, waiting for Crystal to emerge. There was some rustling of cloth, some grunting, and then more rustling, followed by some cursing.

She said, "I'm trapped! It's this damn dress. Can you help me out of here?"

She stuck her hands out of the hollow, flapping them at us. Lopez and I each grabbed one hand and heaved.

There was a moment of suspense, then Crystal and her dress popped out of the tree trunk like a cork coming out of a bottle.

She started straightening her billowing gown. "Damn it! You tore it! How am I going to explain that?"

Lopez said, "I'm sure you have somewhere you should be right now."

"Aren't you supposed to be getting proposed to?" I asked.

"Oh, crap, is it nearly time for that?" She grabbed Lopez's wrist to check his watch. "You're right. Gotta go!"

She lifted her heavy white skirts and dashed off, trotting through the Enchanted Forest toward Solstice Castle. From this angle, she actually *looked* like a fairy-tale princess running to meet her prince.

Gazing after her, Lopez said, "I'm starting to feel like I've fallen down the rabbit hole."

"Yeah, I think that feeling is to be expected around here."

"Does Fenster's keep these people locked away somewhere and just take them out every November, letting them roam the fourth floor for a few weeks before they go back into cold storage for another year?"

"Please don't suggest that to the family," I said. "It sounds like something they'd consider trying."

"Why are *you* working here?" he asked.

"I had some auditions, but I didn't get hired for anything after *The Vampyre*."

"What about Stella's?"

I looked at him in surprise. Since Bella Stella was a notorious mob hangout where several murders had occurred in recent years—one of which I had witnessed from about two feet away—Lopez had been candid about hating the fact that I worked there. Back when he and I had been dating oh-so-briefly in the spring, it had wound up adding a little strain to our budding romance that his bureau had my place of employment— and, by extension, me—under surveillance.

"Suddenly you're in favor of me working at Bella Stella?" I asked dubiously.

"Actually . . ." He shrugged and admitted, "I just need to know why you're *here.*"

I frowned for a moment, puzzled; and then realization dawned. "We've just had a scene change, haven't we? This is my police interview."

"Yeah," he said apologetically. "It is. I need to know—"

"Heads up! Coming through!"

Startled, we both fell back a step as a guy in coveralls came through the door in the west wall, behind which was a maintenance and storage area, pushed aside the dark netting that masked that wall, and entered the Enchanted Forest with a toilet plunger in his hand. "Don't panic! I'm here!" he announced. "Where's the trouble?"

"Maybe we should go somewhere else?" I suggested to Lopez.

"Good idea."

9

I knew we couldn't expect to talk uninterrupted in the break room, so I suggested going into Miles' office; the manager was likely to be making the rounds on the floor the rest of the night, given the disruption we'd had. His office was a plain, stark, small room with two uncomfortable chairs, which Lopez and I used, that were placed opposite the desk where Miles sat when he was here.

"Am I in trouble?" I asked suspiciously.

"No, you're not," Lopez said. "But I need some clarification."

"Of what?"

"You were a material witness when a Gambello *capo* got whacked. Now you're working for a company that's experiencing a series of hijackings in which the Gambellos are the prime suspects. So I need to know—"

"What?" I said in surprise. "The Gambellos? Really?"

"You didn't know? It's been all over the news," he told me.

"I haven't seen the news," I said irritably. "I'm always here! I haven't seen any Gambellos lately, either. By the time I finished *The Vampyre* and needed to go back to work at Stella's, she was already overstaffed for the season. She hardly has any shifts available for me until after the holidays, when the kids go back to college. So I haven't been to the restaurant since I worked a lunch shift there early last week."

"That's why you took this job?" Lopez asked. "Because you couldn't get enough hours at Stella's this month?"

"Yes. Satsy—Saturated Fats, from the Pony Expressive—told me there were jobs available here because performers keep quitting. In fact, some of them don't even bother to quit, they just stop showing up," I added, blaming Moody Santa, in part, for the rough morning I'd had. "So I was able to get a job here right away. Solsticeland is covering my bills until Stella can give me full-time work in January."

I noticed Lopez's relief at how logical my account was, and I recognized the significance of his interest in my reasons for working here. Feeling incensed, I added, "I resent the implication that I'm involved in the hijackings!"

"I'm not implying that you're involved," he assured me. "But as soon as your name popped on the list of Fenster employees—"

"My named *popped?*" I repeated, not liking the sound of that. "Am I in some sort of OCCB database or something?"

"Of course, Esther," he said, as if this should be obvious to me. "You witnessed a mob hit seven months ago. We don't keep your name pinned to a bulletin board or anything, but we didn't throw away those reports after we closed the case."

"Oh." I admitted, "I guess that makes sense."

"But it didn't pop that way," he added. "I meant that *I* saw your name. We're just starting to look at company employees, so we haven't run any matches yet. There's a separate, shorter list of seasonal employees, which I looked at as soon as we finally got it today." Lopez paused before continuing, "Your name jumped out at me. And I figured this investigation would go better for both of us if I took the lead on clearing up exactly what you're doing here."

"I'm helping Santa," I said. "And paying rent."

"Okay."

"Is this why you turned up on the fourth floor today while I was being strangled by a tree?"

He nodded. "After my meeting with the Fensters, I came down here to look for you, so I could ask you about this."

"Am I going to be grilled by your colleagues?"

"No. You're not under suspicion of anything. You were a witness to a hit, not a criminal accomplice."

Apparently not wanting to rake up old arguments,

Lopez tactfully avoided mentioning my friendship with certain members of the Gambello family. Nor did he mention my involvement, of which he had vehemently disapproved at the time, in exposing the culprits in that murder investigation.

He continued, "But if Gambello soldiers are the hijackers, then your connection to a previous Gambello case means that I need to know what you're doing here, and I need to be able to explain it to my lieutenant and the other investigators."

"Oh. All right." I definitely preferred being asked this by Lopez to being questioned formally by his colleagues, so I nodded. "Fair enough. Um, is that the end of the interview?"

"Pretty much." Seeming more relaxed now that he'd gotten an explanation from me which he could credibly share with OCCB, he leaned back in his chair, trying (without success, I suspected) to get comfortable. "Unless, that is, you've seen something unusual around here that you can tell me about?"

I wouldn't pick up that cue for all the Ben and Jerry's ice cream in the world.

Lopez had stubbornly conventional views about mystical matters. Although he liked me and cared about me, he thought I was a crackpot for believing in supernatural phenomena, let alone for attributing various mysterious, disturbing, and criminal events to paranormally empowered perpetrators.

I found his attitude frustratingly rigid for someone

who was, after all, a fairly religious Catholic. I didn't
know the extent of his faith, but I knew he'd been
raised in the Church and still attended Mass regularly.
And it's not as if religion is a bastion of logic and consistency, after all, or as if spiritual faith is based on reason and evidence.

Then again, human nature is rarely founded in logic
and consistency, either. And Lopez's dismissive attitude about the supernatural was a common position,
after all. Besides, it wasn't as if he'd witnessed the sort
of undeniably magical acts and events that had made
me a believer. There were certainly times when I
wished he would just take my word for something; but
I wouldn't have taken anyone's word for it, after all, if
I hadn't experienced powerful mystical phenomena
myself, up close and personal.

Lopez's conventional beliefs about this sort of thing
were also a big factor in his ambivalence (on a good
day) about Max. Which was pretty ironic, since Max
thought that Lopez might be gifted with mystical
power of which he was unaware. By now, I had started
to think that Max's suspicions about this had merit. I
wasn't sure, of course; and neither was Max. We certainly wondered, though . . . But Lopez himself clearly
hadn't the faintest notion of any such thing, and I knew
he would (depending on his mood) just be exasperated, bemused, or amused if we suggested it to him.

So there was no way I was going to tell him that Evil
was haunting Fenster's. I knew from experience that it

wouldn't get us anywhere. And I couldn't think of anything I'd seen or heard here that might be relevant to the hijacking case.

So I said, "Unusual? Hmm, do you mean something like—oh, for example—an enchanted tree attacking me?"

"That was a pretty disturbing experience." His expression changed and he looked concerned again. "I think I should get a police car to take you home now."

Since I didn't intend to go home, I shook my head. I also didn't want to explain to Lopez why I urgently needed to go down to Greenwich Village now to see Max, so I said, "I don't need a ride. It's an easy trip to my place from here." And that was perfectly true, in fact. Fenster & Co. was in the West Fifties, a couple of blocks south of Central Park; I lived in a shabbily comfortable rent-controlled apartment in the West Thirties, which was very convenient from here by subway.

Lopez was familiar with my apartment and knew this, but he still seemed concerned. So I added, "Look, it's not as if I'm afraid the tree will follow me home. I'll be fine."

"Hm."

I could practically see his thoughts in subtitles as he gazed at me, wondering whether he should insist on an escort or just drop the subject. We'd had conversations in the past that followed this route, and the scenery was getting familiar.

I was a creative, imaginative person (he was thinking), working in a weird and surreal place, suddenly endangered by a huge apparatus with spooky features and an audio program. I'd experienced a powerful combination of fear, adrenaline, and oxygen-deprivation in confusing and violent circumstances. All of which accounted for my high-strung behavior in the aftermath, as well as for my claiming some very peculiar things had happened during the incident.

The question in his mind now was whether I'd be all right, or whether I was more distraught than I realized.

I decided to get his mind off this question, which wouldn't lead either of to any place productive, by changing the subject. "Do you really suspect the Gambellos in these hijackings?"

He blinked, obviously having been lost in his thoughts. "Huh? Oh. Well, we're busily tearing apart their lives in an effort to find out, one way or the other. Pressure from the media and the Police Commissioner have put the family—and also OCCB—under a bright spotlight, so we're bringing a whole new meaning to the phrase 'thorough investigation.' By the time we've arrested someone, I'll probably know how often the Shy Don gets up to use the bathroom at night."

Victor Gambello, the Shy Don, had been the head of his crime family for decades. A contemporary of Constance Fenster's, he was now in poor health and extremely frail. We had met briefly once, after I'd helped expose a killer who was trying to start a mob war that would consume his family, and he'd declared his friendship to me.

"God knows the Fensters seem convinced the Gambellos are responsible for this," Lopez continued. "Hijacking trucks is certainly one of the Gambellos' favorite pastimes. It's sort of a family tradition with them. And they have a history with the Fensters, after all."

"They do?" I knew both families now, sort of, but hadn't had the faintest idea that they knew each other.

"Oh, sure. It goes way back. Hijacking trucks, knocking over warehouses, extortion. This all happened back when this place was still Fenster and Powell's." He paused, evidently remembering that I was from Wisconsin. "But an out-of-town girl like you probably doesn't remember that or know about the Powells."

"I've heard," I said. "Elves talk."

That made him grin. He continued, "A joint task force was assigned to the case. They made arrests, got convictions, and shut down the whole thing. So it all ended a long time ago. But because that history is there, now that someone is hijacking Fenster trucks again after all these years, the media have convinced themselves—and the public—that the Gambellos are the culprits." He added with a touch of exasperation, "Which is interfering with the investigation and which will also make prosecution a big headache, no matter who we arrest."

"So you aren't convinced it's the Gambellos?" I asked curiously.

"I'm looking for more evidence before I fall in love with a theory," he said. "But . . . I'm a little skeptical. There was a hot spotlight on them and on the hijackings by the time the third truck got taken. I think that made the heist feel . . ." He shrugged, looking for the right word. "Too daredevil for the Gambellos. Too flashy. Too *risky*," he added with a nod. "They're crooks, but this is business to them. And one of the reasons the Gambellos are so successful is that they know it's not good business for them to attract that much attention. So this just doesn't seem to me like the way they do things." He shook his head and concluded, "Their usual pattern would be to drop this plan like a hot rock the moment they realized every TV news camera in the city was suddenly trained on them—not to go knock over a third truck."

"So it *is* three trucks? Not two?"

Lopez nodded. "The media doesn't know yet about the first one, but that's bound to change any minute. And then the heat on NYPD will get even hotter, what with Fenster's being a Christmas favorite and all."

"The police kept the first heist out of the news?" I guessed.

"No, the Fensters did," Lopez said, his voice dry. "And they didn't call the cops."

"Seriously? Why?" Calling the cops struck me as a pretty self-evident thing to do after an armed robbery. Surely even someone as dim as Freddie Junior knew that?

"Esther, I just had a two hour meeting with that family and I *still* don't know why they didn't call the cops after the first heist," he said wearily. "*Or* the second one."

"They didn't tell you about the second robbery, either?" I said incredulously.

"Nope. The police found out the way everyone else did—when news of that hijacking got plastered all over the media," Lopez said, his face darkening with anger. "So we *started* the investigation with two trucks already hit and the media screaming blue murder that we weren't doing anything. And then the next truck got hit."

"Merry Christmas," I said.

"It's been a hell of a week."

"How did the press find out about the second truck, if the Fensters weren't reporting the robbery?" I asked.

"Freddie Junior told people about it. He's also how the press first got 'tipped' that the Gambellos are behind this."

"Why did he tell people?" I asked in confusion. "If the Fensters were trying to keep this a secret—"

"*I* don't know why!" Lopez realized he'd snapped at me and said, "Sorry. But have you met Freddie? It's like talking to porridge that's been sent to an expensive prep school."

"Yes," I agreed with a startled laugh, "that's exactly what it's like."

"Preston Fenster is in favor of letting the police handle this now." Lopez scowled as he added, "But he doesn't have control of the family, and they're not all on board with the crazy notion of bringing in cops to investigate a series of armed robberies."

"Why not?"

"Because they're idiots!" He added, "But you can't tell anyone I said that."

"Are they giving you any reasons?"

"For being idiots?" he grumbled.

"For not wanting the police involved," I said patiently.

"Well, Helen Fenster-Thorpe seems to think that *negotiation* is the way to deal with armed robbers, and the police should just stay out of it and leave this problem to the professionals. So I suppose she's one big reason no one called us."

"What would she negotiate *for*?" I asked in puzzlement. "I mean, it's not as if the hijackers are trying to do business with Fenster's, is it? They just disappeared with all the merchandise, according to Arthur."

"*Arthur*," Lopez said with a scowl. "I can't help feeling he's got to be the evil mastermind behind this whole thing."

"Evil?" I blurted involuntarily, having the subject on my mind today.

"It seems like he *has* to be the bad guy. He's the least likely person, which is always the one whodunit." He added sheepishly, "And you especially can't tell anyone I said *that*, Esther."

"I won't," I promised. "It's not a convincing theory, it's just evidence that you read too much Agatha Christie."

"I like Agatha Christie," he said. "I find her books relaxing."

I leaned back in my chair, also trying (without success) to get comfortable. "Tell me, Miss Marple, is there anything other than Arthur's cunningly obsequious personality that makes him a suspect? Does he—do any of the Fensters—have a motive?" A bright idea occurred to me, courtesy of *Crime and Punishment*. "Hey, could this be an insurance scam?"

"No, they're having trouble with their insurance claim because they didn't report the first two heists." He shrugged. "And our accountant thinks they're under-insured, anyhow. This seems to be due to cash flow problems—problems that are being made worse by losing three big loads of merchandise in the busiest shopping weeks of the year."

"So I guess it's not an inside job?" I said. "Not unless the Fensters are trying to commit collective fiscal suicide."

"In all honesty, I think their business acumen will ensure their collective fiscal suicide," he said. "But I do think there must be someone on the inside. These heists are *very* smooth. Planned and executed well. Someone knows which trucks have the most valuable merchandise, when they're on the road, and which part of their route is the most vulnerable—where no one will see the hijacking. It's not easy to escape in a huge, heavily loaded truck, after all, if someone witnesses you seizing it at gunpoint and calls the cops right away."

"That's why you're looking at Fenster employees," I realized. "You think someone who has access to that sort of information could be involved."

"So we've got to analyze Fenster's operations," he said with a nod. "Figure out how many different ways there are to access that information and then figure out who can get to it . . ." Lopez started to look discouraged. "In a flagship store the size of a small country, with hundreds of employees and lax security, plus satellite stores and an internet business . . ."

"I'm guessing you might not be home for Christmas?" I said.

"I won't be home for Christmas anyhow," he replied. "I'm scheduled for a ten-hour shift that day."

"Who did *you* piss off?"

Lopez smiled and shook his head. "I'm single and don't have kids. That pretty much makes Christmas Day my shift, along with any Jewish cops on the squad."

"Oh, I see." He may not have a wife and children, but I knew his parents still lived in Nyack, a suburb across the Hudson River, where Lopez had grown up. They probably thought his living so close to them, here in the city, meant they'd get to see their youngest son on holidays. "Are your parents disappointed?"

"They're used to it by now. It's been this way most

years since I joined the force. I always go out to their place right after I get off work, so I'm there for Christmas night. That's when we have dinner and exchange gifts."

"You go out to Nyack after a ten hour shift?"

"It's better than hearing the recriminations if I *don't* go," he said with a wry smile. "Anyhow, I like to go home at Christmas. I don't mind the trip."

I knew that his family was close, so that didn't surprise me.

There was a long moment of companionable silence, and I realized, not for the first time, how much I missed him.

But I didn't seem to be good for him. And, more to the point, I had nearly gotten him killed at least twice. Maybe three times, depending on how you looked at things. In any event, there *was not going to be* another time.

"Would he be lying in agonized paralysis awaiting his death now if not for you?"

I drew in a sharp breath when my imagination replayed those memories, sending a familiar and unwelcome chill through me.

Get out of my head, you murdering bitch, I thought.

"Are you all right?" Lopez asked me, noticing my sudden shift of mood.

"Huh? Oh. Um, tired, I guess." I glanced at the clock. "I think I'll hang up my pointy ears for the night and go."

"You're sure you don't want a lift home?" he asked, standing up. "Because I can easily—"

"No. I could use some air. The walk to the subway will do me good." That statement had the merit of being true.

Thinking of another bitch who had rattled me tonight, I said to Lopez as we left Miles' office, "And thanks for, you know, helping me out with Elspeth. She . . . she kind of gives me the creeps. And not just because she's one of the crazy people who made my life so needlessly interesting during *The Vampyre*."

Lopez grunted in agreement. "Meeting a girl like her almost makes me scared of having kids. I mean, what if they turn out like her?"

"Is your mother still nagging you for grandchildren?" I asked, guessing what had put the thought of having kids in Lopez's mind.

"Oh, only every time she gets the chance. It's become a mania with her. Especially since Tim and Michael are sticking to their stories. Those bastards."

I knew that he had two brothers, each of whom had invented a pretext to shut their parents up about grandkids. One had recently decided to claim he was gay, and the other said he was contemplating the priesthood. These lies struck me as short-term thinking, destined to be unmasked over time; but apparently they were holding up so far. Which left Lopez to bear all the parental pressure alone on this front.

"But I have to admit," I said, "meeting Elspeth's father makes me appreciate my own dad." I wasn't close to my father, but he was an okay guy. We didn't really connect, but I knew he meant well. "Actually, meeting the whole Fenster family makes me glad to have the family I've got—which doesn't happen that often. I might even call Wisconsin when I get home and say hello to my parents."

Probably I'd come to my senses and do no such thing; conversation with my mother usually makes me so tense I can't relax for hours afterwards. But it was rather nice to feel a nostalgic twinge of missing my family. It was a rare event, and rather pleasant.

I smiled as I added to Lopez, "Or maybe the sentimentality of your gentile season of love and joy is just getting to me this year."

"It must be the Christmas spirit at Fenster's," he said dryly. "Oh! By the way, Happy belated Hanukkah, Esther."

"Thank you." It had been over for a week.

"Did you do anything special for it?"

"I was working here the whole time. I sang Hanukkah songs for the crowds, but I only know three. Well, two and a half, really. So it got a little monotonous."

"Oh. I'm guessing you have to know more Christmas songs than that for this job?"

"Yes. Luckily, I do know a lot of those. I went to public schools, and I sang in the choir every year." I shrugged. "And it would be just churlish to try to pretend that Christmas doesn't have lots of great music, after all. I like Christmas carols."

"Do you do anything for Christmas?" he asked curiously.

"Well, given the hours I've been working lately, I think this year I'll probably just sleep all day. But I usually follow the Diamond family tradition of watching some movies and then getting Chinese food." I added, "Christmas is kind of a bond between Jews and Chinese for that reason."

"Well, at least you'll eat better than I will," he said with a grin. "I love my mom, but she's not much of a cook, to be honest."

"And, of course, eating Chinese food on Christmas day also keeps me in touch with the theme of most Jewish holidays, which is: 'They tried to kill us, but they failed, so let's eat.' Except for Yom Kippur, the Day of Atonement, when it's: 'Let's celebrate being Jewish by fasting.' You missed a *lot* of fun by being raised Catholic."

"Obviously." He walked beside me down the hall toward the ladies locker room as he asked, "So when you were growing up . . . No Santa, no tree, no presents?"

"No Santa or tree, certainly. I don't think my father would care either way, but my mother would probably burn down the house rather than let Christian symbolism in the door. Jewish identity is very important to her." I added, "But my parents understood that being Jewish children at Christmas could be a strain, so we did get presents. Mom called them 'holiday gifts for good behavior,' but since my sister and I were getting *presents*, we went along with that."

We paused outside the locker room.

"I guess this is your stop," Lopez said.

"Yes. Um, I . . ." I tried to think of what exactly I wanted to say in farewell. Although he had been the one to break up with me, I was the one who later decided we should stay apart when he seemed to be thinking maybe we should try again. And since memories of nearly getting him killed haunted me, I was still inclined to stick with that decision. So I definitely didn't want to say something that might lead him on. But I also wanted him to know . . . "It's good to see you."

"I'm glad to hear that, since I'll be a fixture around here for the time being," he said. "Investigating shipping warehouses, abandoned Fenster trucks, and hijacking sites is chilly at this time of year, so I *thought* being assigned to investigate here at the store meant I was pulling the lucky straw. But that was before I met the Fenster family."

"Armed robbers would probably be easier to work with," I agreed.

We said goodnight, and I went into the ladies locker room to change into my street clothes and get my purse. Then I realized I still hadn't clocked out. So I went into the break room to do that.

An older man in Fenster maintenance coveralls was hovering near the coffee machine in there, standing with his back to me as I entered the room. He was average height and very stocky, and the short hair under his duckbill cap was nearly white.

I walked over to the punch clock on the wall and reached for my employee card. The man turned his head to look at me. Then, moving swiftly, he seized me by the shoulders, startling me.

"Finally!" he said. "I been waiting for you."

I found myself staring into the face of a notorious Gambello hit man.

10

"Lucky?" I said incredulously. "What are *you* doing here?"

"Oh, you know, at Christmas, *everyone* comes to Fenster's," he said with elaborate casualness.

"Huh?"

"What do you *think* I'm doing here?" Now he was exasperated.

"Um, Christmas shopping?" I guessed in confusion.

"You mean you don't know about the hijackings we're being accused of?" he said. "Where have you been? It's all over the news!"

"Yes, but—"

"And OCCB sure ain't hovering around this place because they suspect Santa of loan-sharking."

"No, but—"

"With the cops snooping all over *our* business, who's going to catch the bozos who are *actually* pulling these heists and getting away with the swag while every-one's busy casting unfair aspirins on the family?"

"Aspersions," I said. "You cast *aspersions*, not—Never mind. What family do you mean? The Gambellos?"

"What other family *would* I mean?"

I took a steadying breath. "Wait. Back up a step."

He did so.

"No, I meant . . ." I cleared my throat. "Let me see if I have understood you correctly."

"We ain't got time for that!"

"We'll have to *make* time for that."

"No, we gotta get out of here before I'm recognized. I just been waiting for *you.*" He added accusingly, "And you sure took your sweet time! What the hell were you and Detective Lopez *doing?* No, don't tell me, I don't want to know. None of my business."

"Wait!" I said as he grabbed my arm and tried to drag me toward the door. "I have to clock out."

Lucky hovered impatiently while I did so, then pulled his cap low as he led the way into the hall after checking to make sure the coast was clear. Then we descended to the ground floor via the stairs, at my insistence, rather than taking the elevator. At the bottom of the stairs, with no one else around, Lucky unzipped the coveralls and stripped them off, revealing winter clothing underneath.

"Ah, no wonder you looked so stocky," I said.

"Let's go."

We exited the building through the employee entrance and started heading toward the subway station. It was damp and cold out here, but I was glad to be outside, under the real night sky, and not dressed as an elf who never felt the cold.

Alberto "Lucky Bastard" Battistuzzi was a semi retired hit man in the Gambello crime family. Due to the strange twists and turns of fate, he was also friends with me and Max.

Lucky had acquired his nickname due to surviving two attempts on his life as a young man, both times because an attacker's gun jammed. Earlier this year, I had been present on a third such occasion, too, when a killer stuck a gun in his face and pulled the trigger— and the gun jammed rather than firing. This old guy really *was* lucky.

"All right," I said, "let me see if I interpreted your garbled comments correctly back there. You're telling me the Gambellos are not responsible for hijacking those three Fenster shipments—"

"Three?" he repeated in surprise. "There's been a third heist?"

"Yes, there have been three, not two," I said, looking at him with interest. "It'll probably be in the media soon."

Apparently the cops hadn't revealed the first heist to the Gambellos. Lucky's surprise about the number of trucks seemed to confirm his claim of the family's innocence. But I hadn't thought he was lying about that, anyhow.

Oh, sure, if I walked up to Lucky and asked him if he or his associates were committing felonies, he'd lie to me and deny it. Of *course* he would. But it would make no sense for him to risk waiting around for me tonight in a place where he might be seen and recognized by an OCCB cop like Lopez, all so he could lie to me about something he certainly knew I would never hunt him down to *ask* about. (I did not make a habit of prying into Gambello business, after all.)

I continued, "And you've evidently come to Fenster's to investigate this matter, because you don't think the cops will solve the case as long as they keep looking at the wrong perps, i.e. the Gambellos."

"Yeah." Lucky pulled a knitted wool cap out of his pocket and put it on his head as we walked along. "That's what I said."

"That's not at *all* what you said, but I guess I got the gist of it anyhow." I added, "So you infiltrated the staff by impersonating a maintenance man?"

"That disguise was a mistake," Lucky grumbled.

"Because you don't know how to fix things?" I asked.

"No, because it don't seem like *those* guys ever fix things."

"Ah. Yes, that much is true."

"I couldn't get much investigatin' done today, because *every* place I went in that store, as soon as anyone saw me, they practically did a full body tackle to get me fix something for them." Clearly scandalized, he added, "That place is really falling apart, Esther. You should be careful there."

"You don't say?"

"Then, late in the day, some big prop on the fourth floor went haywire—"

"I know."

"—and everyone on maintenance was rounded up for that. When I got there, I looked around for you. Stella told me you're working in Holidayland until she's got more hours for you."

"It's Solsticeland these days," I said.

"It didn't used to be like that," he said in a negative tone.

"Nondenominational?"

"*Dark.* They should call it Gloomyland. I liked it better the way it was back when we used to take my daughter there." Lucky was a widower, with one grown-up daughter who lived in California with her husband. "Oh, by the way, before I forget. I ate at the restaurant yesterday. Stella sends her love and says right after New Year's, she'll have plenty of shifts for you, so hang tight."

"Okay."

"Anyhow, where was I? Oh, yeah, Gloomyland. So I spotted you, but I couldn't get near you, because you were with OCCB's golden boy, the one who solved them doppelgangster killings in spring." He added, "Well, you, me, and Max solved them, actually. But your boyfriend did a pretty good job, too. Made his bones at OCCB, and all that."

Since Lucky had been around on the day Lopez broke up with me, he knew he wasn't my boyfriend anymore. Lopez hadn't *ever* been my boyfriend, really. We had only gone on a few dates. But I let the phrase pass, rather than distract Lucky from his account by digressing into that subject.

"And what with the OCCB so unjustly determined to pin these hijackings on the Gambello family, I didn't exactly want to announce my presence in Fenster's to the cops."

"They could so easily get the wrong idea," I said. "What with the Gambello family's history with the Fensters, and all. How petty of the cops to cling to that old stuff."

"Yeah," Lucky said indignantly. "It would be just like them to think I'm casing the joint for the next hit, instead of trying to find clues to expose the perpetrators."

With so many maintenance men milling around in the general confusion after the enchanted tree had attacked, I wasn't surprised that I hadn't noticed one who was keeping a low profile and trying not to be seen by my companion. And Lopez was certainly observant enough that it was wise for Lucky to stay out of his sight.

"And, Esther, was that a *zombie* I saw you talking to?"

I frowned for a moment, trying to figure out what he meant. "Oh! No. That was Elspeth Fenster."

"That dead-looking girl is a Fenster?" he said in amazement. "Jeez, old Connie was really losing her grip on things in her declining years, wasn't she? Back in her prime, no *way* would she have let a family member go around looking like a messy corpse!"

"It's the goth look, Lucky. It's a thing."

"It's a *creepy* thing. I got a strong stomach and I ain't scared of corpses, but I swear if that girl snuck up on me in the dark, I'd scream like a girl."

"You called her grandmother Connie," I noted. "Did you know Constance Fenster?"

"Only by reputation—and that old broad had quite a rep, let me tell you."

I paused at the entrance to the subway station. "I'm going down to the Village. I have to see Max."

"Ah. Right. About the . . . whatever it is that's haunting Fenster's? Good idea." Seeing my surprised look, he said, "Oh, come on, sure I know."

"*How* do you know?"

"Well, I grant you, it's not obvious in the public parts of the store, where you work—"

"Oh, actually, it's gotten *very* obvious in some instances."

"—but sneaking around in the empty back halls and guts of that place, like I was today, you feel it *real* quick. Well, I did, anyhow." He nodded. "There's something at Fenster's that didn't used to be there. Something that don't belong there."

I recalled that Lucky's grandmother had been a

white witch back in Sicily, and that he accepted supernatural phenomena with equanimity. I supposed he
was more sensitive to mystical energy than I was; I
hadn't sensed anything until the enchanted tree had
tried to *eat* me.

"Yes, that's what I'm going to see Max about. Whatever is . . ." I nodded, realizing that Lucky had used the
right verb. "Whatever is haunting Fenster's, it's very
dangerous. It tried to kill me today."

"What?" His eyes widened in alarm.

"Or if it was just trying to scare me, then it certainly
did a great job of that." I added, "It also terrorized one
of the Santas today, and I think it may have threatened a
little boy." Considering what had happened to me, I was
no longer at all sure that Jonathan had been frightened
by a harmless gnome statue due to his overactive imagination. It seemed entirely possible that what he'd described to us this morning was *exactly* what he had seen.

"We gotta go see Max," Lucky said with conviction,
all business now. He took my elbow and accompanied
me down the steps of the subway station. "I won't put
up with something evil threatening Santa Claus and
little kids. That's crossing the line." After a moment, he
added courteously, albeit as an afterthought, "I won't
put with something killing you, either, kid."

"Thank you, Lucky. I'm touched."

Zadok's Rare and Used Books occupied the first floor
of a charming old townhouse on a quiet street in the

West Village. Max lived on the second floor, and his laboratory was in the basement.

Specializing in occult books, the shop had a small but devoted clientele. I didn't think it earned much money, but it was only a sideline for Max, in any case. His real work—his lifelong vocation for over three centuries—was confronting Evil in this dimension. And although I was unfamiliar with the specifics of his financial situation, he certainly seemed to have a healthy cash flow. I supposed that if he had invested prudently back in the eighteenth century and then let his assets grow, he was reaping comfortable dividends from that strategy by now.

Although it was getting late, the shop was still open for business. As Lucky and I approached it, we encountered a couple of people leaving, their arms loaded with their purchases. Apparently Max was enjoying some good holiday trade.

We were about to enter the shop when Max toddled up to the front window to hang up the "Closed" sign. His face broke into a smile when he saw us, and he opened the glass door.

"My friends! What an unexpected pleasure. Come in!"

Dr. Maximillian Zadok (Oxford University, class of 1678) was a short, slightly chubby man with innocent blue eyes, longish white hair, and a tidy beard. Looking at him now, I wondered if his resemblance to Santa Claus played a role in Lopez's overall suspicion and dislike of him. I found this an intriguing theory, which merited further exploration at some point.

Fluent in multiple languages, Max spoke English with the faint trace of an accent, reflecting his origins in Central Europe centuries ago. Although he was nearly three hundred fifty years old, Max didn't look a day over seventy.

"Come sit! I've made a pot of tea," he said. "Unless you'd like something stronger?"

I agreed to accept a cup of tea and some cookies. Lucky didn't want anything but a chair.

Alerted to our presence by her trusty canine hearing, Nelli came trotting down from the second floor to greet us.

Nelli was Max's mystical familiar. She had emerged from another dimension in response to his summons for assistance in fighting Evil. A relatively new arrival in this dimension, she was still working out some of the details of her partnership with Max—such as the conflict between her pleasure in chewing on his things and his desire that she should refrain from doing so. And once Nelli chewed on something, the game was pretty much over, since her jaws seemed big enough to fit around my whole head. Fortunately, though, she was a sweet-natured beast. Well, unless she was confronting Evil. Or possessed by a dark spirit. Or facing a boa constrictor. Or encountering a mystical phenomenon which she found threatening. Or . . .

"Hello, Nelli!" I patted her head. "How are you?"

Roughly the size of a Shetland pony, Nelli was well-muscled beneath her short, smooth, tan fur. Although her long, square-jawed head was very large, her immense, floppy ears nonetheless seemed much too big for it. And when she wagged her long, bony tail with reckless abandon, no one was safe.

Nelli greeted me with a burp and drooled a little.

"Oh, dear," Max said over his shoulder while pouring a cup of tea for me. "I'm afraid we're out of cookies, Esther. That's odd. I could have sworn . . ." Realization dawned, and he turned to look accusingly at Nelli.

She returned his gaze innocently, wagging her tail. Then she bounced around a little, greeting Lucky with delight. He was a favorite of hers, and he hadn't been around for a visit lately. Her long, pink tongue hung out of her mouth as she presented him with her head, imperiously waiting for him to scratch her behind the ears.

Lucky and I sat down in a couple of comfortable, prettily upholstered chairs that were near the gas fireplace. Max rummaged around in the little refrigerator where he kept refreshments for customers, hoping to find something else to offer me in place of the vanished cookies. The fridge sat near a large old walnut table that had books, papers, and other paraphernalia on it.

Max said, "A chocolate muffin perhaps, Esther?"

"Oh, yes, thanks," I said eagerly. I was hungry.

"It may be just a tad stale . . ."

"I don't mind."

The shop had well-worn hardwood floors, a broad-beamed ceiling, dusky-rose walls, and rows and rows of tall bookcases overflowing with volumes about all aspects of the occult. Some of the books were modern paperbacks, but many were old hardback volumes that smelled musty, and a few were rare leather-bound books printed in dead languages. I typically found this store a comforting place. Partly because it was nice to be surrounded by books in such a cozy, comfortable setting. And partly, of course, because this was Max's home.

"Esther, I'm glad you stopped by! I was just thinking about you today," Max said, pulling a chair up to join us near the dormant fireplace. "Christmas is in just a few days. And since you are a person of the Hebraic faith—a religion whose emphasis on learning has always won my most enthusiastic admiration—it occurs to me that you may not have plans for that day."

"Oh, right," Lucky said, nodding. "Christmas is probably kind of a bust for you, huh?"

"Pretty much," I said. "No, I have no plans, Max."

"Then I hope you will join me in the Saturnalia feast which I propose to host?"

"The *what* feast?" Lucky said.

"Saturnalia," said Max. "It's the ancient Roman festival from which Christianity has derived many of its Christmas customs. Saturnalia, of course, was derived, in turn, from even older mid-winter festivals whose

periods of celebration clustered around the solstice—
literally, the days when the 'sun stands still.' Since before the dawn of history, people in many cultures and
societies have sought to ward off the frighteningly
long, dark, cold nights at this time of year with festivals
which celebrate light, fire, life, and the imminent,
longed-for return of spring as we—"

"I would be delighted to be your guest," I said,
knowing that he could go on in this vein for some time
if I didn't distract him. "What time does your feast
start?"

"Why an ancient Roman festival?" Lucky asked
with a puzzled frown.

"It seems suitably ecumenical," Max said. "Although I was baptized as a Christian for simple reasons
of self-preservation . . . That is to say, the world used to
be an even more intolerant place than it is now—"

"That's true enough," said Lucky, who believed Max
to be roughly a contemporary of his. "Ain't no denying
some things is a lot better now than they was when I
was young."

"In any event, while I admire a great deal about the
teachings of the individual commonly known to history as Jesus Christ, and whereas I have the most sincerely profound admiration for those who actually
practice what he preached—which includes, of course,
far, far fewer people than *call* themselves Christians . . ."
Max paused for a moment, trying unravel his own syn-
tax. "Er, well, the fact is, I do not and have never con-

sidered myself a Christian. Indeed, although I have traveled far from my origins, I was actually raised in the Hermetic tradition, rather than in any—"

"You were raised as a hermit?" Lucky asked.

"No, my family practiced Hermeticism." Seeing our blank looks, Max explained, "It is a collection, one might say, of philosophical and mystical beliefs, albeit with an emphasis on the healthy spirit of inquiry, largely based on writings somewhat loosely attributed to Hermes Trismegistus."

"Oh, him," I said. "Of course."

"I considered hosting a Hanukkah feast, since that would be in keeping with Esther's inherited traditions, but then I realized that the Jewish festival of lights is already over."

"Oh, yeah." Lucky asked me, "Why *does* that move around so much? I never know when it's supposed to happen."

"Jewish and Muslim holidays are determined by lunar calendars," I said. "Christian holidays are determined by a solar calendar. And eastern and western Christianity use different calendars, too."

"I always find it so confusing," Lucky complained. "They couldn't all get together on this? Would that be so hard?"

I replied, "Oh, I think the calendar is a fairly minor matter in the things that Christians, Jews, and Muslims have never really all been able to get together on, Lucky."

He gave a sort of Talmudic shrug in acknowledgment of this point.

"So I thought that Saturnalia would be a fittingly inclusive theme for my holiday feast, since the Romans celebrated it on the same day that Christmas is now celebrated."

"A Jewish elf, a Hermetic mage, a pagan festival . . ." I nodded with approval. "It works for me. I think it's a lovely idea, Max."

"Would there be any chance," Max asked Lucky, "of a Roman Catholic joining us for this celebration?"

"Well, now that you mention it," Lucky said with a pleased smile, "my daughter and that schmuck she married aren't flying in for the holidays. And since I can't go out there this year, on account of I gotta clear up this problem the Gambello family has got with Fenster's . . . Thank you, Doc. I'd love to come. I'll bring the cannoli."

"Excellent!" Max said, pleased that his guest list was shaping up.

"Speaking of Fenster's . . ." I said.

"Ah, yes," said Max. "How are you faring at Fenster and Company, Esther? And, Lucky, what's this about a problem between your *famiglia* and the store?"

"Actually, Max, something pretty strange is going on there. Something . . ." I glanced at Lucky, wondering exactly where to start the story.

"I was thinking about this on the subway," Lucky said to me. "And I got a theory."

"Well, since I certainly don't," I said, "the floor is all yours."

"Doc," he said to Max, "do you think it's possible that Constance Fenster, the Iron Matriarch, is haunting Fenster and Co.?"

11

Jeff said to me, "Has it occurred to you—because it has certainly occurred to *me*—that this might be the very worst idea you've ever had? And I am including the time you convinced me to meet your parents."

(They hadn't minded that my boyfriend was black; they minded that he wasn't Jewish. And whenever Jeff brought up that occasion, I still automatically apologized to him for it. As I did now.)

Wearing his Santa costume and ready to go on the floor, Jeff gave a weary sigh. "Esther, I know from long and bitter experience that I'm wasting my breath on you, so I suppose I'm really just saying this for the sake of my conscience: Don't do this."

"Don't we look suitable?" Max asked with concern.

"You look fine," I said. "All of you."

"Esther, Esther . . ." Jeff shook his head. "Okay, you asked for some help, I gave you some help. Now let's agree that I don't know anything about this. Fair enough?"

Lucky was studying his reflection in the mirror of the men's locker room at Fenster's. "Kid, don't listen to Mr. Negative over there," he said to me. "We're gonna be fine. My own mother, God rest her soul, wouldn't know me in this get-up."

"Indeed, I hardly recognize you myself!" Max said enthusiastically.

During our discussion last night, the three of us had agreed that Max and Lucky should meet me at Fenster's today to infiltrate the store in search of whatever entity was wreaking havoc here. Given the high turn-over of seasonal staff, as well as the large supply of old costumes that I had discovered yesterday up on the sixth floor, it had seemed obvious to me during our late-night discussion that my friends should disguise themselves as elves.

Now that I looked at them, though, I was fighting a morbid fear that Jeff might not be entirely wrong about the quality of this idea.

The two covert undercover investigative elves both turned and faced Jeff—along with their faithful rein-deer companion, Nelli.

Jeff, who had agreed today (after a little shrill nag-ging on my part) to help me with their costumes and makeup, took a long look at them. Then he made a hor-rible little sound of mingled dread, pity, and grief. He turned around and trudged out of the room, saying over his shoulder, "I'll be on the floor if anyone needs . . . No, actually, I'll just be on the floor. Period. Full stop."

"Ignore him," I said. "This will work."

God, I hoped I was right. Lopez, who'd be poking around the store again today, knew both of these men, and he was certainly observant enough to recognize them even in costume and makeup. We had concealed their features as best we could, but I wouldn't want to risk close scrutiny by a cop who would unquestionably misinterpret their reasons for being here.

"Just be wary, and make sure you avoid contact with Detective Lopez," I said.

"Gee, y'think?" said Lucky.

"Understood," said Max.

Finding costumes upstairs that fit them had not been easy, since neither man was shaped like a young, fit actor, which was the body type that most of the elf costumes had been made for over the years. It would be much easier to find a good fit, of course, if I could liberate a couple of Santa costumes for them . . . But there were too many logistical problems with that identity, since only one Santa at a time could be on the floor, and he was confined to the throne room. Any deviation from this pattern would instantly attract attention to the, er, undercover operatives.

I also hated to imagine what would happen if Lopez stumbled across a furtive Santa Claus who was sneaking around the basement or hiding in a closet at Fenster's. The poor man might never recover from a shock like that.

Anyhow, unlike Father Christmas, there were quite a few elves in the building, and we weren't confined to any particular spot—or even to any particular floor. In their counterfeit elf identities, Max and Lucky could move around the whole building with relative impunity.

It was a shame, though, that I'd been unsuccessful in finding costumes in which they looked more credible. Then again, I was also in costume now, and when I looked at my own reflection and saw Dreidel, "credible" certainly wasn't among the first thirty words that came to mind.

Unfortunately, the fitted tunic, shorts, and tights that characterized the standard male elf outfit at Fenster's mercilessly revealed Lucky's bony legs and poor posture, as well as Max's tendency to slight chubbiness. The cruel truth was that elf costumes did not lend dignity to gentlemen of a certain age.

I had also confiscated Jeff's ruined Santa beard, the one that he had bled on yesterday. He'd collected a new one from the costumer today, and I draped his damaged one over Lucky's face, after concealing the spots of dried blood with some white chalk.

Looking at it now, though, I said, "Oh, I'm not sure about the beard, Lucky . . ." It had looked absurdly fake on Diversity Santa; on a sixtysomething man in an ill-fitting elf-costume, it seemed almost tragic.

"Nah, it'll work," the old mobster said with confidence. "Hides my face. That's what we need."

I hadn't expected Max and Lucky to bring Nelli with them today; I suppose I should have, though, since she was a mystical familiar who had entered this dimension to confront Evil—and that was certainly what we seemed to be haunted by at Fenster's. Nelli was wearing a festive Christmas doggy jacket of red and green, brightly decorated with sparkling silver accents. Max (who tended to spoil her) had also bought her a matching red leash with jingling silver bells on it. At his urging, I had found a reindeer headdress for Nelli in the costume storage room. It was made for a human head rather than a canine one, but with some ingenuity and a stapler swiped from Miles' office, Jeff and I had managed to fit it to her so that it stayed on. So now she sported an impressive pair of squishy fake reindeer antlers.

"She still looks like a dog," I pointed out to Max. "That'll be a problem." We had managed to sneak her into the building via the staff entrance and back stairs, but she was bound to be noticed if Max took her exploring with him. And upon being noticed, she would be evicted, since dogs weren't permitted inside Fenster's.

"Never fear," said Max. "I anticipated this problem." With a flourish, he pulled out a pair of dark sunglasses and donned them.

I stared at him blankly for a moment, then I got it. "A blind elf?"

Max bobbed his head. "She's my reindeer guide!"

I nodded in acceptance of this, and I hedged our bets by pinning an index card to Nelli's jacket with the words "I'm Working" printed on it.

Last night, when explaining to Max and Lucky exactly what had been happening at Fenster's, I drew a map of the store for them, pinpointing the sites of the mystical phenomena or questionable incidents. They pulled that map out now and formed a plan of action.

"We should attempt to find an epicenter," said Max. "A specific spot where mystical activity or dark energy is focused. If we can do that, it might help us narrow down the precise nature of what we're facing."

I was unconvinced by Lucky's suggestion last night that the ghost of Constance Fenster was haunting the store. Solsticeland had been a pet project of hers, and Fenster & Co. had been her life's work. Although the Iron Matriarch sounded formidable enough to reach out from the grave if she chose, I was very skeptical that she would do so to sabotage her own creation.

As I told Max and Lucky, I was more inclined to go with Satsy's interpretation: whatever was here now, it hadn't dared to mess with Fenster's while Constance was still alive.

As we conferred now in the men's locker room, Max said, "The seeming randomness of the activity, combined with its violence, might suggest a poltergeist."

"That's a kind of ghost, right?" I said.

"Yes. The roots of the word are German, and it essentially means 'noisy ghost.'"

"Well, I never met Constance," I said, "but having met two generations of her descendants, I'd say that 'noisy' seems to be a family trait. So maybe she is our ghost."

"'Noisy' is used in a more figurative sense here," said Max. "There may be rapping, tapping, knocking, and even human voices associated with a poltergeist—"

"Or laughter?" I asked. "That's what Satsy heard in the elevator. That and growling."

"Yes, these are also possibilities. But the key element is that a poltergeist is typically much more physical in its influence than a traditional spirit or ghost."

"Physical?" Lucky repeated. "As in trying to suffocate a young lady with the branches of a fake tree while knocking people around with the other branches?"

Max nodded. "Exactly. If we *are* dealing with a ghost or spirit—which may or may not be the case—then that sort of physical activity points directly to a poltergeist. Rather than revealing itself as a shadowy apparition, a poltergeist throws a plate at you, makes your radio explode, sends a wagon speeding down the street when there is no horse pulling it, and so on."

Max paused and frowned in thought before adding, "We should certainly proceed with caution. If we are facing a poltergeist, then the phenomena which Esther and Satsy experienced indicate an unusually powerful one."

"So the way the enchanted tree fought off a bunch of

people while attacking me," I said. "That wouldn't be considered standard mojo for a poltergeist?"

"No, indeed. Poltergeists are usually just a nuisance. Occasionally, they're dangerous. But they rarely have the level of power and sustained control that characterizes the event in the Enchanted Forest—a locale which, obviously, we'll need to scrutinize thoroughly today, Lucky."

"If this is a poltergeist," I asked, "then how do we issue it an exit visa?"

"You mean invite it to leave?" Lucky asked. "Good question."

"Well, that can be complicated," said Max.

I sighed. "Of *course.*"

"Hey, you knew it wouldn't be easy," Lucky said. "It never is."

"A poltergeist may operate according to a variety of parameters and patterns, but one of the interesting features of this particular type of entity is that it usually haunts a person, rather than a place."

I thought this over. "So the epicenter, in that case, would be some*one* rather than some*where?*"

"Precisely."

"Hey . . . Now that's interesting!" said Lucky. "Max, could the poltergeisted person be a criminal mastermind?"

I said, "You're thinking there's a link between the strange phenomena inside Fenster's and the heists?"

He nodded, making the bells on his elf cap jingle.

"Think about it. *Very* smooth hits. No witnesses. The hijacked drivers can't give the cops any useful information."

"How do you know that?" I challenged.

"Because if the cops were getting any decent information at all, they'd have a lead on the robbers and leave the Gambellos alone, instead of continuing to frisk the family so thoroughly that I'm worried OCCB is going to tell the boss to bend over so they look up *there*, too." Lucky added gloomily, "Victor Gambello don't need this kind of stress at his age."

"Okay, so they're very smooth hits that leave no evidence trail," I said. "That doesn't really connect them—"

"And someone here at the store has supernatural mojo. Someone who really hates Fenster's, I'd say." Lucky paused before continuing, "I've thought about it, and what you said last night is right, kid. If she were still around, in a spiritual sense, old Connie wouldn't be causing trouble in Solsticeland or scaring Santa. No way." Lucky's bells jangled again as he shook his head. "The Gambellos got *La Cosa Nostra*. Our thing. And this company was *La Cosa Sua*. Her thing."

"Yes, I can see that." It seemed like a fitting description.

"She was a tough woman, old Connie Fenster. The cops think it was all their arrests and indictments that put a stop to the, uh, stuff that went on all those years ago, when the Gambellos decided to leave Fenster and

Powell alone." Lucky snorted. "Nah. You know what it was?"

"What?" I asked, increasingly fascinated by Constance, despite feeling no regret that I never got to meet her.

"It was Connie. *She* put a stop to it," said Lucky. "She went to Don Victor Gambello herself, against the wishes of the Powells, and cut a deal with him. A *tough* deal, too. She was a real negotiator. That society widow went to the *capo di tutti capi* to do business, and she didn't go to him with her hat in her hand or begging for mercy. She went to him as an equal. And you what? He wound up treating her like one."

That must be why Helen Fenster-Thorpe, who believed the Gambellos were behind the hijackings, thought she could negotiate with the thieves. Because her mother had done so—successfully. I suspected, though, that Helen overrated her own abilities, whereas Constance Fenster had not.

"The boss has always said that Connie Fenster was the strongest, shrewdest, most ruthless person he ever met—and if she ever decided to get into *our* thing, then he'd retire and move to Florida." Lucky grinned. "I guess we're lucky she stuck to the retail world."

I recalled something else I'd heard during my accidental visit with the Fenster family yesterday. "Lucky, the deal that Constance made with your boss . . . What happened when she died?"

He shrugged. "It went the way of all flesh."

"When I met the Fensters yesterday and they were talking about this, it sounded to me like they think the Gambellos are hitting the trucks in order to pressure them into making another deal."

"The boss respected their mother," said Lucky. "So if he wanted to get the Fensters' attention, this sure ain't how he'd go about doing it."

"They don't seem to know that. Then again, I think Lopez nailed it when he said they're idiots." I added, "You can't tell anyone he said that."

"Who would I tell?" Lucky said, "Anyhow, to return to our current situation . . . It seems like these weird things happening here are probably caused by someone who hates Fenster's. And although the hijackings *could* be just a matter of business, maybe they're being pulled off by someone who hates Fenster's, too. They're doing a lot of damage, after all, right? So if there's an inside person involved in the hijackings . . ."

"Ah," said Max. "Yes, I see your point. The inside person might be the same individual connected to the mystical activities. However, a criminal mastermind is not the sort of personality typically associated with poltergeist phenomena."

"Too bad. Then we'd have a whole new field: polter-*heist* phenomena." I enjoyed a little chuckle over this.

Lucky gave me a peculiar look before asking Max, "So what sort of person are we looking for then?"

"The afflicted individual is very often a troubled young person," said Max.

"Oh, I have a candidate," I said instantly.

"Ah." Lucky's bells jingled as he nodded. "The dead-looking girl."

"Pardon?" said Max.

I explained about Elspeth Fenster.

"Hmmm." Max stroked his beard. "Yes, she does sound like a viable candidate for affliction by a tormenting spirit." After a moment he added, "But we mustn't leap to conclusions. Lucky and I should launch our investigation. We have a big job ahead of us!"

"And I should go to the Hanukkah station," I said, feeling glad this job would be over in two more days. "Miles is bound to come looking for me any minute."

The door to this room swung open. Max immediately donned his dark glasses. Lucky and I looked at the newcomer.

I relaxed a moment later and said, "Hello, Eggnog."

"Dreidel." His brows rose in silent inquiry. I recalled that I was in the men's locker room.

"I was just helping the new elves settle in," I said.

"New elves?" he said in surprise. "This late in the season?"

"Well, we're so understaffed, you know . . ."

"Ah. Yeah. People just keep disappearing. It's getting weird, actually."

"I know," I said. "Like that Agatha Christie novel where they're all trapped on an island and keep getting bumped off one by one, until there are none. Well, except for the killer."

Eggnog looked at Max, then at Nelli. "A blind elf?" he said dubiously.

"Fenster's is an equal opportunity employer," I said.

"How do you do, sir?" said Max, nodding in Eggnog's general direction. "I'm Belsnickel."

"You're who?" I blurted.

"I have chosen it as my elf name," Max said grandly. "It holds fond childhood memories for me. Belsnickel was a goblin who visited children on Christmas Eve to find out if they'd been naughty or nice."

Eggnog snorted upon hearing those familiar names.

"We've got our own Naughty and Nice," I explained to Max and Lucky. "But you probably want to steer clear of them."

Eggnog introduced himself, then looked expectantly at Lucky.

The old gangster shifted his weight. "I'm, uh . . . Sugarplum."

I blinked. "Seriously?"

Lucky shrugged. "It sounds like an elf name. What's wrong with it?"

"Nothing," I said. "Nothing at all." I added to Eggnog, "And their reindeer is, er, Vixen."

Nelli wagged her tail gently.

"You better get out on the floor, Dreidel," said Eggnog. "Miles is looking for you."

"Right. Of course." I turned to my friends. "So . . . you guys know what to do and also where to find me if you need me, right? I'll see you later."

I exited the room, then went into the ladies locker room across the hall to answer the call of nature and touch up my makeup before going out onto the floor. When I exited the locker room, I practically walked straight into Lopez, who was coming down the hall and right outside the door.

"Oh!" I stared at him in wide-eyed dismay and did my best not to look guilty. I hoped that Max and Lucky had already left this area. "Hi!"

"Hi." He was wearing his coat and looked a little flushed with cold.

"Did you just get here?" I asked.

"Yeah." He was carrying an armload of file folders, which he shifted a little so he could start unbuttoning his coat. "Where are you working today?"

"Up here. Fourth floor. Why?"

"All day?" he asked.

"Yes. I'm at the Hanukkah station this afternoon. Then I'm helping Santa after that."

"For how long?"

"Probably all evening. Why?"

"No reason."

"Where are you going to be?" I asked.

"Down at the docks."

"All day?"

"I don't know," he said. "A big part of the day, anyhow."

"But you're not going to be . . . wandering around a whole lot or anything, are you?"

"I . . ." He frowned. "I don't know. Probably not. Why?"

"No reason."

"You seem a little tense," he observed.

"I am," I said darkly as I looked over his shoulder and saw who was approaching. "Naughty and Nice are headed this way."

Lopez turned slightly to see who I meant—and promptly morphed into a predictable stereotype at the sight of two mostly-naked blonde bombshells walking toward him. Within nanoseconds, his IQ visibly dropped by about thirty points, he seemed incapable of speech, and his jaw hung open slightly.

Freddie's bimbos saw a good-looking man ignoring me to gape at them, and they each gave me malicious smiles before batting their lashes at him and giggling flirtatiously.

Lopez blinked.

"Hi, *Dreidel*," Naughty said.

"Yeah, whatever." I stepped aside so the girls could get past me and enter the locker room.

After the door closed behind me, shutting off his view of them, Lopez looked at me blankly. "What were we just talking about?"

"You have a badge," I said coldly. "So you could follow through and *frisk* them, too."

"Oh, come on," he said. "A couple of half-naked playmates walk right by me, and I'm not even gonna *look?*"

"I don't remember what we were talking about," I said testily. "And I have to get to work now."

"But you're up here all day today, right?"

"*Yes.*"

"Okay."

I heard a noisy sneeze right behind the door of the men's locker room across the hall, so I had a good idea who'd emerge when it opened a moment later. Feeling a little malicious pleasure about what would happen next, I gave a friendly little finger-wave to Wheezy Santa, who was blowing his nose.

Lopez turned to see who was behind him—and flinched, nearly dropping the armload of folders he was carrying.

As Wheezy Santa went down the hallway, sniffing noisily, Lopez rubbed his forehead and said, "Jesus, that is just so *disturbing.*"

12

I made my way to Santa's throne room early that evening, where Eggnog and I were due to relieve the Russian elf and a chirpy redheaded elf whom I had worked with only once. I couldn't remember her name—Tinsel? Ivy? Something like that.

"Hi, Dreidel!" the redhead cried, using suitably melodramatic elf gestures. "Oops! I mean, *shalom!*"

The expression on the Russian's face suggested that the redheaded elf's very existence was an affront to her.

"Hi," I said to them both. "What's up?"

"*Please* try to cheer up Santa while you're here, Dreidel! He seems very *down* today." The redhead pushed out her lower lip to demonstrate sadness.

I resisted the urge to remind her that I was a co-worker, not a five-year-old visitor.

The Russian elf said to me, in a voice that carried,

"Two people this afternoon see black Santa and ask me if they can visit white Santa instead."

"I think that's so mean!" said the redhead.

"Oh, for chrissake. I'm not in a bad mood because of a few garden-variety racist assholes," Jeff said grumpily, making the redhead gasp. "I'm in a bad mood because I'm a grown man whose only two job offers since coming back to New York this year have both involved serving as a cheap diversion for retail shoppers."

"Oh, dear," said Eggnog, "it's going to be one of *those* shifts with Diversity Santa."

Oh, *he* was one to talk.

I said to the two women, "Okay, troops, Eggnog and I will take it from here. You can go to your next post."

As they departed, I took a good look at Jeff and realized he did look pretty morose.

Unfortunately, Miles joined us then, which certainly precluded any possibility of cheering up Jeff.

"Ivy never showed up for work," Miles said tersely to me.

"No, I think Ivy was here ten seconds ago," I said, gesturing in the direction the chirpy elf had gone. "Wasn't that her?"

"No, that was Merry."

"I thought Merry was the elf with the Russian accent," said Eggnog, pointing in the direction the dour elf had gone.

"No, that's Nutcracker," said Miles.

Jeff muttered, "And that name suits her perfectly."

"So which one is Ivy?" I asked.

"Does it really matter?" Miles replied impatiently. "She's not here, and she hasn't called in. She's not coming back. We'll never see her again, Dreidel! Who *cares* which one she was?"

"Sorry I asked."

"And since she's *another* one who hasn't returned her costume, she can forget about being sent her final paycheck!"

"People *keep* these costumes?" I asked incredulously. After I took off this outfit for the last time on Christmas Eve, I'd never want to see it again; it would always be a reminder of this humiliating job.

"No one respects store property," Miles said in aggravation. "Moody Santa, Ivy, Giggly Santa, Poinsettia, Thistle . . ."

"Thistle's gone, too?" I asked. "When did that happen?" The straight elf had seemed pretty reliable to me.

"He hasn't called or come in today, either!" Miles said bitterly. "And his costume isn't in his locker. It's gone, too! Hardly *anyone* who's gone AWOL has returned their costumes this year. I've lost track of how many outfits we'll have to replace for next season!"

"Well, you'll get mine back," Jeff promised. "It's not as if I'd get a lot of wear out of it."

"I'll get *everyone's* costume back from now on, or there'll be heck to pay!" Suddenly struck by inspiration, Miles said, "I'm going to write a memo about this!"

"Oh, no!" I cried. "Not a *memo*."

"You'll find it in your lockers by the end of the shift."

"Which seems very far away right now," Jeff said morosely.

Miles said, "To return to the point—"

"There was a point to this?" I asked.

"To return to the *point*," Miles said, "I need you to go take over Ivy's post, Dreidel. Eggnog will have to manage alone here." He asked the elf, "Can you handle it, Eggnog?"

"I have a master's degree from Princeton," Eggnog said with disdain.

"Thank *God*," said Jeff. "That'll really come in handy when the parents riot because they want a white Santa."

Miles said, "Don't say 'God' on the—"

"No one's going to riot, Jeff," I said soothingly. "They'll just make complaints that all begin with the phrase, 'I'm not a bigot, but . . .' and then say something bigoted about you."

Jeff asked Miles, "Can I make a complaint about having a Jewish elf?"

Accommodating for once, Miles said, "I'll move Dreidel to another department immediately."

"Good," said Jeff. "We need some more time apart. Four years wasn't enough."

"Dreidel, with Ivy gone, I need you to go work the west entrance on the main floor," Miles said to me. "Starting right now."

"Oh, *no* . . ." My heart sank. The west entrance was the coldest spot in the whole store.

Miles ignored my protest. "You've worked there before, so you know what to do, right? Greet people as they arrive, point them toward Solsticeland, and promote Karaoke Bear."

"*Must* I?"

"You must."

I sighed in defeat and resigned myself to singing through chattering teeth as I did karaoke duets with an animated stuffed bear that was dressed like Lady Gaga crossed with a gangsta. Strategically placed at the store's busiest (and—did I *mention?*—coldest) entrance, this elaborate and expensive product was one of Fenster's featured Christmas items for the privileged children of the oligarchs. Many youngsters who saw Karaoke Bear on their way to Solsticeland expressed a fervent desire, when visiting Santa, to find the musical mammal under their Christmas tree—or within the tree's general vicinity, Karaoke Bear and his sound system being too big to fit *under* anything.

"Well?" Miles prodded. "Is there a problem, Dreidel?"

"No. I'll do it," I said in resignation. But I decided I'd go to my locker first and get my coat. Fenster's wasn't paying me enough to freeze to death. If I got too cold down there, I'd put it on and *dare* Miles to fire me when he was so short-handed.

I turned to go off and work my new post, but I

paused when it occurred to me that Max and Lucky would need to know where I was. So I said to Jeff, "If, um, anyone asks for me . . ."

"Who'd ask for you?" he said crankily. "It's not as if anyone we know is going to come here."

"At Christmas, *everyone* comes to Fenster's," Miles reminded him.

I stared hard at Jeff, trying to get him to wise up. "I *mean*, if the new elves want my help . . ."

"What new elves?" Miles asked alertly. "We don't have any new elves."

"You didn't get the memo?" I glanced at him briefly, then returned to trying to mind-meld with Jeff. "A couple of, um, emergency elves have come on board for the final days of the season."

"Really?" Miles frowned. "I should have been informed! *I'm* the senior manager of this floor."

"Emergency elves?" Diversity Santa's eyes widened when he finally got it. "Oh! The *new elves*."

"Oh, right," said Eggnog. "Sugarplum and, um . . . Snickerdoodle?"

"Belsnickel."

"What sort of elf name is *that?*" Miles asked.

"A very traditional one." I added, "They have a pretty convincing reindeer with them, too."

Jeff snorted. "*Convincing?* I thought she looked like . . . Um. Never mind." He'd caught my warning expression. "Okay, if they turn up, I'll tell them where you've gone."

Satisfied, I left the throne room and went to the ladies' locker room to get my coat. I put it on but didn't bother to button it, and I headed toward the escalators. I went via the Kwanzaa exhibit and Solstice Castle, deliberately avoiding the Enchanted Forest. (Once strangled, twice shy.)

As I passed the castle, my nostrils stung a little. I noticed a wisp of smoke curling out of one of the castle windows. Princess Crystal was having a forbidden cigarette in the tower.

I reached the escalator and spent the next few minutes riding down to the ground floor. Once I got there, I started making my way through the vast cosmetics department. I use makeup a lot in my profession, as well as having a reasonable supply of it for my daily life, but I always felt overwhelmed by the range and quantity of cosmetic products on display at Fenster's, as well as bewildered by their descriptions.

Did *any* woman—even one who worked as a psychedelic circus clown—need a compact with thirty shades of eye shadow? When had a "revolutionary four-stage process" replaced a tube of mascara for enhancing eyelashes? Was I the only woman here who thought that the lipstick colors "burgundy," "cabernet," and "merlot" all looked identical? Would spending half a week's pay on a three-ounce bottle of moisturizer really "transform" my face—and if so, what would it be transformed into?

"Hi!" a maniacally grinning salesgirl said to me.

"Want to try Compulsion, the scent he won't be able to resist?"

"No, thanks, I'm—Agh!" I staggered backward, coughing hard after she sprayed the cologne directly into my mouth.

"Oh, my God! Sorry, sorry!" she cried. "Are you *okay?*"

My eyes watered as I kept coughing.

"Oh, no! Help! Medic! *Medic!*"

Did we *have* medics at Fenster's?

I waved my hand at the wide-eyed girl, trying to get her to calm down. "I'm . . ." *Cough, cough.* ". . . okay."

A plump, middle-aged woman elbowed her way through the dense crowd of shoppers and demanded, "What's the problem? What's going on here?"

She had applied her makeup with a trowel, and she was so heavily drenched in a rival cologne that one whiff made me start coughing again. I didn't recognize her, but I could tell from her nametag and her manner that she was the girl's supervisor. I wondered whether Fenster's specifically trained its managers to be officious or if that quality was just a standard prerequisite for the job.

"I think I've harmed this figure skater!" the salesgirl confessed.

"I'm an elf," I corrected, dabbing at my watering eyes. "Good guess, though. And at least you didn't mistake me for a hooker."

The scent-drenched manager flinched. "You can't

say that word on the *floor*." She'd obviously realized that my pointy ears signified I was a Solsticeland character.

I said to the girl, "You might want to exercise a little restraint with your spritzer."

"I'm sorry," she said. "I have a quota. I'm supposed to spritz fifty people at every post before I can move on to my next location."

While she spoke, my still-misty gaze beheld a couple of tall, buxom, blonde elves looming behind her, their red-and-green outfits considerably skimpier than my blue one. Their faces bore a familiar combination of vacuity and malice, and I felt a little shiver run through me.

Or maybe that was just from the chilly breeze whipping down this aisle from the nearby north entrance. I pulled my coat more tightly around my body.

In any case, while the girl gestured with her bottle and explained that she still had to spritz nineteen more people before she could move on, Naughty—or maybe it was Nice—gave her a deliberate shove. Foreseeing the inevitable result, I jumped back to avoid being spritzed in the face again when the girl's hand reflexively squeezed the bottle as she stumbled. The floor manager, who had not recognized the imminent danger, shrieked when the girl squirted cologne into her eyes, and clapped a hand over her face. Naughty and Nice giggled and started to slip away, using the dense crowd for cover.

"That *does* it!" I said.

Sniping comments, snickering, and sly looks were one thing, but now they were *assaulting* people. Enough was enough!

While the horrified cologne girl was trying to help her startled, shrieking boss, I tried to get around the two of them to grab those half-naked holiday hags. I didn't really know what I would do once I got my hands on them, but banging their empty blonde heads together until their skulls cracked might not be a bad place to start.

"Come back here!" I shouted as Naughty shoved her way through the crowded aisle.

She looked over her shoulder at me and laughed.

Nice got separated from her, her way blocked by a couple of heavyset women in fur coats carrying a voluminous burden of shopping bags. She turned back in this direction, looking for another escape route.

In my eagerness to shake Nice until her nasty little head flew off, I tried to move the manager out of my way. I was too excited to be gentle, and she shrieked anew, with her hands still covering her eyes, as she stumbled into a customer.

The customer caught her, staggering a little under the sudden impact, then said to me in outraged tones, "What are you *doing?*" I realized she thought the manager was covering her face and shrieking because I was brutalizing her.

"Help!" cried the guilt-stricken salesgirl. "We need help!"

Nice giggled as she dashed behind the manager and the customer. I lunged for her.

"Stop it!" said the customer. "What is the *matter* with you?" She was an older woman, a little smaller than me, and tidily elegant in a forest-green winter coat.

I tried to shove past her. "Move! She'll get away!"

"What's going *on?*" asked the manager, her eyes squeezed shut.

"That's what *I* want to know," the customer said sternly.

Looking over the woman's shoulder, I saw Nice stick her tongue out at me. *Unbelievable.*

Still trying to get past the two women in my path, I pointed my finger at Nice and shouted, "You're *done*, you snarky bitch!"

The manager flinched. "You can't say that on the *floor!*"

Freddie Junior had to get rid of those girls! What if someone really got hurt the next time they pulled a prank?

The salesgirl had given up shouting for help and was now apologizing profusely to her boss.

"Shit! She got away," I sputtered as Nice melted into the crowd and disappeared. I spun around, wondering if I could still spot Naughty in the throng. "Where's the other one? *Damn* it!"

The manager was by now practically hyperventilating over my rapid-fire breaches of store etiquette.

Patting the manager's heaving back, the customer said to me, "Young woman, *control* yourself."

Wondering if I should go in hot pursuit of Freddie's femmes fatales or just deal with them later, I looked absently at the customer who was chiding me. She wore her red hair in a flattering twist and evidently made no attempt to hide the gray that was starting to creep in. Still a beautiful woman, she must have been a knockout when she was my age. She had kept her figure, and *she* certainly didn't make the mistake of troweling on her makeup. She wore only some lipstick, a touch of powder, and just enough eye makeup to flatter her wide eyes, which were long-lashed and very blue.

While keeping a wary eye on me, she pulled a handkerchief out of her purse and handed it to the manager, who thanked her and started dabbing her watering eyes with it. I looked around and realized that some employees behind the nearby makeup counters were staring anxiously at us—or maybe just at *me*.

I said to the cologne girl, "We should take your boss to the ladies' room."

"I can manage," she replied. "You probably need to get back to the rink."

"I'm not a figure skater," I said. "I'm Santa's Jewish elf. I work here."

"You *work* here?" The redheaded lady was clearly appalled by this information.

I decided I should probably make my exit. "Okay," I

said to the salesgirl. "If you can handle this, then I guess I'll go to my post."

The manager said with dread, "Your post isn't on *this* floor, is it?"

"Sorry," I said wanly.

Still dabbing at her watering eyes, the manager said to the redhead, "The seasonal staff are sometimes . . . a little . . . That is . . . She's not a regular here."

"Indeed?" was the crisp reply.

"I'll just go, um . . ." I backed away from them. "Bye."

As I departed, I heard the redheaded lady offering to help the salesgirl take the manager somewhere quiet to compose herself.

I was still fuming about Naughty and Nice when I reached Karaoke Bear's elaborate station, but I knew that Freddie's protection meant those two elves were untouchable. And trying to explain things like professionalism and appropriate conduct to *him* was certainly a more hopeless task than I wanted to embark on. Oh, well. I decided to let it go. There were only two more days in the season, after all.

Chilly air whipped through this area as the doors of the western entrance opened and closed for arriving and departing shoppers. My blue and white striped tights, abbreviated pants, and short sleeves weren't much of a match for that cold air, but I decided to take off my coat, anyhow. I'd be moving around once I started performing, and that might keep me warm enough. I folded up the coat and stashed it beside the karaoke apparatus.

Karaoke Bear awaited me on his sparkly performance platform (included with every purchase of the singing bear). He was surrounded by an elaborate seasonal display (not included); a dense little forest of snow-covered, brightly decorated evergreen trees formed a festive backdrop for the bear's performances. I looked warily at the trees, recalling my asphyxiation incident; but they looked innocuous and inanimate.

I stepped up onto the sparkly platform where Karaoke Bear awaited me in his outfit of sequins, rhinestones, denim, studs, and saggy pants. A little over three feet tall, the bear wore a jaunty cap and had a microphone in his hand, ready to rock. I picked up the other microphone, then turned on the system.

Karaoke Bear jerked into automated motion, blinked his long-lashed brown eyes, brought his mike up to his mouth, and asked if I'd like to join him in a song. I replied, with a lively enthusiasm I was far from feeling, that I've *love* to.

I selected a peppy pop tune released the previous year by Golly Gee, a singer/actress/headcase with whom I had worked on *Sorcerer!*, a short-lived Off-Broadway flop, earlier this year. The song was Golly's only hit, the one that had propelled her onto the coveted D-list of fame. Considering Golly's foul mouth and R-rated persona, I found it odd that a song of hers would be featured in a karaoke program aimed at children; but I had already learned that plenty of kids who came to the store knew this number.

By the time Karaoke Bear and I finished the song, we had attracted an audience—which was the whole idea of having an elf posted here to demonstrate this apparatus, of course. I paused between songs to welcome the shoppers, explain to them how to get to Solsticeland from here, and tell the kids watching this performance how much Santa Claus was looking forward to meeting them. I also explained a little about how Karaoke Bear functioned, and I hinted that Santa would be receptive to requests for the singing bear as a Christmas gift. Then I sang another duet with my mechanical companion. Karaoke Bear only had a few limited dance moves, but he was always in time with the music.

In addition to the people watching our performance, many shoppers passed my platform, coming and going on their quest for Christmas gifts. Some paused briefly to watch the show, but others just shoved their way irritably through the gathered crowd, barely slackening their pace. Some shoppers, while talking to each other or into their cell phones, raised their voices to a shout to be heard above the bear's amplified speakers; I was by now too used to this to let it bother me. Other people asked me questions between songs—sometimes about Karaoke Bear, sometimes about where something was located in the massive maze of Fenster & Co.

I had just answered several such questions and was

about to launch into another song when a neatly dressed man who was holding a cell phone to his ear approached me and asked politely, "Excuse me, miss. Where am I, please?"

"You're at the Karaoke Bear station near the western entrance," I replied.

He looked puzzled. "The *what* kind of bear?"

"Uh, the singing bear."

His English was crisp and well pronounced, but he had a foreign accent—Hispanic, I thought. This impression was confirmed a moment later when he spoke Spanish into his cell phone. He repeated a phrase loudly a couple of times, then switched to English: "The singing bear. Yes. Would I make that up?" He switched back to Spanish and then stepped away from the platform as the next karaoke tune blared through the speakers.

After I started singing, the man finished his call and returned to the platform, standing directly in front of it and watching my performance intently, with a smile on his face. He clapped enthusiastically at the end of the number, then asked me, "Does the bear know any Christmas songs?"

"I'm glad you asked!" I replied with elfin delight. I launched into my next "all about Karaoke Bear" spiel, explaining that the bear had a broad repertoire, including Christmas music, nursery rhymes, pop tunes, traditional songs, and so on. Then, in deference to the courteous Hispanic man, I did a seasonal medley with my fuzzy co-star, including "Jingle Bell Rock," "Winter Wonderland,"and "Happy Holiday."

For much of this medley, I played directly to the man who'd requested a Christmas song. This was partly because the crowd was thinning a bit, with some people leaving and newcomers arriving slowly, while he remained in place. And partly because he was an engaging audience, standing close to the platform, smiling merrily at me, and bouncing along a little to the music. He was a pleasantly ordinary-looking man, somewhere in his sixties, a little stocky and shorter than average height. He had mostly gray hair that had once been black, dark olive skin, a strong, plain face, and an air of gentle good humor. His most noticeable features were his warm, expressive brown eyes.

He applauded again when I finished singing. "You have a wonderful voice!"

"Thank you," I said with a smile, enjoying myself now—an enthusiastic audience makes the day for any performer.

"I must find my wife," he said, looking at his watch. "She would enjoy this." He pulled out his cell phone while saying to me, "Please, let's have another song while I wait for her!"

While I programmed the next song into Karaoke Bear, I heard the gentleman say into his phone, "*Querida*, where are you? No, I'm with the singing bear now. The singing bear . . . Oh, then I think you're very near. Just follow the music and you'll find it . . . No, but

I spoke to him a few minutes ago. Yes, he'll be here any moment."

The man pocketed his phone as I started singing "Let It Snow! Let It Snow! Let It Snow!" Although he was still an appreciative audience, now he was mostly looking around for his wife rather than watching me. A half-dozen small children showed up, wide-eyed with wonder at the sight of the singing bear and his elf friend, and I played to them.

What happened next was confusing and very quick, though it all seemed to occur in slow motion at the time.

The nice man turned away from the stage, so that his back was to me and the bear, and waved to someone in the distance—his spouse, I assumed. At that moment, Karaoke Bear broke out of his mechanical pattern and came to horrible, menacing life. The bear suddenly crouched down, sprouted claws, and grew fangs.

The children who were gathered near the platform saw the transformation and started rumbling in frightened confusion. Karaoke Bear's normally benign expression was a ferocious snarl, and his plastic brown eyes were now red and glowing.

I froze with startled fear and dropped my microphone, staring in stunned horror at the bear.

Apart from the scared children right by the platform, the audience seemed a little puzzled, but not alarmed. With Karaoke Bear crouched down on the little stage, most people couldn't see him now. They seemed to assume the kids were squealing because the bear had over-balanced during his mechanical dance and fallen down.

Karaoke Bear's predatory gaze zeroed in on the nice gentleman who was looking across the store, waving a hand as he tried to catch his wife's attention. The man's back was to the possessed bear, with its dripping fangs and sinisterly glowing eyes.

"Mister! Watch out!" I shouted.

The man started to turn my direction, still not seeing the bear. He looked puzzled rather than alarmed.

The bear lunged for him.

Without thinking, I did a sort of flying dropkick to knock the man out of the leaping bear's path while the children near us screamed. I had never executed a move like that before. It's amazing what a combination of mortal terror and adrenaline can accomplish on short notice.

I hit the floor with a heavy thud and rolled over a few times, carried by my own momentum. People were startled into panicky reaction all around me, and I was trampled by the feet of shoppers fleeing the scene.

I lay there for a moment, winded and dazed.

A woman was screaming, "Carlos! Carlos!"

Then I realized that I might be next on the possessed bear's menu, and I scrambled to my feet, heart pounding with shock and fear.

Karaoke Bear was lying on the stage, as if he had keeled over. He looked normal now, except for the fact that smoke was rising from his garishly clad little body. I stared warily at the bear for a moment, but he didn't move at all. Whatever force had invaded the apparatus was gone. Around his platform, to my relief, the cluster of Christmas trees still looked completely innocuous and inanimate.

I turned to examine the gentleman into whom I had just flown feet first. He was lying motionless on the floor nearby. Shoving my way past a few confused and curious bystanders, I stumbled over to him, stepping on the blue stocking cap and pointy ears that had fallen off during my tumble to the floor, and sank to my knees. I grabbed his shoulder and bent over him, trying to see his face.

"Mister! Mister? Are you okay?" I asked urgently.

He groaned, conscious but dazed.

"Carlos!" a woman screeched right behind me.

I flinched and started to turn around, but something heavy hit me in the head.

"Ow!" I collapsed on top of the man, instinctively shielding my skull from the additional blows that were raining down on me now.

"No! No! No!" the woman was shrieking.

Confused, startled, and in pain, I was trying to shield the man from this attack, too. He was struggling beneath my sprawled weight, conscious but disoriented, while someone continued beating the crap out of me with a solid object.

I think that's her purse.

"Let him go! Let him go!" the woman shrieked.

Then I heard a man's voice. A familiar one. "Jesus Christ! What the *hell*?"

"Let go!" the woman shouted, still clobbering me.

I'm gonna kill her, I decided.

I took an instinctive guess at where her legs would be and lashed out with one foot. I connected with a satisfying thud—but instead of the woman, I heard that familiar male voice howl in pain.

"OW! Goddamn it!"

Oops.

"Connor!" the woman cried, then hit me again.

"Stop! STOP!" he shouted at her. "What are you *do-ing*?"

There was a scuffle, and the pummeling on my head finally ceased. I lay there breathing hard, not sure it was safe to look up yet.

"Let me go!" the woman insisted. "That lunatic is trying to *kill* your father!"

Oh, no . . .

"Mom, will you let *me* handle this?" Lopez snapped.

The struggling man beneath me spoke a few breath-less words in Spanish. Lopez responded in the same language. I heard him call the man "*papá*."

Shit.

A pair of strong hands grabbed me by the shoulders and hauled me to my feet. I faced Lopez and his beauti-ful, redheaded mother.

Lying on the ground at my feet, Mr. Lopez said in

frantic confusion, "What happened? What's going on? *Perrito! Qué pasa?"*

"No one really knows, Pop." Lopez gave a heavy sigh. "Hello, Dreidel. I assume there's a perfectly logical explanation for all this?"

13

She wore just enough eye makeup to flatter her wide eyes, which were long-lashed and very blue . . .

He'd certainly inherited his eyes from her. You could see it easily when they were side by side like this.

Holy crap, I thought, recognizing the customer from the cosmetics section of the store who'd identified me as a dangerous lunatic even before she'd subsequently seen me drop-kick her husband.

Lopez's mother.

I'd always had a feeling that I might not want to meet her. Now I was sure.

Fine-boned, fair-skinned, and elegant in her sensible coat, she thumped her son with the same purse she'd been using to clobber me. "Don't just stand there," she said to him. "Arrest her!"

"Mom, will you please—"

"He *can't* arrest her," said an interested spectator,

stepping on my foot as he moved closer to us. "You need a cop for that."

"Ow," I said, trying to free my foot.

"I *am* a cop." Unaware I was being stepped on, Lopez tightened his grasp on my shoulders when he felt me trying to wriggle away. "Now move along, folks. Nothing to see here. The fun's all over."

A few people ignored this, clearly hoping there'd be more violence. But most of the jostling crowd started to melt away, including the guy standing on my foot, carried along on the tide of busy shoppers rapidly passing through this area.

I asked Lopez hopefully, "Can I go now, too?"

"You were supposed to be upstairs," he said accusingly to me. "You were assigned to the fourth floor for the rest of the shift!"

"You *know* this madwoman?" his mother demanded. "Is she someone you've arrested before?"

Still holding me by the shoulders, Lopez gave me a sharp shake. "What are you *doing* down here? You weren't supposed to be *here*."

"I got reassigned. Stop that!" I jerked myself out of his grasp before he could shake me again. As I staggered backward, I accidentally kicked his father, still on the floor, who groaned in reaction.

"Oh, *nice*," Lopez said to me in exasperation.

"Carlos!" Mrs. Lopez shoved me aside and knelt beside her prone husband. "Are you all right?"

I looked down at the couple, thinking it was just as

well that Lopez and I weren't dating. It could never work out between us. Not after *this*.

"What happened?" Mr. Lopez asked again.

"This crazy person attacked you!"

"What?" he said.

"I did *not* attack him," I protested. "I was trying to . . . to . . ." I glanced at the performance platform, where Karaoke Bear lay innocently on his side.

Trying to rescue him from the possessed ravening bear might not sound entirely sane, I realized.

"Trying to . . . ?" Lopez prodded.

"Protect him," I finished feebly. "I thought he was in danger."

"Of course," Lopez said, to no one in particular.

"Protect him?" Mrs. Lopez raged. "Protect him? You *kicked* him in the *head*—"

"No, no, it wasn't my head, *querida*," Carlos Lopez said placatingly, trying to sit up. "The young lady hit my shoulder."

"Lady? *Lady?*" his wife repeated in outrage.

"Ah!" The gray-haired man winced as his aches and pains started introducing themselves. "And my jaw, too, I think."

"What are you people still doing here?" Lopez said to the few remaining stragglers who'd stuck around to see what else might happen. "Go about your business. *Now.*"

He didn't even have to show them his badge. They did what he told them to do. I envied him that handy skill.

"I'm very sorry, sir," I said, reaching out to help Carlos Lopez off the floor.

His wife slapped away my hands. "Don't touch him!"

Their son looked up at the ceiling and prayed, "God, please let this be just a nightmare. If You're truly merciful, then any minute now, I'll wake up in a cold sweat and vow never again to eat a chili dog so late at night . . ."

As Mrs. Lopez helped her husband rise shakily to his feet, she informed me shrilly, "I intend to press charges!"

Two security guards shoved their way through the crowd of shoppers still entering and exiting the building, *finally* arriving on the scene after being alerted to the commotion. Given how rarely we saw security around here during an emergency, I was starting to think that Fenster's would be a good place to commit a murder.

I regretted the chilling idea as soon as I had it, half-afraid that the Evil menacing the store could hear my thoughts.

I needed to find Max and Lucky, I realized, and tell them what had just happened.

"What's going on here?" demanded a pale, pot-bellied security guard.

"This *insane* woman attacked my husband, and I want—"

"NYPD," Lopez said loudly, giving his mother a

warning glare. Looking distracted, he patted his pockets, searching for his badge, as he said to the two guards, "There was a little mishap."

His mother blanched. "A *little* mis—"

"But it's all under control now." He found his gold shield and flashed it at them. "Detective Lopez, Organized Crime Control Bureau. I'm investigating the hijackings."

"*Hijacking?*" the guard bleated. "Has someone taken Mr. Fenster's helicopter?"

"What? No. I meant . . . Never mind," Lopez said. "We've got it covered. And I'll deal with this situation, too, guys. But I appreciate your alert response."

"Alert response?" I repeated incredulously. "Are you *kidding* me?"

"Not now," Lopez said to me between gritted teeth.

"Oh, yeah, detective, now I recognize you. From yesterday, on the fourth floor," said the other guard, an older man. "Wait a *minute.* I recognize that elf, too! She's the one who caused all the trouble there!"

"That's not fair," I protested. It was hardly *my* fault that I'd been attacked by a possessed tree.

"Did she? Well, I'm not surprised to hear it," Mrs. Lopez said to them. "A little while ago, I saw her attack a store manager!"

Lopez gave me a sharp glance.

"I *didn't*," I told him.

"Good," he said.

"I was attacking Naughty and Nice," I explained.

"What?" he snapped.

"You see?" said his mother.

"Mom, will you please stop?"

"Well, no, I wasn't *attacking* them," I amended. "I was trying to, um, apprehend them, I guess. They . . ." I sighed. "Never mind. It's not important now."

"Then, by all means, let's cross it off our agenda," said Lopez.

"Detective, should we escort this elf from the store?" asked the older guard.

Bridget Lopez gasped in protest. "You can't just unleash her on the general population! I insist that you lock her up!"

"Mom, that's enough."

"I guess we could put her in the holding cell on the sixth floor," said the pot-bellied guard, perking up at the idea of incarcerating someone.

His partner said, too enthusiastically for my taste, "Hey, that's right! That cell is mostly used for shoplifters, but if the elf is causing trouble, we could—"

"*No*," I said, taking a step back as he took a step toward me.

Mrs. Lopez said to them, "That's an excellent idea."

"*Mom*."

"*Querida*, I think you should let your son handle this."

"Thank you, Pop." Lopez said firmly, "No one will be locking up anyone."

"Damn right," I said.

The security guards looked a little deflated. Mrs. Lopez looked miffed. Her son sent me a glance warning me to keep my mouth shut.

Lopez said to the security guards, "Guys, I've got control of the elf. The singing bear. The whole situation. So you can leave it in my hands. Really."

"Well, okay, if you're sure . . ."

"I am. Thanks again for your help."

"Their *help?*" I said.

"Not now, Esther," he muttered as the departing guards left us to our own devices.

"In what way have they *helped?* Now *or* yesterday?" I demanded, attracting curious glances from fresh passersby in the crowded store. "I could have been—"

"Esther!" he snapped, hoping (in vain) to make me shut up. "Let it go, would you?"

His mother drew in a sharp breath. "*What* did you call her?"

Lopez blinked. "Huh?"

"Did you just call her Esther?" his mother demanded.

"Uh . . ." Lopez sighed and his shoulders sagged. "Shit."

His father said, "I don't like to hear you using language like that in front of ladies, *mi perrito.*"

"Sorry, Pop," Lopez said, looking warily at his mother.

"*Esther?*" Mrs. Lopez said, gazing at me with an appalled expression. "The chorus girl with ties to the mob? *That* Esther?"

"Yes," Lopez said darkly.

"No!" I was offended. She'd gotten that description of me from the tabloids after I witnessed Chubby Charlie Chiccante getting murdered at Bella Stella.

Seeing my outrage, Lopez amended, "She's an actress, not a chorus girl, Mom. I told you that."

I was about to add that I also didn't have ties to the mob . . . but since my relationship with the Gambello crime family was undeniably complicated, I decided to leave that subject alone.

"This is Esther?" Lopez's mother said to him in undisguised horror. "*This* is who you . . . you . . ."

"Eh?" Carlos' eyebrows lifted in surprise as he looked at me. Then he asked a few quick questions in Spanish, and his son replied in the same language. The gist of it seemed to be that, yes, I was the woman whom Lopez had told his parents about. His father looked bemused and concerned; but at least he didn't look stricken with simultaneous nausea, vertigo, and stunned rage—the way, for example, that Mrs. Lopez looked right now.

"This half-naked *lunatic* is the woman you've been seeing?" she demanded of her son.

"I am completely clothed," I said irritably. Sure, my costume was uncomfortably brief for that chilly store, but it wasn't as if I was showing a depraved amount of flesh.

"Now, *querida*, your son is a grown man, and—"

"*She* is the reason," Mrs. Lopez continued, pointing at me, "that you wouldn't even *call* Kathleen O'Malley's daughter when I asked you to? That you refused even to *meet* Jennifer Gonzalez when I suggested it?"

"You're still using me as an excuse to get out of dating her friends' daughters?" I asked Lopez.

"It's convenient," he said with a shrug. "Anyhow, just because you and I aren't dating doesn't mean I don't still . . . still . . ." He fell silent as he realized that his parents and I were all three staring at him with varying degrees of surprise, waiting for him to finish that sentence.

His father asked, "Do you mean that you're not still seeing Miss . . . ?"

"Diamond," I said. "Esther Diamond."

"You are no longer involved with Miss Diamond?" Carlos asked.

"I'm still involved with her," said his son. "I'm just not seeing her."

Since that was a pretty accurate description of our relationship, I let it stand.

"I don't understand," said his father.

Lopez sighed. "I'm not dating her. We haven't been on a date in . . . months."

"You lied to us?" his mother exclaimed.

"I lied," he confirmed.

"You *lied?*" she repeated.

"Yes, I lied," Lopez said wearily. "Can we move on now?"

"But why?" his father asked in bewilderment. "Why did you lie, *perrito?*"

"What did you call him?" I asked.

"Oh, why do you *think*, Pop?" said Lopez, gesturing to his mother.

"Ah. Yes." The old gentleman nodded.

"What does *that* mean?" Mrs. Lopez snapped at her husband.

"It *means*," said her son irritably, "that no matter *how* much you nag, I'm not going out with any of the women you try to throw in front of me, Mom! Not ever. *Never.* How can I make this any clearer to you?"

"You shouldn't talk to your mother in that tone," his father chided.

"And, what's more, you can *both* just stop asking me for grandchildren!" Lopez included his father in his diatribe now. "Because you're not getting them!"

"My son!" Carlos exclaimed, looking wounded.

"I mean, not anytime soon," Lopez said more calmly. "So just stop *asking*, would you? Enough already! Because I don't even feel like going *out* with anyone else while I'm still . . . still . . . while . . ."

"Yes?" his mother prodded coldly.

Lopez glanced around the busy store. Happily, people had ceased paying attention to us. After all, now we seemed pretty much like anyone else at Fenster's in this festive season of joy—tense, tired, bickering, and stressed.

"Go on," said Mrs. Lopez, though her tone was not encouraging.

"No, we're stopping there," her son said firmly. "I've just exceeded my annual quota of discussing this subject with you."

"Well, *I'm* not through discussing it," she said, gearing up.

"I had a feeling," I muttered.

"I'll have you know, Connor, I was still recovering from the brawl this woman started in the cosmetics section—"

"I *didn't* start a—"

"—when I got here and found her assaulting your father!"

"Now, Bridget," said her husband, "I'm sure it was just a misunderstanding."

"I can't *believe* this is happening," Lopez grumbled, shaking his head and staring abstractly at the floor.

"And if you think that I will accept this—this—this *deranged elf* as the mother of my grandchildren, Connor Lopez, then you have got another thing coming!"

"Whoa!" I said. "How did you get from 'we're not dating' to me giving him children?" I could see it really *was* a mania with her.

"This is a family matter!" she snapped at me, offended that I had intruded.

"Oh, come on, of *course* this is happening," Lopez

muttered schizophrenically to himself. "Don't pretend you weren't expecting it, one way or another. No, *dreading* it. Be honest. Why else—"

"But at least we know now why you're not arresting her," his mother added critically. "I suppose doing your duty by your father would interfere with your love life!"

"Now, Bridget—"

"*What* love life?" Lopez said morosely.

"I'm very disappointed in you, Connor."

"Yes, I think we've established that, Mom."

"What were you *thinking?*"

"I thought she'd be on the fourth floor," Lopez replied, as if this explained everything.

"What?" his mother said.

He sighed. "Never mind."

I feared we'd be trapped in family hell all evening if I didn't change the subject. So I said, "I hope you're feeling all right now, Mr. Lopez? I didn't mean to hurt you."

"Oh?" said his wife. "Then maybe you shouldn't have kicked him in the head."

"Mom, can we *stop* now? You've made your point."

"It wasn't my head, *querida*, it was more—"

"Connor, I *insist* that you—"

"Pop, maybe you should sit down for a minute," Lopez said loudly, taking his father's elbow and guiding him toward Karaoke Bear's sparkly platform. "You just got kicked—"

"Not there!"

They all stopped speaking and stared at me.

I realized I had sounded a tad hysterical.

I took a deep breath and glanced at Karaoke Bear, who was still lying on his little stage. Thinking fast, I said, "All of a sudden the bear short-circuited and toppled forward, toward . . ." I gestured to Mr. Lopez, then said to him, "I was afraid you'd get a nasty electric shock or something if he fell against you."

They all continued staring at me.

Mrs. Lopez was the first to find her voice—which I suspected was usually the case. "So kicking my husband was your solution? You couldn't just have *said* something to him?"

"I *did*," I said, annoyed that she wasn't receiving my explanation with more grace.

"She did," Carlos said gently to wife. "She shouted, but I didn't understand—"

"The bear short-circuited, too?" Lopez said, examining the prone performer at a safe distance. "Jesus, this whole place is falling apart, isn't it?"

"Too?" his mother repeated alertly. "You mean this has happened before?"

"Yeah, yesterday," Lopez said, still studying the bear. "Up on the fourth floor."

"You see?" Carlos said to his wife. "It was an accident, and Miss Diamond was looking out for my safety."

"Hmph," said Bridget.

"I hope you're okay, Mr. Lopez?" I said.

"I shall be fine," he said with a warm smile. "Thank you."

"Please don't thank me," I replied sincerely, seeing the way his wife and son were looking at me.

But despite the expression of mingled bemusement, speculation, and suspicion on Lopez's face, he asked me with concern, "Are *you* okay?"

"Yes," I said. "Just shaken."

"Connor is right about *one* thing," Bridget said, taking her husband's arm. "You should sit down."

"I just had the wind knocked out of me, that's all," he replied reassuringly. "But, yes, maybe I'll sit for a minute."

Karaoke Bear was near the ladies' winter accessories department, where an empty loveseat awaited a couple of weary shoppers. I watched Mrs. and Mr. Lopez walk over to it and sit down together. Next to me, their son let out his breath in a gush and sagged with relief, like a boxer taking a much-needed break between rounds.

"So those are your parents," I said.

"Those are my parents," he agreed, eyeing them with disfavor.

"Your mom's a little . . ." I didn't know how to finish the thought tactfully.

"I know," he said dryly.

I added, "But your dad's very . . ."

"Yeah. He is." Lopez smiled and started to relax a little.

I had always assumed, in my romantic imaginings, that he got his exotic good looks from his Cuban immigrant father. I had vaguely pictured his dad as a combination between a fiery counter-revolutionary and a sultry tango instructor who'd swept an ordinary New York girl off her feet decades ago.

Now I realized, looking at the couple, that only Lopez's dark coloring and straight black hair were inherited from his sire. (Well, that and his patience—which had quite clearly *not* come from his maternal line.) He got his masculine beauty from his mother, who'd probably been the most stunning young woman in whatever crowd her husband had first spotted her in. In the obvious ways, of course, Lopez looked nothing like his petite, fair-skinned, redheaded mom. But to someone as familiar with his face as I was, the resemblance was evident now that I knew who this woman was.

"I'm still a little unclear," Lopez said, turning to face me, "about why I found you apparently smothering my dad while my mom was whaling on you."

"It was all part of my grand plan to rescue him from the singing bear."

"Ah. Of course." Lopez nodded. "That should have occurred to me."

After a moment, I said inanely, "She calls you Connor." I'd never heard anyone call him that before.

"It *is* my name," he pointed out.

"You don't look like a Connor."

"I know," he said with a smile. "Everyone says that. Even my dad. But it was the name Mom decided on when I was born, and she usually gets her way."

That was easy to believe.

"But your father calls you something else, doesn't he?"

"Oh." He didn't seem pleased that I had noticed. "Yeah."

"I didn't quite catch what it was . . ." When Lopez didn't respond, I prodded, "What does he call you?"

He hesitated before saying, "*Perrito.*"

On his tongue, the word sounded sexy and exotic. I tried to conceal the quiver of pleasure it always gave me to hear Lopez speak in Spanish.

"Is that your middle name or something?" When he shook his head, I prodded, "Why does he call you that?"

Lopez shrugged. "It's just my dad's pet name for me."

"What does it mean?"

It took him a moment to decide to tell me. "Puppy. Little dog."

I was charmed by this. "Puppy?"

"*Sí, yo soy su perrito.*" He looked across the store at his father. "Thirty-one years old, an NYPD detective, and I'm still his little puppy."

"That's so sweet!"

He grunted.

I recalled that both his brothers were older. "Oh,

that's right. You were the baby of the family, weren't you? The puppy trotting around after the big dogs?"

"Uh-huh."

"Well, I'm not sure it suits you any better now than Connor does," I said. "But I like it, anyhow, *mi perrito*."

That made him smile. "My brothers changed it to 'burrito,' which they thought was hilarious. Thanks to them, that's what most other kids in the neighborhood called me."

"Burrito?" I said with a sympathetic laugh. "No wonder you wanted handcuffs and a gun when you grew up."

"Yep."

After a moment, I touched his arm and said, "I, uh . . . Look, it's not really my fault that meeting your parents went so badly, but I'm sorry about it, even so."

Lopez waved away my apology. "No, I'm sorry that they . . . That we . . ." He cleared his throat. "You know."

"I guess it was a shock to the system for all of us," I said. "Will you recover?"

"Hmph. Serves me right for agreeing to let them meet me at the store today, I suppose. But I thought, you know, it's a huge place, half a dozen floors, thousands of people . . . And *you* were supposed to be stuck in Santa's crib all evening. So what could *possibly* go wrong?" He smiled ruefully. "That'll teach me."

"You dad will be okay, won't he?"

"Of course," he said. "See?"

He gestured to his parents, who were still seated together. His mother was fussing over his father, who seemed to be enjoying her anxious attentions. As I watched, Carlos took Bridget's hand from his head (*how many times did she have to be told I hadn't kicked him there?* I wondered irritably), held her hand between both of his, and spoke soothingly, calming her down. Seeing his gentleness and the affection shining in his expression, it was easy to guess what had drawn Bridget to him nearly forty years ago, when she'd probably been a dazzling catch who could have any man she wanted. Then he kissed her hand flirtatiously and teased her about something, and the two of them laughed together.

"All better now," I murmured, recognizing that the storm had passed.

I recalled Lopez once telling me that he came from a family that always shouted noisily over stupid arguments but handled serious problems very quietly. Although it wasn't exactly flattering, I was nonetheless glad that his parents' disapproval of me qualified as just a stupid argument in their family.

Lopez, who was now looking around this area as if seeking an explanation for what had occurred here, noticed my blue stocking cap on the floor. He bent over to pick it up. Examining it, he said, "I think someone's stepped on it." He slapped it against his thigh a couple of times to dust it off, then shook it out a bit, making the attached ears bobble. Satisfied with its condition, he handed it over to me.

"Thanks." I just held it in my hands, not enthused

about suiting back up. I didn't know where I'd spend the rest of my shift, but there was no *way* I was going to keep working with a possessed karaoke apparatus.

"Tell me again what happened to the singing bear," Lopez said.

The phrase brought to mind Carlos' phone conversations near the performance platform, and I realized he had been speaking to his son shortly before calling his wife.

"Oh, *that's* how you showed up here just in time to stop your mother from giving me a concussion," I said, realizing it hadn't been a lucky (or unlucky) coincidence. "This is where you were meeting your parents."

"Actually, I was meeting them in sporting goods," he said, "so we could pick up my eldest brother's Christmas gift. He's getting into town tomorrow. But my dad couldn't find the department, and my mom couldn't find my dad. Then Pop called and asked me to meet him by the singing bear, instead. At first, I thought I'd heard wrong . . ." He looked over at the prone bear. "So what exactly happened here?"

I decided just to tell him. "Karaoke Bear grew fangs and claws and tried to attack your father."

There was a long pause. Then: "That's your story? For real?"

"Yep. And I'm sticking to it."

"O . . . kay." Another pause. "Did anyone else see this?"

"Some little kids. They got scared and ran away."

"Before or after you attacked my father?"

"I *didn't* attack—"

"Let me rephrase that," he said. "Is it possible that *you* scared them away? When you suddenly launched a flying dropkick at a bystander, for example?"

"No! They got scared when they saw the bear turn into something monstrous."

"And that's when they ran away?"

"No, they screamed and ran away when . . . um . . ."

"Yes?"

"When I kicked your dad," I said sullenly.

"So when did the bear short-circuit?"

"He didn't. I just made that up so your parents won't think I'm crazy."

"Oh, I think we already crossed that bridge and burned it behind us," Lopez said in resignation.

"I was trying to sound sane," I grumbled.

"It was a good effort," he assured me. "I appreciated it."

"But you didn't believe me?"

"Well, I had a feeling there was more to it than that—with you, there usually is," he said philosophically. "But I believed that part. I still do. I mean, that bear sure *looks* like its circuits blew."

"Really?" I cautiously stepped closer to Karaoke Bear to get a good look, recalling the smoke I'd seen rising from his body after he keeled over. I noticed scorch marks around his eyes and mouth. "Hmm. Like the tree yesterday . . ."

"Yeah. I'd say they really need to overhaul all their mechanical displays." He thought it over and added, "Or their whole electrical system."

I wondered what to make of this. Maybe the force lurking inside Fenster & Co. was looking for a host—or hosts?—but was so powerful that its energy quickly destroyed the vehicles it tried to inhabit.

Well, the ones powered by electricity, anyhow. I thought about my consistent impression that Naughty and Nice were Evil incarnate . . .

"I want you to promise me something," Lopez said.

"Mmm?"

But what if my metaphor had been more realistic than I'd realized? What if Freddie's bimbos *were* Evil in the flesh? What if they weren't a couple of air-headed bitches whose entire self-worth was tied up in their cheap good looks, but instead innocent victims of the entity inhabiting Fenster's?

"I want you to stay away from anything mechanical around here," said Lopez. "Toys, promotional items, gimmicks, displays . . . Since you're not worried they'll fire anyone at this point, you probably won't lose your job for refusing to work at certain posts."

What if this thing invading the store wasn't starting its insidious conquest via toys and devices? What if it had started by possessing *people*, and we just didn't realize it?

"And even if they do fire you . . ." Lopez continued, "It was only going to be two more days' pay, right?

And you'll be back at work at Stella's soon, after all. I know things are tight, Esther, but if push comes to shove, it would definitely be better to get fired than to get electrocuted. They're obviously not exercising due diligence around here—or even common sense. So I'd feel better if you'd promise me not to do any more shifts with things that could hurt you."

I needed to find Max and Lucky. And Nelli! Maybe the familiar's combined mystical and canine senses could detect whether Naughty and Nice were possessed.

"Esther? Are you listening to me?"

"Uh-huh," I said absently.

With luck, maybe Nelli could *smell* the Evil emanating from those two elves. Or something.

"In fact," Lopez was saying, "until we know how widespread the problem is, maybe you should just avoid touching *anything* connected to the electrical system here. Light switches. The coffee machine or microwave in the break room. Elevator buttons."

"Elevator," I repeated, meeting his gaze when I heard him say that.

The elevator, the mechanical tree, the singing bear . . . Electricity was the common denominator in the incidents we knew about for certain. Maybe that was how we could narrow our search and locate the—the—whatever was here at Fenster's with us, unseen but present. Could the entity be inhabiting the store's electrical power system?

Lopez said, "Your friend Satsy's reality was more than a little altered by the high-quality grass he'd been smoking before he got into the freight elevator, but that doesn't mean the elevator didn't really malfunction."

"How do you know about that?" I asked, startled.

He gave me a funny look. "I was standing right there when Drag Queen Santa said the elevator had . . . Oh." He realized what I meant. "It's my job to be better at noticing things than the guys on the loading docks are at hiding them. Of *course* I know about the weed."

"Oh. Right." I nodded. I should have expected that—especially given that activity on the docks comprised part of his investigation. "Never mind."

"Luckily for those guys," he said, "I don't care about it. I'm looking for a criminal conspiracy to commit armed robbery, not a few tokers."

His cell phone rang. He pulled it out of his pocket, glanced at the screen, and said, "I've got to take this. Excuse me."

I liked that he did that when he took a call. So many people just interrupted me without pause to start yammering into their phones, as if I were chopped liver. Having seen Lopez with his father, I could guess where he'd learned his good manners. (And having seen him with his mother, it was easy to guess how he had learned to exercise his patience.)

"Lopez," he said into the phone. After a moment, he frowned. "*Now?* I thought—Oh. Yeah, okay. So how's it going?" He smiled as he glanced at me. "Well, elves can be feisty, you know. Uh-huh. Yeah, I know who you mean. No, I don't think so, either." He listened for a few more moments, then said, "Right. Okay. Let me know."

As he ended the call, I said with a touch of resentment, "Is there *another* trouble-making elf in the store today?

"Not exactly." He took a breath and informed me, "NYPD has just started executing a search warrant of employee areas throughout the store. And the Russian elf . . ."

"Nutcracker," I supplied.

"Well, *that* name sure fits," he muttered. "Nutcracker was in the ladies' locker room on the fourth floor when the cops entered and started their search. I gather she got a little hostile."

"I have absolutely no trouble picturing that," I said.

"But they're gonna let it pass."

I was annoyed. "Why am *I* the only elf that people want to lock up?"

"I am not touching that with a ten foot pole," he said.

I realized what he'd just told me. "The cops are searching the locker room? The one *I* use?"

"Yes. Well, *all* the locker rooms. And all the break rooms."

"You really think elves and reindeer are involved in the hijackings?"

"I'm more inclined to suspect Santas," he admitted. "But that's a personal prejudice."

I gasped as I realized, "This means NYPD will be looking through my things!"

"The warrant's very specific, Esther," he said reassuringly. "You can't get in trouble for anything they find that doesn't connect you to this case."

"Oh, thank you very much for your confidence in me, *Connor*," I said irritably. "I'm not worried about them finding something illegal. I'm worried about total strangers pawing through my personal belongings! It makes me feel violated."

"Do you want me to do it?" he asked.

"No," I snapped. "Having *you* paw through my belongings—"

"I don't *paw*."

"—would just be . . . *weird*."

"It would be a little weird for me, too," he said. "So let's leave them to it. Okay?"

"Hmph." After a moment, I asked, "You really think one of us is involved?"

"I think it seems like someone has access to more information about Fenster's procedures and shipments than is likely to be available to a short-term seasonal employee. And getting the inside person in position *just* in time to start pulling these heists seems too clumsy to match the skill level that's behind this operation. Which is why I'm more interested in the permanent staff. But I could be wrong." He shrugged. "So we're running background checks on everyone. Which is a big job, given the size of the staff, especially at this time of year. It's taking a while."

"Background checks?" I repeated anxiously. "Um . . . that time I got arrested in Harlem won't show up, will it?"

"No, there's no record of that." He kept his expression carefully blank. "I made sure of it."

"Good." In one of those little misunderstandings that can so easily arise when you're confronting Evil, one night in summer the cops of the 25th Precinct had taken me for a prostitute who was disturbing the peace and assaulting people on Lexington Avenue. Although he had broken up with me several months earlier, Lopez answered my middle-of-the-night cry for help and ran the gauntlet of laughing cops to get me out of that mess. I added, "Thank you."

"My pleasure." He looked over his shoulder to frown at Karaoke Bear as he said, "And now, on top of everything else, I think I'd better get a city inspector in here to check out the electrical system before someone gets seriously hurt." He glanced at his watch and added, "First thing tomorrow. I won't find anyone now." When he caught my concerned frown, he prodded, "What?"

"Nothing," I lied.

If something mystical was in the system, would it attack an intrusive presence—such as an inspector poking around?

"And we need to get Maintenance here right now to disconnect the bear and shut down this display," Lopez added.

"That's a good idea," I agreed.

After he finished that call (and complained to me about how casual Fenster's management was being about a prominent main-floor display short-circuiting and nearly injuring people), he said, "Stay here, okay? Keep people away from the whole karaoke setup, just in case there's a dangerous current."

"Where are you going?" I asked.

He squared his shoulders. "I'm going to get rid of my parents."

I was all in favor of that plan, but I refrained from saying so. I smiled as I watched Mr. Lopez's little *perrito* walk purposefully across the store, his black hair gleaming under the fluorescent lights.

And that's when a Christmas tree spoke to me.

14

"Psst. Esther!"

"Urngh!" I nearly jumped out of my skin and started coughing on the surprised shriek I swallowed.

"Whoa, are you okay, kid?"

I looked around for the source of that familiar voice.

"Over here," said a tree at the center of the display. "No, don't *look*. Act casual!"

"Lucky?" I said hoarsely, gaping at the tree. "What are you doing?"

"Hiding from your boyfriend."

I looked over at Lopez, whose back was to us as he approached his parents. "Oh! Right." I said to the tree, "Good thinking."

"Jesus, look at something *else*, would you? Do you want him and his folks to see you talking to a tree? What are they gonna think?"

"Nothing they haven't thought already," I said wanly. I turned so that my back was to the Lopez family and pretended to be examining my costume for wear and tear. "I guess Jeff told you where to find me?"

"Yeah. I come to report our findings," said Lucky, keeping his voice low. "I got here just in time to see the cop's mom telling the guards to put you in stir. She's a beauty, ain't she? Got a temper on her, though."

"Uh-huh."

Lucky continued, "Wish I'd been here in time to see you drop-kick his dad. That musta been something."

"Yes, if only someone had thought to take pictures," I said. "Then I could share the moment with you."

"Yeah, I been avoiding the elves with cameras," said Lucky.

He was referring to the photo duty elves, whose job it was to capture the joy of Christmas moments in Solsticeland. (I had been permanently eliminated from photo duty after just half a shift; predictably, since I am not good with gadgets, I had mostly captured blurry images of feet or elbows.) The photos were uploaded to computer monitors on the fourth floor, where shoppers could order copies of their fun-filled moments for a "nominal" fee.

The old hit man added, "I don't think anyone would recognize my picture in this beard, but it don't pay to be careless."

"Good thinking," I said.

"So the bear went polter-scary on you?"

"Yes." I realized Lucky had eavesdropped on my whole conversation with Lopez. I tried to remember whether we'd said anything embarrassingly personal.

"His old man calls him 'puppy,' huh?" said Lucky.

Okay, I tried to remember whether *I* had said anything embarrassingly personal.

Lucky added, "It's nice that they're still close."

"Uh-huh."

"And the cops are searching the whole place now?"

I replied to the tree, "No, just the—"

"Don't *look* at me!"

"Sorry." I turned my back to him and gazed absently at the passing crowd—some of whom seemed to wonder why I was speaking into thin air as I said, "Just the employee areas, I think. For tonight, anyhow."

"Hmph."

I suddenly realized whose belongings were being pawed through besides mine right now, and I gasped in alarm. A nearby shopper gave me a surprised look.

I turned slightly toward the Christmas trees and said, "Lucky, please tell me the cops aren't going to find anything, uh, awkward in your locker."

"What am I, an idiot? I'm gonna bring my piece into a store that I know is crawling with cops who are investigating armed robberies that they're blaming on the Gambellos?" He sounded offended.

"Just checking," I said. "What about ID?"

A random patrolman might overlook the name of Alberto Battistuzzi if he checked Lucky's wallet when searching the locker I had unofficially allocated to him today; but if any OCCB detectives saw that name, they'd immediately realize a high-ranking Gambello was in the store and masquerading as a Fenster's employee. Lucky was famous in his world even when OCCB *wasn't* quite so intensely focused on the Gambello family.

"You think I'd bring my *real* ID to a place infested with cops?" he demanded.

"Okay, never mind." And, fortunately, it was very unlikely that anyone but Lopez, who was down here rather than searching the fourth floor locker rooms, would recognize Max's name if his ID was in his locker. Which reminded me . . . "Where is Max?"

"Nelli needed to go outside for a few minutes. The doc asked me to check in with you while he's walking her." Lucky asked, "So what happened with the bear? It looks like it set itself on fire from inside."

He was right. That was exactly how it looked.

I warned a curious kid who was approaching the platform, "Don't go near Karaoke Bear. He's having electrical problems."

The boy's father took his hand and pulled him away, giving me a nod of acknowledgment. I positioned myself closer to the platform so no one could touch it before I stopped them.

Then, not wanting passersby to hear this next bit and report me to a psychiatric ward, I turned toward Lucky's tree and bent over, pretending to adjust my stockings and fiddle with my boot buckles as I described Karaoke Bear's terrifying transformation.

But when I told Lucky my theory about electronic objects—or possibly Fenster's whole electrical system—being targeted by the mystical activity, he said, "No, that won't wash, kid. We had a very *non*-electrical experience up on the fourth floor a little while ago."

"What happened?"

"You know Chérie the Chef? That nice doll on display near the menorah?"

"*Nice?* You think that doll is . . . Never mind. Yes, I know it."

"I like her little kitchen," he said. "I was looking at Chérie, thinking she'd be a good gift for a granddaughter."

Sure. A Madonna-whore complex in a kitchen-porn apron. *Perfect* present for a little girl. Maybe we could throw in a pair of mink handcuffs, too.

Lucky continued, "Well, a nice gift for a grandchild if, you know, my daughter and that schmuck she married would get on the ball and start a family already. I'm beginning to think I'll be in my grave before—"

"I just know there's a point to this," I said, in no mood to hear more complaints about my generation's failure to produce grandchildren soon enough to satisfy our parents' generation.

"Oh. Right. So I'm standin' there, thinkin' what a nice gift she'd make for a kid . . . and Chérie all of a sudden tries to turn me into veal piccata."

"What?" I whirled around in surprise.

"Don't look this way!"

I turned back. "Lucky! What happened?"

"Huh?" said a shopper.

"Nothing." I waited until that person had moved on, then prodded, "Well?"

"All of sudden, from one second to the next, Chérie's eyes start glowing red, and she grows these sharp pointed teeth that are dripping with her drool—and, Jesus, the *smell* coming from her."

"A foul smell! Yes, I noticed the same thing!"

"*What* smell?" asked a shopper, looking ready to take offense.

"Merry Christmas!" I said. "Be sure to visit Solsticeland while you're here!"

"Hmph."

Lucky said, " 'Foul' don't begin to describe it. I'm tellin' you, kid, I've relocated decomposing corpses that didn't smell that bad."

"Moving quickly past that point," I said, "what happened next?"

"She picked up a little knife from her kitchen, and it got all glowy."

"Glowy?"

"Glowy. And then it grew about five inches—big enough to send me down for the dirt nap, believe me."

I believed him. He had more practical experience with lethal weapons than anyone of my acquaintance—except possibly Max. I looked across the store at Lopez, wondering how to explain to him that inanimate objects were arming themselves with deadly intent at Fenster & Co.

Lucky continued, "Then the doll—glowing red eyes, dripping fangs, big knife, and all—gives this sort of cackling screech and leaps through the air at me."

"My *God*, what did you do?" I cried.

"Huh?" said a startled shopper.

"Nothing! Go away." I turned and looked at the tree. "What did you do?"

"Whaddya think? I turned and ran."

"What did the doll do?" I asked the tree.

"She ran after me," Lucky said grimly. "Laughing and screeching and drooling—and trying her best to stab me with that knife."

"Did people see this?"

"Nah. We were near the menorah. Who goes *there*? Not meaning to hurt your feelings or anything, Esther, but no one comes to Holidayland to see a menorah."

"So there was no one around?" I asked.

"Nope," he replied. "Things happened so fast. The doll turns into a monster and leaps at me. I jump and run. It chases. I run past that Viking mural and that big log, and I take a sharp turn toward Solstice Castle—where I bump into a whole buncha people, all standing in my way."

"And?"

"And I turn around to fight the doll . . . But it's lying face down on the floor now, looking normal again . . .

except that Chérie's hair is smoldering and her tiny little knife has melted."

"Whoa," I said.

"Yeah," he said.

While I pondered this horrifying story, a child's voice floated to me from the other side of the trees. "Mommy, there's an elf hiding in there!"

"Oh? Uh, hello, Mr. Elf," said a doubtful-sounding parent.

"Buzz off," said Sugarplum, in a tone that prohibited discussion.

I thought of the little blond boy who'd been so frightened yesterday. "So Jonathan saw exactly what he thought he saw, didn't he?" I mused. "Something with glowing eyes and claws and dripping fangs."

"Yeah, I'd say that little kid gave you the straight dope on that."

"I wonder if that grimacing gnome came to life?" I said. "Became animated. Got possessed. Whatever."

"Well, we know from what happened with Chef Chérie that once they're possessed—or whatever—these things are mobile. Mighta been the gnome. Mighta been a Santa dummy from the North Pole that chased the kid *into* the Enchanted Forest."

"That poor little boy!" A shudder passed through me. "No wonder he was hysterical when we found him."

"No kidding. I hope his mother leaves the lights on at night for him for a while," Lucky said with feeling. "I've faced down some pretty scary things in my life,

Esther, including three different guys who pointed a gun at me and pulled the trigger. But I swear, I don't think I ever seen anything as scary as poltergeist Chérie. I'm a little amazed that I don't need to change my elf shorts now, if you know what I mean."

"So we know this entity, whatever it is, is messing with mechanical toys, regular toys, elevators, displays . . . Oh, and I think it might also be messing with people!" I told him my theory (half-baked, admittedly) about Naughty and Nice.

"Well, if they're evil, then Nelli ain't noticed it," he said. "Those girls was upstairs earlier today, helping keep the fathers under control in the line to see Santa. Me and Max was casing that whole section of Gloomyland with Nelli at the time, trying to pick up a vibe. Our favorite familiar walked right up to those two elves without acting any different at all. One of the blondes is kinda scared of big dogs and the other one giggles a lot, but that was as weird as it got."

"Hmm." All right, if they weren't possessed by something, perhaps they were the *source* of the trouble. "Maybe they're causing the activity. Could they be the instigators, either consciously or unwittingly?"

"That sounds like a question for the doc."

"I mean, those two bimbos seem like disturbed personalities to *me*. So if a poltergeist attaches itself to—"

"We'll ask Max what he thinks."

"Even if Nelli didn't pick up on anything, *I* find it easy to believe those women are—"

"We'll ask the doc," Lucky repeated tersely.

"Huh? Oh. All right."

"In fact, he should be here any minute."

"What?" I glanced anxiously across the store at Lopez, who was still talking with his parents. I was relieved to see that they looked relatively calm now. His mother was straightening the collar of his coat, and he was nodding while listening to his father say something to him. "We don't want Lopez to see Max here!"

"No kidding," Lucky replied. "But when the doc and I decided to meet you at the karaoke bar—"

"It's a bear, not a bar."

"—we didn't know you'd be busy entertaining New York's finest. By the way, I thought you two broke up?"

"We did."

"He don't *act* like a guy who's broken up."

"More to the point," I said, "he don't act like a guy who'll be happy to see Belsnickel here at Fenster's. So we should take steps to prevent their meeting now."

"Well, we can't call Max and tell him not to show up. He don't have a cell. And I can't head him off, because I got no idea which direction he's coming from," he said. "So you'll have to get the cop out of here right away."

"How do I do *that*?"

"I don't know," Lucky said irritably. "Show some ignition!"

"I think you mean initiative," I said. "All right, I'll see what I can do. Then you and Max and I should meet later."

"How about meeting by the menorah?" he suggested. "It's pretty private there, compared to the rest of Gloomyland."

"No, I'll probably be stuck in the throne room. With Karaoke Bear deceased now, I think Miles will want me to go back to helping Santa for the rest of the shift."

"We'll look for you there later, then," said Lucky. "I'm gonna wait here for Max and Nelli, and then we'll keep a low profile until the cops are done with their search."

"All right." I looked across the store again. Lopez was saying something to his mother, then he kissed his father's cheek. That made me smile—until I realized he was saying goodbye to them. "Watch out, Sugarplum. Lopez is coming back this way."

"Someone called for maintenance?"

I jumped at the sound of a voice right behind me and turned to find myself facing a guy in tan coveralls that had a Fenster's logo on the shoulder.

"Uh, yes," I said.

"The message I got was a little garbled," said the maintenance man. "A bear fainted?"

"No, he short-circuited, and we're concerned this whole karaoke apparatus may be dangerous."

"Karaoke?" the guy said. "That *is* dangerous."

"We don't want anyone to get a nasty shock," I said as Lopez joined us. "So you've got this under control now, right? We can leave immediately, *right?*"

"Uh, sure, yeah," said the maintenance man.

I scooped up my coat from behind Karaoke Bear's platform. "Let's go," I said, taking Lopez's arm and pulling, eager to get him out of here before Max and Nelli appeared.

"Wait, Esther, I should make sure this guy—"

"This is his job, not yours," I said, hauling Lopez away from the platform. "What do you know about electricity, after all?"

I turned my head to give him an impatient glance. Behind him, I saw Belsnickel and Vixen approaching us from the western entrance.

Lopez shrugged. "Well, all right. Since I'm still here, I guess I could go upstairs and help execute the search."

"No!" I blurted, fearing that he might find Max's ID up there.

"I won't touch *your* stuff, I promise. Okay?" he said reassuringly. "Believe me, I'd rather not search the belongings of someone I—"

"No, I mean . . ." Max and Nelli were approaching this spot. Max's gaze was roaming the area, but he hadn't seen me yet. "I mean . . ."

Behind Lopez, Lucky stepped out from behind his tree and started making exuberant gestures to Max to go back—*go back!*

Max mistook this for a friendly wave and returned the salute.

Lopez prodded, "You mean . . . ?"

"I'm . . . I'm . . ."

Lucky pointed at Lopez, then repeated his gesture urging Max and Nelli to flee—*flee!*

"You're . . . ?"

Max looked this way and saw me. He smiled and started to wave . . . then apparently recognized the back of Lopez's head. They had met a number of times, he knew Lopez was here, and I guess he made the connection between my companion's build and his shiny black hair, and Lucky's frantic grimacing. Max's eyes flew wide open and dismayed surprise swept across his features. He stood there, stock still, while my heart raced. Lopez might shift or turn around any moment, and both elves were within easy view now.

"I'm . . . hungry," I blurted. "Want to get a bite? Let's go. Come on." I started tugging on his arm again.

Looking understandably surprised at my urgency, he said, "Um . . . sure. I am kind of hungry." Letting me drag him along, he asked, "Where do you want to go?"

"Out!" I said. "Out of the store!"

"All right." He shrugged. "It's not like I *have* to help with the search. I'm off duty now."

"You are?" I asked distractedly, shoving through the crowd of shoppers as I towed him by the hand.

"Yeah. I was supposed to have dinner with my parents. But . . ." He stopped in his tracks. "Hey, Esther, why don't we go out that way? It's closer. And then we wouldn't have to fight our way through this—"

"No!" When he tried to turn around to head back to the western entrance, I tugged on his arm so hard he stumbled into me. "It's . . . We should . . . The north entrance!"

"Huh?" He didn't back away after bumping into me. Just stood very close, looking down into my face.

Gazing up into his eyes, fringed by thick black lashes, I immediately lost my train of thought—such as it was. My heart gave that unexpected, inconvenient little *lurch!* it sometimes did when I looked at him. Especially when he stood so close that I could feel his body heat. The wool of his coat brushed against my skin.

He smiled and murmured, "What *about* the north entrance?"

"It's, um . . ." Much to my surprise, a coherent thought entered my head. "It's closer to the park."

"You want to walk in the park?" he asked in surprise. "Now?"

"No, but I really want to get some air, you know? And walking up to the park is nicer than . . . walking the other way."

"Okay," he said easily. "Sure. Let's go."

I turned and led the way. The herd of shoppers was by now so dense that I could easily crowd-surf my way to the north entrance, if they'd cooperate. So we just moved along with the throng, not saying much until we were outside on the sidewalk.

It wasn't mind-numbingly cold outside tonight, but it was certainly brisk. I was still carrying my coat, so Lopez took it from my grasp and held it open for me as

I slipped my arms into it. While I fastened it, he asked if I wanted to go anyplace in particular to eat.

"It'll have to be someplace quick," I said. "I only get a half hour for dinner." I wasn't supposed to go on my meal break without telling anyone, and I especially wasn't supposed to leave the store for it—let alone go outside in my costume. But removing Lopez from the scene had been an emergency measure. Besides, it wasn't as if I feared Miles would fire me for this; not with a skeleton staff and two days left in the season.

Lopez pulled on his gloves as he said, "Well, you said you wanted to get some air, and it's not that cold tonight. Want to see if we can find someone selling chili dogs by the park?"

"All right." I smiled and took the arm he offered me. "I gather you've got a weakness for those?"

"I'm in control," he said as we turned and headed toward the park, which was so close to Fenster's we could see it from here. "I can quit whenever I want."

"Hah! I've said that about Ben and Jerry's ice cream, but I spiral into a panic if there's an emergency and I haven't got that stuff handy to keep me calm."

He grinned at that. "But as vices go, it seems like a harmless one."

"Not if you have to parade around in an elf costume," I said gloomily. "Every extra bite shows up in this outfit."

"That thing is disturbingly sexy on you," he said, which made my heart give a little skip. "Are Santa's elves really supposed to have that effect? I think it might have rocked my world if I'd met Dreidel at a tender age."

As we approached the light at West 58th Street, we came upon a Santa Claus who was ringing a bell and soliciting donations for charity.

I said, "Speaking of things that evidently rocked your world at a tender age . . ."

Lopez grimaced as he dropped a dollar into Santa's bucket, and he said grumpily to me, "God, they're *everywhere* at this time of year."

15

As we crossed 58th Street, our arms still linked, I asked, "So what's that all about, Lopez? Why are you phob . . . Why do you find Santa Claus so startling? Did you have a bad experience when you visited him as a child?"

"Well, yes, but I had a . . . a *thing* about Santa even before that."

"Why?"

"Hey, look at that." He pointed to an upscale store window on the corner. "Who pays fifteen hundred dollars for a purse?"

"People like the Fensters," I said. "Don't change the subject. When did your *thing* about Santa start? Do you remember?"

He sighed, realizing I wasn't going to drop it. "Okay. As soon as I was old enough to understand the concept, I found it very suspicious. I don't really remember this, but my parents say I was full of questions about why we were allowing a total stranger to roam our house at night while we slept."

"That sounds exactly like you," I said, laughing.

"And I was very disturbed about the notion of some-one, um, breaking and entering via the chimney."

"Wow, you haven't changed a bit since you were a little boy, have you?"

"So I tried to booby-trap it."

"Booby-trap the chimney? I'm impressed! How did you do it?"

"I made a big pile of sharp things in the fireplace. You can't expect something elaborate," he added defensively. "I was three years old."

"Three years old and trying to do grievous bodily harm to Santa Claus. Does the NYPD know about this?"

"Oh, there's plenty they don't know about my youth," he said with a gleam in his eyes.

He's really not *the altar boy he pretends to be, is he?*

I heard her voice in my head again; the woman who had nearly killed him, because he had come to Harlem that hot, storm-tossed night looking for me, trying to save me from her. She'd been correct in her observation that Lopez wasn't exactly what he seemed—in more ways than she realized, too. But I really wished I could banish her, once and for all. I felt cold all the way through for a moment.

"Are you okay?" He'd noticed that shiver and misunderstood its cause. "Do you want to go back? I guess it's colder out here than I—"

"No, elves are made of tough stuff," I said. "We live in the North Pole, along with You Know Who."

"You're sure?" he asked, rubbing my hand to keep it warm.

"So Santa survived your attempt to perforate him, and he left Christmas presents under the tree that year, I assume?"

"I think if I'd been an only child, my parents would have let me think I'd succeeded in keeping him out of the house. Apparently I was very . . . *focused* on this problem."

"I can see this whole story so clearly," I told him in amusement.

"But my brothers both wanted Santa Claus to visit, of course, so my parents kept trying to get me to come round."

"And *that* always works so well on you."

He smiled wryly. "So the next year, when I was four, my parents decided to bring us all into the city to visit Holidayland at Fenster's, where I'd meet Santa in this fairytale setting and finally realize what a great guy he was." Lopez paused before continuing, "You know how some kids have a bad reaction to clowns?"

"Clowns are scary," I said with a nod.

"That was pretty much my reaction to Santa Claus. I thought his bright outfit was creepy and his jovial behavior was sinister. I thought the way he hid behind that obviously fake beard and wig was suspicious and menacing. I imagined an evil face lurking behind all that fake hair."

The word *evil* reminded me. "Actually, since learning of your Santa, uh, startle reflex—"

"I just don't like it when they creep up on me."

"—I've developed a theory."

"I don't want to hear it," he said as we began crossing 59th Street, with Central Park right in front of us now.

"I think you dislike Max because of his resemblance to Santa Claus."

Lopez looked surprised for a moment, then amused. "Actually, I never noticed a resemblance. I still don't. He seems too small for Santa. I always think of Max as looking like a mad professor, or maybe like the ancient wizard in an old fairytale. What's wrong?"

He'd noticed my startled reaction to *that*. "Nothing," I said.

"But Max as Santa?" Lopez shook his head. "I don't see it."

"Even so," I persisted as we reached the curb, "I think your unconscious reaction to his round face, with his white beard and hair, is why you have such a negative attitude about him."

"No, I have a negative attitude about him because I think he's a whack job who encourages you to believe crazy things and, more to the point, to *act* on those things—and to get into a lot of trouble, as a result."

Well, that was direct. And hardly a surprise. I decided to revert to his childhood.

"So what exactly happened when they put you on Santa's lap in Holidayland?" I prodded. "Being one of Santa's helpers, I ask this strictly out of professional interest, you understand."

"Well, that's where the story resembles a criminal investigation: Everyone remembers it differently."

We were on the sidewalk at the edge of the park, which spread lush and romantically dark before us, its glowing lamps peeking through the bare branches. People passed us, entering the park, maybe going to Wollman Rink to watch the skaters or to take a spin on the ice. On the next block over, we could see a hot-food cart under the street lights, so we started walking that way, arm in arm.

He explained, "My mother remembers me hyperventilating and then passing out, I was so overcome with fear of the red-clad menace. My father is still guilt-ridden about the visit because he remembers me crying until he thought I might need to be tranquilized. And my brothers remember me throwing a screaming tantrum and deliberately ruining their visit to Holidayland."

"What do you remember?" I asked curiously.

"I remember finding Santa Claus suspicious and threatening, and then asking to leave."

"Yes, that does sound like the way *you* would remember it," I said.

"What does *that* mean?"

"Oh, look, we're in luck," I said as we approached the food stand. "Chili dogs."

"I am a very reasonable person," Lopez insisted.

"But between this tight costume and the difficulty of getting away from Santa's throne if nature calls, I'd better not risk it. So I'll just have a hot dog . . . Oh, what the heck, with cheese, please." I added to Lopez, "I thoughtfully left my purse in my locker, so your colleagues could paw through it at their convenience—"

"Esther, we don't *paw*—"

"—so you'll have to pay."

"If you want me to buy your dinner, you should be a lot nicer to me." He pulled out his wallet and told the vendor, who was ladling cheese over my frankfurter, that he'd have a chili dog. We also got bottled water, one order of fries, and some napkins, and then we found an empty bench—which wasn't a challenge, despite how crowded the whole area was tonight, since it was too cold, really, for sitting outside. But in his company, I scarcely noticed.

"So was the visit to Holidayland the experience that cemented your Santa phobia?" I asked.

Lopez gave me a frosty look for using that word. "Christmastime at our house was a little tense that year. And the year after, my father found me asleep by the chimney on Christmas Eve with my brother's Jedi lightsaber in my hands."

"Of course," I said before biting into my deliciously messy cheese dog.

"By the following year, when I was six, Michael was nine and Tim was eleven, and they didn't believe in Santa Claus anymore. So my parents decided we could dispense with all the Christmas trauma now, and they told me the truth."

"That doesn't seem to have resolved your Santa issue," I noted.

"No, I was furious. They had *lied* to me my whole life. They'd scared me into believing a suspicious, weirdly dressed perp was infiltrating our house annually. They had even forced me to meet someone who was impersonating that character! And now they were telling me they'd made it all up?"

"You know, I didn't exactly hit it off with your parents tonight—"

"Oh, I'd say my dad thought you were okay." He offered me this faint praise as if it were rubies beyond compare.

"—but as this story unfolds, I feel the most profound sympathy for them," I said.

"Hmph. Anyhow, I realized I could never trust anyone in my family again, and I didn't speak to them for . . . Well, the stories vary there, too. My brothers say this lasted about a day. My mother claims it was at least a week. My father just gets teary-eyed and can't talk about it."

"I'm starting to feel a little sorry for your brothers, too," I said.

"Those bastards," he grumbled.

"And ever since then . . . ?"

"I just find Santa . . . startling. It's not a big deal. So can we *drop* it now?"

"Of course not," I said. "You know, it's unusual to carry this fear into adulthood—though you've obviously changed so little since earliest childhood that I guess I'm not that surprised in your case. But Rick says quite a few kids have a negative reaction when they first visit Santa. And I certainly see it in the throne room every day."

"Who's Rick?" he asked.

"Super Santa. The psychology grad student."

"Oh, right." Lopez rolled his eyes. "The self-proclaimed good listener."

"He was trying to be nice," I chided.

"Aren't you supposed to be a student of human nature?" he said critically. "That guy was not trying to be nice, Esther. Your friend Satsy was trying to be nice. Rick was trying to play on my insecurities."

"No," I protested. "I think you've got him all wrong."

"He's not a healer, he's an opportunist."

"What makes you say that?"

"I've spent plenty of time interrogating people like him. I've learned to spot them."

"I think you just feel defensive because he zeroed in on your . . . *thing.*"

"He's a psychology student?" Lopez asked, backtracking. "I thought all of the Solsticeland staffers were actors."

"Mostly, but not all. I don't know what Eggnog *does*, really, but if you're in the same room with him for five minutes, you find out that he's—"

"Got a master's degree in literature from *Princeton*." Lopez did a fair imitation of the way Eggnog said it, which made me laugh.

"And I think Twinkle studies computer science."

"Well, that fits." He added, "Is it just me, or does Twinkle seem like he's still in the closet, despite wearing red leotards in public?"

"You think he's gay?"

"Sure." Lopez shrugged. "What straight guy would agree to being called Twinkle?"

"That's what I said! But Rick thinks Twinkle's being ironic with that name."

"And Rick, being a grad student in psychology, must necessarily be right in all things."

"No, I didn't mean that, I meant . . . I think he seems insightful."

"Hmm." Lopez didn't say anything else, just sat frowning absently at his half-eaten chili dog as if it might contain the secrets to the human heart. I was familiar with that expression and knew that it usually meant something had triggered a thought or connection in his mind, and now he was examining scattered pieces of information inside his head, trying to figure out how to fit them together into a coherent picture.

Maybe he was thinking about the hijacking case. Or maybe he was thinking of asking Rick if I thought

Karaoke Bear had grown claws and fangs because I was still traumatized by yesterday's enchanted tree attack. Would I think I saw something supernaturally spooky *every* time an electronic device malfunctioned at Fenster's? And so on.

Whatever it was, I decided to let him think about it while I finished eating, since I had to go back to Fenster's soon. So we sat in companionable silence for a few minutes. I ate while Lopez stared blankly at his dinner, his thoughts turned inward.

"Don't you like your supper?" I asked at last, picking at the French fries now that I'd finished my cheese dog.

"Huh? Oh. No, it's fine." He took another bite and relaxed again.

We talked some more about my fellow Solsticeland employees, Fenster's, and my various experiences there.

After we both had finished eating and drinking, he threw away our garbage, then sat back down on the bench with me as he commented, "That many people have just stopped coming to work? It seems like a high attrition rate even for a seasonal job with bad pay and obnoxious policies. I mean, I can tell you're not happy working there, and I can understand why—"

"I am *so* glad Stella will have steady shifts for me after the holidays," I said with feeling.

"—but is it really *that* bad?"

"Well, I *much* prefer being a singing waitress for a

nice boss in a restaurant where the clients tip well, and where I rarely get mistaken for a hooker or a figure skater."

"A *what*?"

"But I've had worse jobs than Solsticeland." I shrugged. "Maybe the employees who quit without even giving notice or returning their costumes—which means no final paycheck—just don't need the money as much as I do. Or as much as Jeff does—*boy*, does he hate this job! Actually, he's been so down lately, I'm a little worried about him. But he keeps coming to work, just like I do. Because no one pays our bills for us."

It wasn't really an explanation, though, since I had chatted with at least of few of the AWOL employees and knew they actually did need the money as much as I did. Had they all gotten better job offers on the spur of the moment? It didn't seem that likely, only days before Christmas. Certainly there was no new acting work being offered between now and January, let alone enough to account for the exodus from Solsticeland.

I checked Lopez's wristwatch and said, "I should go back. Miles will be looking for me."

"Wait. Stay a little longer." He slipped his hand into mine and stroked my knuckles with his thumb. "I'll tell him I detained you on police business."

Feeling his touch, sensing the shift in his thoughts, my heart picked up the pace.

"I'll be late." My voice was faint.

"Don't go yet." So was his.

I saw the look in his eyes. And a moment later, I knew he saw the look in mine.

My voice shook a little as I said, "No, I should go . . ."

"Stay," he urged softly. The streetlights shone on his black hair and shadows shifted across his face as he leaned closer to me. "This is nice. You. Here . . . with me."

I was breathing faster, aware that his gaze had shifted to my mouth. Aware of what he wanted. What I wanted, too.

Lopez's hand tightened on mine as he leaned very close, so that his breath was tickling my lips as he whispered, "I miss you."

His lips were warm, full, and soft. I fell into his kiss like I was tumbling into a dream, losing all sense of reality and my surroundings as soon as his mouth touched mine. I could have been floating in outer space or sinking underwater, rather than sitting on a hard park bench in a public place, surround by people and traffic. I wouldn't have known the difference.

I hadn't forgotten that he *really* knew how to kiss, but it had been a long enough drought that I had forgotten the effect his kisses had on me. Now I clung to him and whimpered a little, my mouth opening to invite him in, my head spinning, and my hands reaching for his coat to pull him closer.

He was all silky heat on the inside, his mouth seductively hot compared to the cold air on my skin, his stroking tongue making my pelvis quiver reflexively. And on the outside, he was all cuddly warmth, my shelter in the cold night, his arms cradling me as he nipped and nuzzled me affectionately.

When we came up for air, I murmured, "You taste like chili dogs."

We both laughed breathlessly, our hands grasping each other like swimmers trying to survive a riptide together.

"Esther . . . now that you know the worst . . ." he whispered.

"The worst?" I rubbed my forehead against his.

"My parents."

We laughed again.

"Couldn't we . . ." he breathed. "I mean . . . Us not seeing each other . . . It's not really working out, is it?"

I started to pull away, coming to my senses now that he had mercifully paused in kissing me.

Lopez didn't stop me. "Am I wrong?"

"You're not exactly . . . wrong." I scooted a little away from him, unable to think or talk sensibly when he was that close.

"But . . . ?" he prodded.

"I don't think I'm very good for you," I said in a rush.

He looked around, as if searching in our vicinity for an intelligent response to this. Finding none, he said, "Does that matter so much?"

"Are you listening to yourself?"

"Not really," he admitted and tried to kiss me again.

"Wait! No, *wait*." He could probably tell from the excited breathlessness in my voice, as well as my innate inability to move away from him again, that I was trying to think rather than rejecting his touch.

Lopez let out his breath in a gush, held up his hands, and nodded. He scooted back, putting a little safe distance between us on the bench.

After a moment, he said, "I know I'm the one who broke up with you, and—"

"No, it's not that."

"Are you sure?"

"It's not that," I said firmly.

A swift, sharp intake of breath. "Are you seeing someone else?"

"No. It's not that, either."

"Oh." He sagged with relief. "Okay." A pause. "Then, what?"

"I nearly got you killed," I blurted. "More than once. It was because of *me*. I can't go through that again! I *can't*. I won't be the reason you get–get—" Now that I had said it aloud, I was surprised to hear my voice break.

Yes, this was a fraught subject for me; but I hadn't realized I would cry if we talked about it. I felt tears spill down my face, and I couldn't go on. My throat was too choked with emotion. I put my hand over my mouth and started whimpering with distress now, rather than passion.

He was clearly taken aback. Whatever he had imag-

ined I might say, it had obviously been nothing re-
motely like *this*.

"Oh, Esther. Hey. Come on. Shh, shh." He slid across
the bench to put his arms around me, comforting now
rather than seductive. "What's all this, huh? Shh. Everything's okay." He kissed my hair, murmuring soothing things while he used one hand to fish around in his
pockets. After a moment, he produced a crumpled
handkerchief that had seen better days.

That snapped me out of my bout of sniffles. I shied
away from it when he tried to press it into my hand.
"Where has this been?"

"Sometimes I use it to pick up evidence. When I
don't want to get fingerprints on—"

"Ugh! I can't touch *that*. Put it away!"

"You're already sounding better," he noted, pocket-
ing the sad piece of cotton.

I scrubbed my hands over my face and took a deep
breath. "I just get very emotional thinking about you
lying in the basement of the Livingston Foundation,
dying of an ordeal poison."

"Yeah, I get pretty emotional when I think about it,
too. That was grim." He added, "Mostly, though, I remember seeing Dr. Livingston go off to kill you, and I
couldn't move a muscle to stop her. That was the *really*
grim part."

"See? You wouldn't have been there if it hadn't been
for *me*. You never would have gone to Harlem that
night and confronted that evil, demented, deadly—"

"Well, sure, I would," he said, sounding puzzled.

I paused. "Huh?"

"She was a *killer*, Esther. And she was about to kill again. Yeah, it made me crazy-violent that it was *you* she going to kill. And since she's dead and I hope I can trust you not to repeat this, I will candidly admit that I violated some of her civil rights when questioning her and tearing apart her place in search of you. But Esther . . ." He brushed my hair off my face. "I would have gone to the Livingston Foundation that night no matter *who* she was trying to kill. That's my job. It's what I do. You know—that whole 'protect and serve' thing. I don't get to say, 'Well, I don't really feel attached to the person that demented bitch is going to murder tonight, so I guess I won't try to stop her.' I have to go even if the victim is a total stranger—which is usually the case, and frankly a lot easier for me to deal with." Apparently hoping to lighten the mood, he added, "Esther, listen to me. I'd have to go to the Livingston Foundation in those circumstances even if the victim was Max."

That made me snort with laughter, even though I was actually, at that moment, thinking about how much alike he and Max were. These two men, centuries apart in age and living in such different realities; yet both so unwavering in their purpose and selfless in their mission. And both so dear to me.

"By the way," Lopez added, continuing to shift the

mood away from my brief bout of tears. "What the hell did Max *do* to me that night? Or *for* me? If anything?"

"If anything?" I repeated indignantly. "He saved your life!"

"I thought so, too. But when I got to the hospital later . . . Uh, you do remember that's where I decided to go once I found out what some of the *revolting* ingredients were in that potion he poured down my throat?"

"Yes."

"They couldn't find anything wrong with me. They couldn't find evidence that anything *had* been wrong with me, either. There was no trace or evidence at all of whatever Dr. Livingston had done to me, or of whatever Max gave me. Nothing, *nada*, zip."

I hadn't realized this, but I wasn't surprised by it. Medical practitioners weren't trained to look for mystical means of killing and curing, after all. And for all I knew, when Max's cure restored balance to Lopez's body, perhaps it even eliminated all mystical traces of what had happened to him that night.

I tried again to explain my fears. "But if you hadn't been so upset about knowing she was holding *me* captive somewhere, she wouldn't have been able to catch you off your guard and—"

"That's flattering," he said. "And maybe it's a view of my prowess that I should encourage in a woman I want see naked."

"Oh!" Well, *that* had caught me off guard.

"But I'm not Superman, Esther. Dr. Livingston was a very clever and devious woman, with extensive knowledge of exotic ritual poisons—about which I know exactly nothing. I had no *idea* she could kill me just by touching me with a topical poison. And I don't understand why, in that case, it didn't kill her, too." Lopez blew out his breath hard enough to make the hair on his forehead flutter. "*If* that's what happened. I'm skeptical by now. I wonder if that 'poison' was just some weird short-term hallucinogenic that she'd developed a resistance to, since I was completely fine later, as if nothing had ever happened."

I didn't bother trying to explain that Dr. Livingston had been a bokor, a dark sorceress indebted to very powerful and dangerous spirits. It was the sort of explanation that never got us anywhere. I wondered if I should even try to broach my concerns about nearly getting Lopez killed on other occasions . . . but when I thought about it, those were cases he was already involved in, and—based on what he had said tonight—those were risks he would have taken as part of his duty, regardless of whether or not I was involved or in danger.

He put his hand on my cheek and met my eyes. "So . . . are we okay? You know I care about you. But you get that I do my job even when I don't care, right? Well, don't care in a personal way, I mean. So this stuff you were crying about a minute ago . . . which, *God*, that's painful! I really, *really* can't stand making you cry, so let's agree—"

"Shh," I said, and I kissed him.

He was still cooperating enthusiastically when his phone rang a few minutes later. Breathing fast, he rested his forehead against mine and murmured, "That's work calling . . . I have to take it . . . I'm sorry. They must have found something in the search."

I stiffened, thinking of Max and Lucky. "You'd better take it, then," I said breathlessly, wanting to know right now if either of my friends was in trouble, rather than wondering what Lopez would learn when he checked his messages later.

He nodded, kissed me quickly again, and answered the call. "Lopez."

As he did so, I probed and prodded in vulnerable places inside myself, waiting to hear Dr. Livingston's nasty voice scaring me yet again. But she remained silent. I had a feeling that Lopez had finally shut her up for good.

Snuggled next to me on the cold park bench, he sat up so alertly I was startled.

"What?" He listened to his caller. "Say that again . . . *Jesus.* This will be a three-ring circus. Yeah, you *bet* I do. Where is he? Okay, I'm on my way."

He ended the call and stood up, helping me rise from the bench as he put his phone way. "I'm sorry, I've got to go. Right now."

"Okay." Thinking of Max and Lucky, I asked warily, "What's happened?"

"There's been another hijacking. About an hour ago."

"Oh!" No wonder he had to go.

"And this time, someone shot the driver."

"What?" I exclaimed. "Is he alive?"

"He is." Lopez added with relish, "And he's identified the shooter."

16

Back at Fenster's, I wanted to find Lucky and Max to tell them the news right away. Lopez wouldn't say anything to me about the identity of the shooter, who was still at large, though he told me it would probably be all over the news once the gunman was apprehended. So this was the break in the case that Lucky had been hoping for.

Depending on who the shooter was and what could be learned once the news broke, this might also assist with our mystical problem at Fenster's, if our poltergeist was indeed connected to a nefarious scheme to commit polterheists. (Well, *I* thought it was clever.)

The cops were done searching the locker room and all gone by the time I got back there—which was to be expected, I thought, when I saw the time. I'd been gone longer than I'd realized. Time really flies when you're lip-locked with a man about whom you've fantasized far too much.

I took off my coat, donned the elf ears-and-cap which I had shoved into my pocket earlier this evening, and checked my reflection in the mirror. I looked disheveled and excited . . . and my ears were a little smooshed and bent. Oops. Oh, well. They only needed to last for two more days.

With less than an hour left before closing, I decided not even to bother touching up my makeup, and I left the locker room as I was. I realized that after I got out onto the floor, I probably wouldn't be able to leave it again until closing time. So, just in case Max and Lucky had gotten tired of searching for me (or had gotten hungry and thirsty), I popped quickly into the break room to see if they were there.

"Oh, hi!" I said, startled. "Um, sorry," I added, realizing I had interrupted something. Followed by, "Uh, is everything all right?"

I was looking at Rick and Elspeth. This late into the shift, no one else was in the break room—everyone who wasn't on the floor now had clocked out—and they were alone together in here.

And this wasn't just happenstance, I realized; they were clearly *together*. But not in a good way, it seemed.

Rick was holding Elspeth by the shoulders, and he looked furious with her. I saw the way his fingers were digging into her flesh when I walked in on them, and I thought she'd have bruises tomorrow. Elspeth looked . . .

oh, pretty much the same as always. Sulky, sullen, angry, snide, slouching. And . . . triumphant, I realized with surprise.

Maybe she was glad she had made Rick angry—which, for someone like Elspeth, probably counted as an achievement. Or maybe she had the upper hand in their argument, whatever it was.

"Hi, Esther." Rick took a breath and released Elspeth.

"Hi." I noticed that Elspeth didn't move away from him. He must have been hurting her a moment ago, or perhaps trying to intimidate her, but she didn't seem to be upset with him. Mostly, I thought, she just seemed annoyed that I had intruded on their scene. After an awkward pause, I asked, "What's up?"

Rallying, Rick said casually, "Miles couldn't find you before he left for the night, so we all thought you went home and forgot to clock out or something."

"Oh, I had sort of an unexpected detour this evening after Karaoke Bear malfunctioned," I said vaguely. "I'll talk to Miles tomorrow and explain." Actually, Miles would do most of the talking, and since I didn't really expect to get paid for kissing Lopez, I'd go along with having my pay docked for the time I'd been missing.

"The singing bear malfunctioned?" Rick said alertly. "What happened?"

He and Elspeth exchanged a glance. She looked smug. Rick's face—unusually, for him—was unreadable.

"Yes, what happened?" Elspeth asked me.

I hadn't realized these two were more than scant acquaintances; but it was obvious from their body language and eye contact now that there was a relationship between them. The extent or the nature of the relationship wasn't at all clear to me, though.

"He short-circuited or something, I think," I said.

At Rick's prodding, I elaborated a little; but I didn't hint at what had really happened. Not with Elspeth in the room, watching me with those simultaneously hostile and avaricious eyes. There was actually something vampirish about this ardent *Vampyre* fan, I realized. This was the way she had looked at me when asking me what it had been like to be embraced by actor Daemon Ravel, and also when later asking me how I'd felt upon thinking I might die. It was as if, lacking access to her own emotions, she fed off of other people's.

"That's all there is to tell about the bear," I lied with a casual shrug. "Short circuit. Smoke. Pop! Keel over. Dead."

"Dead?" Elspeth repeated—exactly the way I might involuntarily repeat Lopez's name if someone said it right now out of the blue.

Well, no, not *exactly* the way. I had never been and sincerely hoped I never would be that creepy. But it did make me think of the way a woman would respond to hearing her absent lover's name unexpectedly said aloud.

Stop right there. He's not your lover.

Well, not yet. But he said he wanted to see me naked.

God, how did he make such a bald statement sound so hot?

I thought again of his lips on mine, his breath brushing my cheek, his hands . . .

"Oh, calm down," I said aloud.

Seeing their startled expressions, I felt embarrassed. Until I realized they thought I meant that Elspeth should calm down.

Rick chuckled and gestured to the goth girl. "She gets a little excited by death." He tried to make it sound like a joke. He failed.

"And men get excited by genitals," she said with open disgust.

Well, she must be tremendous fun in bed.

Given Elspeth's consuming interest in Daemon Ravel aka Lord Ruthven, I assumed she was heterosexual, at least in theory. So I wondered if she was extremely disappointed in her sex life—with Rick? Or resentful of not getting sex from Rick? She'd certainly had a clumsy way of expressing her attraction to Lopez, followed promptly by being resentful when he didn't reciprocate.

Then I wondered if "excited by death" meant . . .

No, not going there, I decided firmly. These were not thoughts I had any interest in pursuing.

In any event, I would not have said that the sullen, emotionally stunted, poor little rich goth girl seemed to be Rick's type . . . But then, I hardly knew Rick. Maybe she was exactly his type. His clean-cut appearance and wholesome persona weren't necessarily evidence of his sexual tastes or emotional needs, after all. Maybe his intellectual passion for psychology translated into a personal passion for deeply troubled women . . .

Certainly he had seemed passionate when I'd entered the room. But not in a good way. I glanced at Elspeth, recalling that moment and wondering whether I should leave them alone together. But it was clear that she considered my presence an annoying intrusion. So I said that I needed to go finish the shift on the floor, and I left the room.

As the door closed behind me, I thought of Lopez's unfounded and probably unfair assessment of Rick as an opportunist. And it occurred to me that, especially for someone who had insight into the way people's minds worked, the rich, unhappy, and insecure Elspeth might be very easy to manipulate . . .

When I got to the throne room, I found Diversity Santa, Belsnickel, Sugarplum, and Vixen all waiting for me.

Jeff took advantage of the fact that things were slow this late in the shift to start berating me immediately. "Where have you been? I've been stranded here in holiday hell with Belsnickel the blind elf, his drooling reindeer, and the meanest Santa's helper who's ever lived! Do you have any idea how many people Sugarplum has frightened away this evening?"

"I thought you liked kids?" I said to Lucky.

"I do," said the Santa-bearded elf. "I just don't like their parents. What a buncha whiny schmucks."

"Where do you *find* these people?" Jeff said.

I still thought it best, as I had thought earlier today when asking for his help with makeup and wardrobe, not to tell Jeff where I had found Lucky.

"Diversity Santa's been a little cranky all evening," Lucky told me.

"Oh, he's been cranky for longer than that," I replied. "Don't take it personally."

Lucky made a dismissive gesture that indicated he hadn't let it bother him. In his line of work, after all, he had dealt with more much difficult personalities than an actor who was unhappy about the wasteland his career seemed to be stuck in.

Hoping this news would distract Jeff from his doldrums, I told the three men about tonight's hijacking, the shooting, and the possibility that the shooter would soon be identified.

"This is great news! I gotta go out to Forest Hills and tell the boss in person. The family's problems with Fenster's might be almost over!" Lucky added to Max, "Doc, Nelli's had a hard day. Do you want me to take her for a walk and drop her off at your place, since I'm heading out now?"

I glanced at the familiar and realized she looked weary and worn. Her fuzzy antlers looked floppy, her head was drooping, and she was panting with fatigue.

"Thank you, my dear fellow. That is most considerate." As Max handed Nelli's leash over to Lucky, he removed his sunglasses. "It will also be a relief to me to cease wearing these. It's been almost impossible for me to see anything in Solsticeland today!"

"There is a sense in which that's a blessing," I said, thinking of the Hanukkah-goes-Vegas display.

Lucky said to me, "Kid, I guess the doc will catch you up on what we been doin' today. I'll talk to you both tomorrow."

"Goodnight, Lucky," I said as he left.

Jeff stared after him with a thoughtful frown. After a long moment, be turned an accusing gaze on me. "Oh, my *God*, Esther."

"Max," I said quickly, "maybe we should—"

"*Lucky*. The *family*. Forest Hills?" said Jeff, each phrase getting louder. "The *boss!*"

"Hello!" I said brightly to a child who was approaching the throne. "Are you here to see Santa?"

"*'The family's problems with Fenster's'?*"

The kid and her parents took one look at the bellowing Diversity Santa, changed their minds, and left.

"Are you *insane?*" Jeff demanded. "Do you know who that man is?"

"Well, I gather *you* know now," I said.

Jeff was a pretty voracious news consumer. I had hoped he wouldn't put it together, but I really hadn't counted on that. Mostly, I had hoped to be in another part of the building when he figured out who Lucky was.

"There is a valid explanation for Lucky's presence here today," Max said to Jeff. "As there is for mine."

"Yeah, yeah, your poltergeist." Jeff rolled his eyes dismissively.

Unlike Lopez, Jeff wasn't stubbornly conventional and obsessively prone to seeking rational explanations in terms which adhered to his established belief system; he was just obtuse.

"Dreidel!" Twinkle came trotting over, his bells jangling as he bounced along. "I didn't know you were still here!"

"Nobody did," I said. "And I'm starting to wish it had stayed that way. Are you working the throne room with me now, Twinkle? I warn you, Diversity Santa is in a bit of a snit."

"Isn't he always?" said Twinkle.

"You brought a Gambello hit man here?" Jeff raged. "You got *me* to help you smuggle a wiseguy into Fenster's?"

"Lower your voice, would you?" I snapped.

Realizing this was good advice, he did so. "You brought a Gambello . . . Have you lost your mind, Esther?"

Twinkle gave Jeff a puzzled look, then said to me, "No, I'm on photo duty, Dreidel. The store's clearing out now, of course—"

"Well, it is getting late." I said to Diversity Santa, "Just a little longer until we clock out for the night. So let's all try to stay calm in this highly public place!"

Twinkle continued, "So I've just been uploading to the system the candid shots taken this evening. Probably no point, really. We fell hours behind today—we're so understaffed! So I'll bet all of these people have already left the store."

"It's all right, Twinkle," I said reassuringly. "We're bound to fall behind on things."

"Especially when a wiseguy-fraternizing elf doesn't even show up for her shift!" Jeff snapped.

"I came as soon as I could." I added primly, "I was detained for a police matter."

"Anything to do with smuggling a famous mob hitter into Fenster's today?" Jeff muttered.

Twinkle continued, "And what I found when I was uploading was so . . . so *weird*. Photo after photo."

Max said to Jeff, "The two problems may be linked. But even if they're not, Lucky recognizes the danger of the mystical evil haunting Fenster's—"

"Do we still think it's a ghost, Max?" I asked. "A poltergeist?"

"A ghost?" Twinkle asked doubtfully, tapping on the computer monitor to bring up some images. "Do you really think that's what this is?"

Max said to me, "I'm leaning away from that theory, now. I'm theorizing in a bit of a vacuum—"

"But that won't stop you from talking," Jeff grumbled.

"—but I suspect that Nelli's reactions today, which were at times dramatic, were not consistent with a ghostly presence at Fenster's. I think the entity we're investigating may be something else entirely."

"Good, because I don't think it's a ghost, either," said Twinkle. "I think it looks like . . . something a lot worse, don't you?"

He turned the flat screen monitor so that we could all see it.

We fell silent and stared in stunned alarm at the twenty or so digital photos he ran past us in a quick slide show.

In picture after picture, ordinary people smiling for the camera—in front of Solstice Castle, posing with Prince Midnight, greeting an elf, or visiting Santa— were unaware that, within easy reach, something indistinct and shadowy, with glowing red eyes and dripping fangs, was reaching for them with sharp, grasping claws.

When we got to the last picture in the batch, Twinkle said unnecessarily, "Here's one of you, Jeff."

"Holy *shit*," Jeff said with feeling, looking at the glowing eyes that peered over his shoulder as he posed with a wailing toddler on his lap. "What the hell is that?"

"That is not a poltergeist," Max said apologetically to us, as if taking responsibility for the problem being bigger than we'd feared. "It's a solstice demon."

"This is the worst idea you've ever had," Jeff said.

I replied, "That's what you said to me this morning

about a different idea. Make up your mind. Anyhow, this is Max's idea, not mine."

"I wasn't talking to you," Jeff said. "I was talking to myself. What was I *thinking* when I agreed to do this?" After a moment, he added, "But, just to be clear, though it wasn't your idea, I do blame you for this."

"Of course."

"*Why* do I let you talk me into these things?" he moaned.

"Because I'm much stronger-willed than you are."

Also, he hadn't needed much convincing at the time. Jeff had been really spooked by seeing a demon peering over his shoulder.

Now, of course, he was rationalizing it, speculating that Twinkle—who was safely outside the store now, serving as our lookout man—had probably digitally altered those photos to enjoy playing a gag on us. Never mind that a possessed tree had nearly strangled me the other day while vocally craving flesh and blood. No, we were the dupes of a silly joke pulled on us by a college kid.

I had seen Jeff do this before, so his change of heart didn't surprise me. I had expected it.

But it was too late now. Max, Jeff, and I had remained hidden in the store after closing to confront whoever was, Max believed, planning to raise a demon at midnight.

As he had explained it to us earlier, after dropping his bombshell about the solstice demon, "Since before the dawn of history, going back to the long-ago eons when men gathered around the fire at night—"

"And women," I said.

"When men and women gathered around the fire at night to ward off the menacing darkness and protect themselves from the creatures, both mystical and mundane, which lurked in the shadows, beyond the light," Max had told us, "many cultures have feared these days of deepest winter, when night is longer than day and the barriers between dimensions crumble and give way."

"Wow," Twinkle had said to me, transfixed. "Your blind friend is one good storyteller."

"He's not blind," I said.

"On the longest night of the year," Max continued, "the winter solstice, darkness tumbles into darkness, the night is too long for the fabric of this dimension to easily withstand, and that is when demons can emerge from their hell dimensions to enter this world!"

Looking back now, as we waited for midnight, I was pretty sure that was where Max began to lose Jeff, who had started shifting restlessly and looking skeptical.

"Winter solstice demons go by many different names in many different cultures, but they all impart an almost identical sense of dread. *They* are the reason that so many ancient faiths, dead and still surviving, created a midwinter celebration of light—to ward off the demons trying to break through to our world on the longest night of the year!"

"But Max," Jeff had interrupted then, "those festivals occur all over the calendar. Hanukkah is already over. Christmas isn't for three days. Winter solstice was last night. Other cultures—"

"Well, it's not as if demons keep digital calendars in their hell dimensions," Max said prosaically. "These events happen *around* this time."

"Wait, what about what Jeff said? Digital calendars notwithstanding, is that why we saw this thing in these pictures *today?*" I asked then. "Because last night was winter solstice, so this thing is already here? We're too late, and Hell has come to Fenster's?"

Well, it turned out that the good news, so to speak, was that winter solstice was actually tonight, December 22nd. I objected vociferously to this information, since everyone knew that solstice fell on the 21st of the month.

"Only sometimes," Max had said.

"That's right," said Twinkle, treasurer of his astronomy club.

The cosmos and the earthly calendar used for tracking time weren't in perfect harmony. So just as we have Leap Year once every four years to straighten things out, it also happens that once every few years, winter solstice actually falls on December 22nd rather than on the 21st.

Which meant that *tonight* was the longest night of the year. And all of this mystical activity at Fenster's over the past couple of days indicated that the barrier between dimensions had already been pierced and weakened, so to speak, and that the store was the epicenter of whatever was coming through the dark veil tonight.

"Someone is actively helping this demon," said Max. "Someone is *inviting* it here. That is terribly dangerous."

So, *naturally*, we had decided to stay in the store after closing and hide in the dark to confront it.

Actually, I was just hoping to confront Elspeth, who struck me as the most likely person to try raising a deadly solstice demon, given her interest in death, her flirtation with vampirism, and her easy access to Fenster's after hours, as a family member and a stockholder.

Of course, Arthur was another possibility. Lopez had influenced me more than I liked to admit with his sheepish "least likely person" theory. But Arthur seemed sad and harmless, whereas there was something genuinely disturbing about Elspeth, though she was also adolescent and seemingly ineffectual. She was a grown woman who appeared to live under her father's thumb as if she were still fifteen. She was the sort of person who'd had the time to be at *The Vampyre* night after night for weeks, since she had no job, vocation, or personal life to occupy her.

That somehow struck me as a ripe personality for falling into the mad notion of raising a solstice demon for kicks.

But it wouldn't be a kick. According to Max, these creatures were horribly destructive; people had been sensible to fear them for millennia.

I was scared by the prospect of the three of us taking on this thing alone and without preparation, but Max had reassured me. "It is a relatively simple matter to prevent a solstice demon from entering this dimension and to force it to return to hell—or some abstract variation of that concept—where it belongs."

"Okay, what's the secret?" Jeff asked.

"There is no secret," Max said. "It's the same tool that has been used for millennia."

"Fire!" I guessed.

"And light," Max added. "That is how solstice demons are kept out of this dimension. Fire and light on the darkest nights of the year."

So after closing, we had gone sneaking up to the home and garden department on the fifth floor (I'd never even known it was there until Twinkle mentioned it tonight), careful to avoid being seen by the occasional—*very* occasional—security guard, and we had collected flashlights, strobe lights, and patio torches. Although there had been menacing mystical activity in several areas of the store, Max believed that Nelli's increasingly erratic behavior when investigating the fourth floor suggested that Solsticeland itself would be the site of the dimensional rift.

It was a fitting setting, since the entire exhibit was murky even when all the operational lights were on. It was always supposed to seem like the darkest night of the year in Solsticeland. We planned to throw the main switch for the operational lights when the time came, to help illuminate the scene . . . but that certainly wouldn't suffice, Max had said. Hence the additional lights collected from elsewhere.

So Max, Jeff, and I huddled together nervously in the throne room with our torches and bright lights. We planned to make the demon, when it tried to break through to this dimension, feel like it was entering our world on the pitcher's mound during a night game at Yankee Stadium—which should force it to turn around immediately and go back to where it damn well belonged.

It seemed like a workable theory—right up until about 11:00 PM, roughly an hour before we were expecting trouble, when the first stuffed teddy bear in the toddler's play area started cackling madly as it raced across the floor of Solsticeland toward us, fangs bared, eyes glowing red.

I shrieked and fumbled with my flashlight, my hands shaking so hard that I dropped it. Jeff turned his strobe light on the possessed bear.

It keeled over instantly and lay there silent and inert.

"Oh, thank God," I said, shocked and trembling with reaction. "Is it—*arrggh!*"

Another one came rushing at us, then another—then another!

Then a dozen little Chef Chéries appeared out of the

dark, having freed themselves from their packaging. They were chattering and cackling, racing toward us in their porn aprons with their little kitchen knives in their clawed hands. We shone our lights on them, but as fast as they lost animation and fell, others rose and appeared to replace them.

If we shone our lights one way, something attacked us from the other direction. I was screaming my head off, terrified, turning on flashlight after flashlight, then fighting off leaping, shrieking, *stinking*, drooling toys as I tried to light the patio torches.

"Esther!" Jeff screamed. "Watch out!"

I turned in the direction of his horrified gaze and saw an old-fashioned mannequin of Santa Claus coming at me, looking exactly as little Jonathan had described him to me yesterday morning—eyes glowing, claws reaching for me, fangs dripping with saliva. He had entered this area from the North Pole—where, to my horror, I saw other displays coming to life, too. Maniacal elves were heading in this direction, bloodlust in their glowing eyes, evil grins on their sharp-toothed, drooling mouths.

Sweet old Mrs. Claus was racing toward us, grinning with homicidal intent, shrieking, "Kill . . . kill . . . *kill* you! I want *flesh!* And *blood!*"

She chased me, cackling and screeching, as I ran around in circles, trying to light my patio torch. I'd lined up a row of flashlights to keep the Chef Chéries and teddy bears under control, but I had nothing left to defend myself from the elves, Santa, and Mrs. Claus if I couldn't get this torch lighted.

Max was fighting off demonic toys from every direction as best he could with his mystical power, but I recalled with a sinking heart that fire was his weakest element—and we hadn't anticipated an attack like this. We had expected to face one big demon that would cower when we showered it with light. Not dozens— hundreds?—of attackers from all over Solsticeland who were replacing each other as fast as Max could strike them down with his Latin incantations, flaming spears of light, and powerful waves of invisible force knocking them back like a giant, unseen hand. They still came at us, in wave after wave.

"Turn on the lights!" Jeff was screaming, pounding on the main power switches. "The lights!"

The Solsticeland lights were on. They were just too dim to affect our attackers.

I'd *always* thought the dim light in here was a terrible idea, I thought furiously. Now it was going to get me killed!

I got a torch lighted—and then I did the only thing I could think of to forestall annihilation. I started setting things on fire—starting with the hideous gold lamé curtains in the Hanukkah display. If we could create our own massive bonfire, as the ancients had done for millennia, maybe we could hold off our attackers.

"It's working, Esther!" Max shouted, realizing what I was attempting. "It's working!"

The room was filling with bright, fiery light! As it did so, the demonically possessed toys, dolls, stuffed animals, and mannequins started keeling over, falling down onto the floor, inert and harmless.

"Stop!" Jeff shouted. "Stop, Esther!"

"What?" I set a Christmas tree on fire.

I heard Jeff coughing and turned around to look at him. A small mountain of dead toys and elf mannequins lay in front of him, but he was coughing hard as smoke billowed toward him from the hideous Hanukkah exhibit, which was now entirely in flames. I realized the whole room was filling with smoke as well as with light.

"Oops."

The smoke alarms went off at that moment, screeching shrilly overhead. They were industrial strength, intended to alert the whole department store to the fire. We couldn't even hear each other shouting over their high-pitched clamoring.

A moment later, the sprinkler system came on, drenching us in water. The sprinklers also started dousing the fire. We all picked up strobe lights, terrified the demonic toys would rise and renew their attacks . . . but nothing happened.

I heard yelling behind me and whirled in that direction, pointing my strobe light at what I thought was another attack.

Then I realized that powerful flashlights were pointing at me. I also realized that the voices were shouting, "Hands up! Hands UP!"

I dropped my strobe light and squinted against the lights shining in my eyes. I gradually made out the shape of several security guards. Three of them were pointing flashlights at me. One was pointing a gun.

"Oh . . . *no*," I said.

They, of course, saw two elves and Diversity Santa, standing amidst a mountainous wreck of ruined toys and vandalized displays, in the smoldering wreckage of the fire we had started inside Fenster & Co.

17

"You know what's interesting about this?" Max said.

Jeff asked, "There's something interesting about this?"

"What's interesting is that we're not dead."

"Fascinating," Jeff said wearily.

"I need to use the bathroom again," I said. "Sir?"

"Let the next guy take you," he said. "It's almost the end of my shift."

We had been locked up inside the holding cell on the sixth floor at Fenster's for more than eighteen hours. I strongly suspected this wasn't legal; but since they were treating us humanely (food, water, bathroom visits, a television), and since I wasn't at all eager to face the police—let alone Lopez—I was disinclined to rock the boat.

"We should be dead," Max mused. "A solstice demon from a hell dimension should have arisen in Solsticeland approximately one half hour after we were incarcerated, and it should have promptly begun destroying, devouring, and demolishing everything within its range."

"*Should?*" I repeated. "Can we choose a different word, Max?"

The security guard seated at the desk near our cell was looking at Max intently by now. "What is this thing's range?"

"Initially?" Max said, "Midtown Manhattan, I would say."

"*Initially?*" the guard repeated, clearly unsettled.

Always pleased to lecture, Max strolled over to the corner of the cell closest to the guard and explained, "There are a wide variety of solstice demons, some of them very strong and voracious, some of them rather weak and fleeting. So I hate to theorize without more data—"

"No, you don't," Jeff said irritably.

"—and therefore I'm using a mid-range estimate. It's possible the demon would only have the strength to destroy this city block before it would lose its ability to hold back the light—"

"Hold back what light?"

"The sun," Max replied. "This genre of demon needs darkness to function. The greater the demon's strength, the longer they're able to keep this dimension—or, at least, a very localized portion of it—shrouded in darkness, and the longer the demon is therefore able to go on feeding and increasing its strength, thereby creating a cycle of—"

"Feeding?" the guard blurted. "Feeding on what?"

"Mostly on people," Max said. "But not exclusively."

"Holy crap!"

"So you can understand why we felt we must confront this demon last night and send it straight back to its hell dimension," said Max, "before it had time to wreak untold havoc on our world."

"Absolutely!"

"And given the intensified level of mystical activity last night here at Fenster's," Max continued, "I believe there is no question but that the danger is still imminent."

"Really?" I asked in dismay.

"Oh, yes." Max nodded emphatically.

"What do we *do?*" the guard cried.

"The most advisable first step," Max said sincerely, "would be to release the three of us, so that we can determine why the demon did not arise last night—the longest night of the year—and re-plot its trajectory for entry into this dimension."

"Release you?" The guard paused for a long moment, then laughed. "Let you go? Good one, buddy!" He seemed genuinely delighted. "You really had me going there! That was *great!* Hey, they didn't say you were a con. Just an arsonist, vandal, burglar, blah blah blah. I had no idea. Got any others? I *loved* that one! Really gave me chills!"

Max sighed and turned away from him. He said to me, lowering his voice to avoid engaging the guard's amusement again, "I think we need to narrow this down. Exactly what is being raised, why, and when?"

"I hate my life," Jeff moaned.

"Oh, please, Jeff," I said irritably. "Are you going to try to rationalize what happened to us last night? Pretend that someone accidentally animated—"

"No, I'm on board with the whole 'demon rising and infiltrating Fenster's with evil forces' thing," he said. "And I will be seeing last night in my nightmares for years to come. I just don't see why this has to happen *here*."

"Here?" I repeated. "You mean Fenster's? Actually, I have a theory that Elsp—"

"No, I mean here in New York. Why now? Why when *I'm* here? I was living in LA for over three years. Why couldn't a solstice demon have struck New York then? Why did it have to wait for me to come back? Or why can't it go eat Los Angeles? After all, I'm done with that town. But, noooo, this thing waits to destroy New York until *I'm* back. And it does it right when I'm at the absolute nadir of my life, playing Diversity Santa in Solsticeland. I mean, Christ, could this year turn into any more of a nightmare for me?"

I stared at him for a long moment, not wondering why I had broken up with him, but why I had ever dated him in the first place. "You're right," I said at last. "This is all about *you*."

"We're going to prison," he said to me. "You know that, don't you?"

"Not necessarily," I said gloomily, gesturing to Max. "New York may be shrouded in eternal darkness and devoured by a demon from hell, instead. So cheer up, Jeff."

The guard opined, "Santa is right. I saw the damage in Solsticeland. Jesus, you guys went to town! There's gonna be a lot of charges for what you did. A *lot*."

I wasn't sure if staying at work after closing counted as "breaking and entering," but I thought it seemed very likely we would be charged with vandalism, arson, destruction of property, and perhaps attempted burglary. For starters.

I wasn't mentally ready to face criminal charges and a prison sentence, so I hadn't yet objected to being kept in limbo inside this cell with Max and Jeff.

Max's prognosis about the demon was a terrifying prospect, but since I sincerely doubted that anyone would free us to go deal with it, my thoughts mostly kept galloping toward being charged with various felonies and disgraced in front of Lopez. I felt sad when I thought of that. Also very queasy.

"You really won't take me to the bathroom?" I asked the guard.

"I took you twice already," he said. "Wait for the next shift."

We had been brought here immediately by the security guards who'd apprehended us last night in Solsticeland. They said they were going to call Mr. Fenster, and then we would be turned over to the authorities.

Jeff and I had spent all night pacing the cage and occasionally sniping at each other. Max was very anxious about the demon, I now realized, but he accepted the prospect of prison with relative equanimity. Probably because he didn't expect to live long enough to be tried and imprisoned if he wasn't freed to confront the demon soon.

Thoughts like this had kept me wide awake since being placed in this cell—as had the absence of any place to sleep. There were some chairs here, but no bed. The cell wasn't meant to hold people for long. It had been constructed to contain newly apprehended shoplifters until the police could pick them up. It was never intended to hold prisoners overnight.

This was also why we all had to keep asking to be escorted to the bathroom. The cell contained no facilities of that sort.

Max had attempted to use his mystical power to get us out of here, but all that had fizzled and flopped. He was depleted from last night's battle. I hadn't been in favor of staging a jailbreak, anyhow, which I thought would just make our problems worse . . . but now that I understood how imminent Max thought death by demon destruction was, I was rethinking that. However, I suspected he wasn't likely to regain sufficient strength for more mojo unless he could get some sleep. He didn't look a day over seventy, but 350 years do take their toll.

So here we sat. It was now dinner time of the following day, and we were still in this cell.

However, we had at least discovered a couple of hours ago *why* we were still here. There was a TV in the holding area, and the guards ran news programs most of the day. A couple of hours ago, the big local story of the day broke—and it wasn't that half of Solsticeland had been destroyed or that a demon had pierced the dimensional barrier.

Freddie Fenster had been arrested as the shooter in last night's hijacking.

No *wonder* the Fensters were a little too preoccupied to ask the cops to come pick us up! And given the scale of what had happened, apparently no one on duty here wanted to do an end run around the Fensters without knowing their exact wishes in this matter.

I had a dark moment of wondering if this meant that having us quietly executed was one of the possible choices. But then I realized the most likely scenario was that the Fensters wanted to control all the media spin about their company, so they didn't let anyone else make decisions in a messy situation.

It was a management strategy that didn't take into account the possibility of three employees destroying a substantial portion of the store on the same day that a member of the family was arrested for armed robbery. Moreover, surely the way the Fensters had handled the first couple of hijackings demonstrated that they'd be very wise to start leaving their decisions up to others.

Meanwhile, Freddie Fenster was not commenting, nor were any members of the family, nor was his lawyer. The police and the DA weren't saying much, either. In the absence of anything resembling facts or information, the media didn't waste its valuable time actually investigating this juicy case. Pundits just jumped straight into the fruitful practice of speculating, then stating each other's speculations as if they were facts. After about an hour of this, I had begged the guard to turn off the TV, threatening to have him charged with prisoner abuse if he didn't.

My elf suit was getting rank enough that I was about to start lobbying for a change of clothes when, to my astonishment, Elspeth Fenster entered the holding area and announced that she was letting us go.

"She let you go?" Lucky asked us incredulously. "Why?"

"She claims her father doesn't want the scandal of pressing charges against three unhappy employees who had a drunken bacchanalia inside the store," I said.

"I'm not even an employee," Max said. "But I certainly did not protest my liberation on that basis."

We were in the bookstore, where Max and I had come after being released. Jeff had gone home. Lucky, who had realized by mid-morning that we were both missing, had somehow found out what had happened to us (Gambellos had a way of getting information that

was not necessarily available to everyone), so he had
spent the day here at the bookstore, taking care of Nelli
and making a gazillion phone calls, he said, in hopes of
finding some strings he could pull to get us set free.

"Preston Fenster just . . . ain't pressing charges?"
Lucky frowned. "That don't make much sense."

"I didn't think so, either," I agreed. "But since Elspeth is a Fenster—and the only Fenster they'd heard
from after eighteen hours of holding us—the guards let
us go when she told them to."

Max asked, "So that was not your doing, Lucky?"

"Nope." The old mobster shook his head. "Back
when Connie Fenster was alive, the Shy Don could've
worked something out quick. He's been trying all day
to help you, too. He ain't forgot what you done for our
family in the past. And him and Connie had a lotta mutual respect. But since she died this year . . ." Lucky
shrugged. "We really ain't had contact with the family,
and today turned out to be a bad day to try to establish
it. So I don't think we're the ones that helped you out
there." He thought it over. "Maybe the girl was telling
the truth about her old man's decision. The Fensters do
got a lot on their plates right now. Maybe dealing with
you three was just too much for them to add to the
load."

"Or maybe Preston was actually relieved that someone's destroyed so much of Solsticeland," I reflected. "I
wonder if letting us disappear without charges is his
way of thanking us. When he had his heart attack, you

know, he was in the middle of saying that he wanted to shut that place down immediately, after all."

"So he's stuck in the hospital still, his nephew is in stir, and his sister and brother are scrambling to do damage control on every front and keep the company going in the middle of this mess," mused Lucky. "Yeah, I guess it makes sense that he sent the dead-looking girl to get you out, though she wouldn't normally be anyone's idea of a seminary."

"I think you mean emissary," I said.

Elspeth had been her usual sulky, sullen, socially inept, and rather creepy self when setting us free. She also seemed very pleased about something—insofar as Elspeth seemed capable of pleasure. I supposed she was experiencing schadenfreude over Freddie's felonious disgrace and her loathed family's steadily spiraling situation—the expensive hijackings were now exposed (the press claimed) as an inside job staged by a key family member, a big portion of Solsticeland was in ruins today, and her father was still in the hospital. This was an immense downturn in the family fortunes within just a few days.

I really didn't think, though, that in the throes of her sly pleasure over all this, Elspeth took into account that she was ill-equipped to live without her family's millions supporting her, in the event that they *kept* sinking in the world.

It occurred to me that the other people who were probably enjoying the Fensters' spectacularly fiery descent didn't have that inherent conflict of interest: the Powells. Bullied and marginalized for years by Constance, finally ejected from their own company, and then defeated in their various attempts at legal redress or restitution . . . They had not lived to have revenge on the Iron Matriarch, but they were probably delighting in the Fenster train wreck which had begun so soon after her death and seemed to be piling up by leaps and bounds now.

"Actually, it makes you wonder . . ." I said.

"What?" Lucky prodded.

"Whether the Powells could have engineered any of this."

Lucky seemed skeptical. "I only knew them by reputation, too, but they seemed like a family that thought of lawyering up as big mojo, not cooking up polter-heists, kid. Their biggest talent, as far as anyone could tell, was slinking away with their tail between their legs after every tangle they had with Connie—for years before she kicked them outta the company, as well as after."

"Hmm." Max stroked his beard. "They are a couple of tragically unhappy and unappealing families, it seems to me."

"They make me appreciate my family, that's for sure," Lucky said with feeling. "I'm gonna go visit my daughter when this is over."

Max and I looked at each other.

Lucky noticed. "What?"

"There's some stuff we need to catch you up on," I said. "Something we figured out last night right after you left Fenster's. This isn't so much a polterheist situation, Max now thinks, as it is a demon-devouring-us situation."

"That don't sound good," Lucky said. "I think I liked this thing better when it was a poltergeist."

"I liked this thing better when it was just a humiliating day job," I said.

Dimension-crossing demon or not, I *had* to get some sleep. I insisted that Max did, too. We had worked a full day at the store yesterday, had barely survived a terrifying confrontation with mystical Evil last night, and hadn't slept in at least thirty-six hours. I was so exhausted that I'd keel over if a toddler gave me a firm tap, never mind being assaulted by a battle-ready solstice demon.

My fatigue was such that I treated myself to a taxi to get home from Max's. It was an extravagance I regretted as soon as I got to my apartment and discovered some bills in the mailbox. It occurred to me then: destroying about one-third of Solsticeland last night undoubtedly meant I had lost my job, and it probably also meant I wouldn't even get my final paycheck.

Damn, damn, damn.

This gloomy thought stayed with me as I stripped off my ruined elf clothes, took a hot shower in my chilly bathroom, and then went straight to bed. I couldn't face the problem of paying my bills this month—or any other problems—right now. Like Scarlett O'Hara, I would think about that tomorrow. I also couldn't be bothered to check my phone for messages. I didn't want to know if Lopez had called to tell me he'd found out about last night. I didn't want to know *anything*. For now, I just wanted to sleep . . .

And I did so. For almost twelve hours.

When I woke up the following day, I felt rested and peaceful for almost ten seconds. Then I remembered that we might all be killed soon by a solstice demon.

I also remembered that if New York was not shortly devoured by something from another dimension, I wasn't sure I had enough money to live on for the next few weeks.

Shit.

These thoughts were depressing enough to make the possibility of getting chewed out by Lopez seem positively sunny by comparison. So I checked my messages. There was one from him yesterday afternoon saying he was working long hours due to the case breaking with such a high profile arrest, but let's talk soon. Nothing since then . . . so I supposed it was possible he didn't know I'd accidentally destroyed part of Fenster's fourth floor a few hours after he'd kissed me in the park.

The next message was from Twinkle, who had called yesterday afternoon, too, while I was still incarcerated. "Dreidel, I got your number from Miles' file cabinet. I hope you guys are okay? I still don't know what happened, except that part of the fourth floor got demolished and three people were locked up on the sixth floor—which has been off-limits to everyone since late last night. So I'm guessing that was you guys?"

He continued, "But I swear, no one went in or out of the building last night . . . I'm a little punchy. Sorry. Just hoping you're okay. Oh, and maybe you heard? Freddie Fenster has been arrested. The way *we* found out around here was that Elspeth Fenster came down here and fired Naughty and Nice. Told them about Freddie and sent them packing. Naughty's going back to stripping, she says. Nice thinks she might have to move back home with her parents now that she's off Freddie's payroll."

Couldn't happen to a couple of more deserving elves, I thought.

"We're keeping Solsticeland open for the final day of the season," Twinkle said. "Well, sort of. About half the place is still intact. Solstice Castle, the Enchanted Forest, the solstice mural . . . Probably not much chance of running my lunar eclipse display, though, since things are in chaos and we're so understaffed. Drag Queen Santa didn't come to work today. So that's makes *another* one. I've lost count by now. Of course, you and Diversity Santa are being counted as no-shows, too, but I know that's not true."

After a pause, he concluded, "Well, call me when you get this, okay? Just to let me know if you're all right? It's getting weird, the way everyone just disappears around here."

And that's when I knew. It all came together in my head at that moment, thanks to Twinkle's rambling.

The final message on my phone was from my friend Whoopsy Daisy, who worked at the Pony Expressive with Satsy. It was from yesterday afternoon, too. As soon as I heard Whoopsy's voice, I knew I was right. I didn't really understand what was happening, but I could see the shape of the scheme now.

"Esther, sweetie, gimme a call when you get this. Satsy didn't show up for her show last night, and she's *never* missed a performance. I've left her three messages, and she hasn't called me back. Honey, this is not like her! You're working at that department store with her. When did *you* last see her? I'm really worried. All the girls here are. *Call* me."

I put down the phone and looked at my Dreidel costume. It was a wreck. I couldn't possibly work in that outfit. Besides, Dreidel would probably never be allowed on the floor at Fenster's again. Nor would Esther Diamond, I realized.

But I knew with sinking dread what I had to do. So I called Twinkle and left him a message. He was probably on the floor right now, but I hoped he'd check his phone regularly and get this soon: "Twinkle, it's Dreidel. I'm fine. We're all fine. But I need you to do something very important for me. Tell Princess Crystal she's been fired—too many smoking violations. Tell her

Miles wants her off the floor *right now*. Then get her costume—I don't care how—and meet me in the employee stairwell. I'll be there in three hours, so get this done by then."

Then I phoned Whoopsy, who picked up my call, and said I hadn't seen Satsy for two days, but I thought I'd be seeing him tonight, and I'd tell him to check in.

No reason to worry Whoopsy with the details. Hopefully this would all work out. And if not . . . well, why make him grieve sooner than he had to?

After that, I called Max. I was glad he answered the phone, since he didn't always.

"Max," I said, "they *are* related—the mystical phenomena and the heists! She's using *employees* to do the hijackings. She just used Freddie as a cruel joke on the family—or maybe because she hates him. Anyway, I don't understand *how*, but that's *why* Solsticeland employees keep disappearing with their costumes! We thought they were quitting without giving notice. No, they're being waylaid when they get off work! That's how she's recruiting her robbery crews. She's culling temporary staff in Solsticeland, where people hardly know each other and don't ask questions if someone stops turning up for work."

"I think I know her ultimate plan, Esther," he said. "I did some research last night—before I fell asleep on top of my books. Tell me again what that enchanted tree said to you when it tried to kill you."

"The same thing Mrs. Claus said: 'I want flesh! And blood!'"

"Yes, that's it! She has promised sacrifices to this demon. She's going to make *sure* it's powerful enough to hold back the light and wreak terrible destruction," Max said. "And she's going to do it tonight!"

"Tonight, yes, I thought so! Two magic words," I said. "Lunar eclipse."

18

I sat hiding in Solstice Castle, dressed as Princess Crystal, for several hours. A big advantage of this role was that Crystal spent most of her time up on the ramparts or in the tower, where it wasn't easy to see her face. Another big advantage was that her costume had a hood. The actress who usually played Crystal didn't use it often, but I'd kept it up ever since confiscating the costume, via Twinkle's subterfuge, and entering Solsticeland in this guise.

It was handy that my build and coloring were similar to the original Crystal's. And it was *very* handy that, unlike Dreidel, Crystal actually still had a job here.

Solsticeland was the last place on earth I wanted to be this evening . . . but since I didn't want this to be my friend Satsy's last evening on earth (nor mine, nor anyone else's), this was where I had to be, since someone needed to let Max, Nelli, and Lucky into Fenster's after closing time, which was surely when Elspeth planned to make her blood sacrifices and raise her demon in Solsticeland.

To my dismay, Twinkle insisted on helping us. I really didn't want to get the elf killed. But it is everyone's right to choose whether or not they're ready to confront Evil; and since he clearly felt his fantasy role-playing games had prepared him for tonight, who was I to deny him this chance to make a cosmic difference?

My stomach was roiling so much that I was afraid a few times that I'd toss my cookies on Crystal's bulky gown as I sat in the castle tower, waiting for the closing gong to sound. Fenster's was shutting down at eight o'clock this evening, Christmas Eve. (Nothing like waiting until the last possible minute to buy that special someone a gift from the heart.)

A lunar eclipse on Christmas Eve.

Of *course* Elspeth couldn't resist that symbolism when plotting the destruction of her family and, incidentally, a substantial portion of New York City. I didn't know what had led her into dark magic and demon summoning, which is not exactly an inevitable destination for those who start out as goth girls and/or vampire groupies. But there was a big, dark hole inside that girl, and I could see that she had repeatedly tried to fill it with more darkness.

So how could she possibly resist making *this* her night for summoning ultimate spiritual darkness? In the deepest part of winter, this night which was holy to the gentiles—of which she was one—would become the darkest Christmas Eve in over four hundred years.

It almost seemed as if tonight and Elspeth were meant for each other.

I stifled a shiver and hoped there was also something in this oppressively dark night that was meant—in a good way—for a nice Jewish elf from Wisconsin who was dressed as a princess and just trying to do her part to confront Evil, keep the city from being consumed in a demon's fiery belly, and pay the rent on time.

Was that so much to ask?

Before ending our call earlier today, I had asked Max what to expect if the demon broke through the dimensional barrier tonight. He replied by asking me if I'd ever seen Walt Disney's *Fantasia*.

"The segment known as 'Night On Bald Mountain' is an excellent representation of what awaits us if we do not succeed tonight," he said.

I tried not to tremble as I contemplated the night ahead of me. That movie depicted an immense, terrifying, dark demon, shrouded in night, with glowing eyes, fangs, and claws. It took pleasure in torturing and tormenting other creatures.

I had worked myself into quite a state of nerves by the time the closing gong finally sounded at Fenster's and a canned voice on the intercom asked all shoppers to depart, wishing them Happy Holidays. Finally! I wouldn't have to keep hiding from Miles or preventing

Prince Midnight from getting a good look at my face when he popped by to propose to Crystal. That part of this ordeal, at least, was over now. Fenster's was closing, and the holiday shopping season was finished at long last.

The plan was that Twinkle would clock out, change into his street clothes, and appear to leave. In reality, he'd let our friends in through the employee stairs, and they'd make their way to Solstice Castle to join me. We would then prepare for Elspeth's arrival with, we suspected, her sacrifices.

Since we had a better idea of what we were facing tonight, Max had ensured that we also came better prepared. I was wearing a protective amulet pinned inside my gown. It would shield me from collateral attacks— the sort of thing we had experienced in recent days, and particularly the other night, when the demon's energy was piercing through the increasingly permeable dimensional barrier, testing its powers in this world the way you might dip your foot into the water from a boat to test the temperature and the current. This was the time of year when barriers crumbled between this world and dark dimensions, and the demon had been looking forward to tonight, unable to wait until now to start toying with its new victims.

What could Elspeth *possibly* be thinking? Did she understand what horrors she was about to unleash? No matter how awful her family was, did *anyone* deserve this? And what about those of us who weren't even related to her?

Waiting here alone for Twinkle, Max, Lucky, and Nelli to arrive was unnerving. This store had become a terrifying place to me. My heart was pounding so loudly, I had trouble listening for the reassuring sound of their footsteps in the eternal starlit night of Solsticeland—or what was left of it. Then I heard them coming at last.

"Esther?" Max called.

I tensed, thinking he should lower his voice . . . but then I remembered how light the security staff was expected to be tonight. Christmas Eve. I doubted there were any guards on this floor at all.

"This place gives me the creeps," Lucky said. "I hope to God these amulets work, Doc."

"So do I," said Max, which was not the reassuring answer that I had hoped to hear.

"I'm up here," I called. "I'll come down to you. I've been stuck in this tower all damn evening."

The lunar eclipse was due to occur shortly before midnight. That, too, seemed like symbolism that would have appealed to Elspeth when plotting her revenge on her family.

We didn't know how soon she would arrive. She would no doubt need time to prepare her ritual. I realized we should get ready right away to confront her. She might be here very soon.

I reached the bottom of the tower's spiral stairs,

where I could still hear the reassuring sounds of my friends' voices in the dark. Twinkle was lamenting the lunar eclipse he'd programmed but hadn't gotten to display in the Solsticeland sky. Lucky told him to shut up, we had enough eclipses already. Nelli growled suddenly.

"What is it, Nelli?" Max asked.

Beneath my bodice, I touched the amulet I wore, reassured to feel it there. The other night's experience here was *not* something I wanted to repeat.

"This place is makin' her jumpy, too," said Lucky.

I exited the castle, then gasped and fell back a step when a large figure loomed before me. I turned on the flashlight I'd brought with me today and found myself staring at my purple-lashed friend.

"Satsy?" I said in surprise.

The blow came from behind. I never saw it or knew who delivered it. I dropped my flashlight and staggered forward into Satsy, whose arms caught me in a ruthlessly tight embrace. I tried to call for help, but Satsy squeezed me so hard I couldn't breathe. He gazed down into my face without expression, his eyes unblinking in Solsticeland's dim light. Elsewhere in the building, I heard cries of alarm and the sounds of physical violence. My friends were being ambushed.

Trap.

As I slipped into unconsciousness, I finally understood why Elspeth Fenster had released us from her family's private prison.

So that we would come here tonight and become her sacrifices.

"Esther, wake up! Esther, can you hear me? Esther."

There was an annoying whispering in my ear. My head was pounding fiercely. And that chanting was so loud . . .

Chanting.

My eyes flew open.

"Oh, my God," I said, appalled by the spectacle before me.

Elspeth Fenster had painted a bright red symbol in the fake snow on the floor outside of Solstice Castle. Based on the knife in her hands and the blood flowing from a cut in each of her arms, I gathered that the blood was hers.

Okay, stay calm, at least she's not cutting anyone else, I thought. *Such as me.*

Elspeth was also, incidentally, stark naked.

Although I really don't like to judge my own gender on the basis of appearance, public nudity was not a look that I thought anyone would ever recommend for this girl.

Given the ardor on Elspeth's face as she raised her bleeding arms and chanted to her dark lord, offering the solstice demon (who, fortunately, had yet to make an appearance) her body, I thought that her disappointments with sex were perhaps due to focusing a little too much of her sexual energy on *this* sort of thing, rather than on the simple pleasures of the flesh with an earthly partner.

She was surrounded by Solsticeland employees, all stone-faced and chanting with her. I saw Satsy, Poinsettia, Moody Santa, Thistle, Giggly Santa, and several other people whose names I didn't know—some of whose faces I didn't even recognize, so they had apparently gone missing even before I had been hired. Elspeth had been collecting victims for a few weeks. And she had gotten away with it, because (as I had thought from the start) it seemed perfectly understandable that someone might just stop showing up for this job. Still, it had taken people in Satsy's life less than a day to realize he was missing and to start worrying and making inquiries. I wondered if he was Elspeth's only miscalculation, or if she was leaving a trail of Missing Persons that led straight back to Solsticeland.

"Esther," that whispering voice said from behind me again. "You're awake? Good. No, shh! Don't say anything, and don't turn around."

I finally recognized that voice. "Rick?" I whispered. "What are you doing here?"

"She's gone insane," he whispered back. "We have to stop her. Will you help me?"

"Of course!" I blurted.

"Shh!"

Fortunately, my outburst had not been audible above the chanting. I noticed the bloody symbol in the snow was starting to glow a dark red. That struck me as a bad thing.

I started to move, then realized I had been tied up. Without turning around, I whispered, "Can you untie me?"

"Yes. I have a knife."

"Be very careful with it," I instructed.

As soon as I felt my bonds loosen, I said, "Now free Max—um, Belsnickel."

"That crazy old blind elf?"

"He's not what he seems," I said. "He can stop El-speth."

I noticed with anxiety that Max appeared to be un-conscious. This was not going well.

I supposed the first thing we should do was disrupt the chanting. As soon as Rick appeared to have freed Max, who was not yet awake, and then moved on to Lucky, I leapt to my feet with a blood-curdling scream and launched myself at Elspeth. Using a move similar to the one which had worked on Lopez's father, I drop-kicked her out of her enchanted circle and clear into the Enchanted Forest.

Damn, I'm good. I should study kung fu or something.

"Lucky, wake up Max. He's got to stop the demon from breaking through!" That red circle appeared to be glowing more robustly now. The thing was on its way.

Twinkle cried, "Untie me! Untie me! I can help!"

Freed from his bonds, Lucky crawled over and

started shaking and slapping Max, shouting into his face.

I heard Nelli barking excitedly and looked around. I saw her tied to a fake tree. "The dog, Rick! Free the dog!"

"The *dog?*" he repeated incredulously.

"It's important! Free the damn dog!"

"Untie me! Untie me!" Twinkle shouted.

Without Elspeth directing them, the missing Solstice-land actors seemed unthreatening now. But they kept chanting. I wondered how to make them stop.

Max staggered to his feet. He took one look at the glowing red circle and said, "The demon is coming! It's arriving! We must stop it! Nelli!"

Freed from her tree by Rick, the familiar came running over to the circle and promptly began racing madly around it, going widdershins, trying to reverse the direction of its energy. She was howling at the top of her lungs as she did so, doing a fair job of drowning out the chanting.

With Max awake and on the job now, Lucky turned his attention to Twinkle, who was still demanding to be untied. As soon as that task was achieved, the two of them began flinging themselves at the chanters, trying to get them out of formation, startle them, interrupt their chant—*anything* to weaken the demon's attempt to break through the dimensional barrier and emerge here in all its power and ferocity. Max started bellowing out a chant of his own.

Cold wind filled the room, heralding the demon's arrival. The most unimaginably foul stench came with it.

"Aw, Jesus, that *smell*," Lucky said.

I realized that I hadn't seen Rick since he had followed Elspeth into the Enchanted Forest to free Nelli. Who knew what Elspeth might be doing to him in there? I went running after them, lifting my heavy skirts and praying that my amulet would protect me from being attacked by a frisky tree again.

But when I found the two of them, Elspeth wasn't torturing or tormenting Rick. The two of them were fighting. Like partners. Co-conspirators. A *couple* . . .

"You've ruined everything!" Rick raged. "We had a perfect plan!"

"You have betrayed me!" she screeched into his face. "How *dare* you interfere!"

"Interfere? When you're about to get half the city devoured? Including yourself! And, more to the point, *me!*"

"Death is the ultimate glory!" she proclaimed, indeed sounding insane. "The ultimate reward!"

"No," he shot back, "the ultimate reward will be getting back every penny of what your family stole from my family, you demented, frigid bitch!"

"Oh, my God," I said, as realization dawned. "Rick . . . you're a *Powell*."

He looked stunned to see me—and appalled to realize he had been exposed.

"No one noticed when you applied for this job?" I asked in surprise. We had to use our legal names on our employment forms, and people were *very* sensitive about the name "Powell" around here.

"He's a Powell on his mother's side," Elspeth said contemptuously. "And, *God*, if I have to listen to him whine even *one more time* about what my family did to the pathetic losers in his family."

"So Elspeth had the mystical mojo," I said to Rick, "and you knew how to apply it to human nature to get control of various employees' minds and turn them into drones in your hijacking scheme."

"And that's all it was supposed to be!" he screamed at Elspeth, beside himself with anger now. "Not *this* shit! I just wanted the money! I'm sick of my family doing nothing about what was taken from us!"

"Oh, for God's sake, Rick," I said in disgust. "It was a long time ago. Move on. Go out and get a job like the rest of us."

"Oh, that's great advice coming from you, *Dreidel*."

"You thought you could control her," I said to him with malicious satisfaction. "But once you got her going on the idea of revenge, of humiliating her family, of exploring her mystical gifts . . . You had no *idea* what you had set loose, did you? You've just been finding out in the past couple of days how far she's strayed from your plan and how little control of her you actually have."

"What kind of demented lunatic wants to destroy all

of Midtown?" he shouted. "I thought she was only talking about destroying Fenster's—and I mean the *business*, not the damn building!"

We heard a horrible bellowing roar from Solstice Castle, so powerful that it blew a hot fetid wind through the Enchanted Forest. Max's chanting rose in volume. I heard Twinkle scream aggressively as he barreled into someone else, trying to break the demon's power circle. The kid was really showing his mettle tonight.

"I didn't know about *this!*" Rick insisted. "All I wanted to do was rob the Fensters!"

"Somebody got *shot* the other night, Rick," I pointed out. "That's what tends to happen once you dabble in *armed robbery*, you jackass!"

"No, that tends to happen once you dabble in an idiot like Freddie Fenster!" Rick shouted as another hot, grotesquely foul wind blew through this area. The grad student turned his ire on Elspeth again and raged, "What were you thinking? On top of everything else, using your idiot cousin has led the cops *straight* to us!"

I was about to say that the police seemed a minor matter at the moment, compared to a solstice demon. But then there was a long, loud, enraged demonic *scream* from the next room, and a prolonged flash of white light so bright that we had to shield our eyes, even though we were screened from it by fake trees. This was followed by a stunned moment of silence . . . And then I heard the chatter of confused human voices as Elspeth's victims regained their senses and started demanding to know what the hell was going on.

Nelli was barking again—but joyfully now, announcing their victory.

"Oh, thank God," I said. "The demon has been sent back to hell."

"Noooooo!" Elspeth wailed. "*No, no, no, noooooo. . . .*"

Naked and weeping hysterically, she collapsed to the floor. I immediately heard a bunch of feet stampeding this way, coming from the direction of the solstice mural. I tensed as I looked that way, and was surprised to hear heavy, authoritative voices shouting, "NYPD! *Freeze!* Police! Get down on the ground! FREEZE!"

"Lopez!" I cried, seeing him among the officers running in this direction. He was wearing a bullet-proof vest, which struck me as an odd thing to wear to a demon's summoning.

"*Esther?*" he stopped in his tracks, looking stunned.

Then I felt the barrel of a gun against my temple as Rick grabbed me from behind, his hand around my throat, choking me so hard that my eyes watered and I felt dizzy. He started dragging me backward, using me as a shield, telling the approaching cops to back off or he would kill me.

Lopez looked horrified, but he didn't drop his gun or stop pointing it at Rick. "Let her go!"

Other cops were screaming things at Rick like, "Freeze!" and "Drop it! *Drop it!* DROP IT!"

Given how agitated my captor seemed as he jammed

his gun against my head, I really questioned whether all this screaming was a good idea.

I tried to scramble away from Rick, but my ball gown made my movements slow and clumsy.

He tightened his grip on me and said, "I like you, Esther, but I'll shoot you if I have to."

Breathing hard with fear and adrenaline, I shifted a little to look into his eyes . . . and I realized that I believed him.

"And *he* wouldn't like that, would he?" Rick added to me as he flicked a glance at Lopez.

I started shaking all over. *Oh, my God, this manipulative, demented, greedy bastard is going to shoot me in the head*, I thought. It was easy to see now how Rick had tried to manage the volatile situation in recent days, create an impression of himself as innocent in all matters, distract my attention, and convince me that nothing strange was going on at Fenster's. And *now* the lying, thieving bastard was going to shoot me in the head.

"I want out of here!" Rick said. "Esther comes with me!"

Lopez just shook his head; I could see the fierceness of his expression from here, even in Solsticeland's gloomy light.

"I'll shoot her," Rick warned. "*I'll shoot her!*"

"No, you won't," Lopez said coldly, his eyes hard. "You know what I'll do to you if she dies."

There was a short, very tense silence . . . and then we

all collectively flinched as the sky started moving above us. I looked up and saw Twinkle's lunar eclipse taking place overhead. He had uploaded the program after all, hoping there'd be a chance to use it. He must be running it now, trying to create a life-saving distraction.

Lopez tried to use that moment of surprise to get a better angle to take a shot at Rick; but Super Santa was ready for that and kept me safely in front of him, his gun still pressed against my temple.

I was shaking all over and seriously starting to fear I'd become a long-term hostage. Or a fatality. I couldn't stop trembling.

"Hold still!" Rick screamed, terrifying me.

For a moment, I thought I saw Lopez's eyes flash like blue fire. And then the next thing I knew, Twinkle's lunar eclipse exploded directly overhead. It noisily showered shards of Solsticeland's sky all over us, along with tiny electrical stars, bits of flaming debris, and torrents of floating sparks. Rick flinched and backed up a step, losing his hold on me. Determined not to let a cumbersome ball gown be the cause of my death, I threw myself bodily in the opposite direction.

By the time Lopez was scooping me off the floor to check me for injuries (none), Rick was on the ground, face down, being handcuffed.

Breathing hard in reaction, Lopez looked up at the sky. "Who turned on that display?"

"Twinkle," I said with certainty. "It was his idea. His design."

"It was good thinking," Lopez said. "It almost worked."

His hands were clutching me hard enough to hurt, but I didn't protest. He hugged me for a long moment. Then he looked up at the ruined Solsticeland sky again, a wreck of shattered parts, sizzling wires, smoking sockets, and exploded little lights.

"Jesus," he said, "this place really *is* falling apart."

I thought I knew better, though. There had been other incidents. Other bizarrely fiery moments, such as the exploding sewer tunnel that killed a homicidal vampire while mysteriously leaving Lopez and his colleagues unharmed. And tonight, I was looking right at him when the sparkling lunar sky of Solsticeland had exploded in a lifesaving shower of fire and sparks, heat and smoke . . . and I thought I had seen something powerful pass through his eyes a split second before that happened.

There was also the time my bed burst into flames, while we were in it together.

I suddenly needed to sit down, feeling very shaky.

Lopez called another cop over to sit with me while he went around securing the scene. Elspeth was still screeching and weeping hysterically, which was getting on my nerves. The police had custody of her and were evidently calling for a stretcher.

Lopez went through the forest and over to Solstice Castle, where Max and Nelli had contained the demon and freed the actors from their psycho-mystical thrall to Elspeth and Rick. I could hear Satsy's voice from all the way in here, and it made me smile.

At some point, feeling as if I was experiencing everything through a fog, I asked Lopez how he had found us.

The answer was absurdly simple. NYPD thought that a hit on the store on Christmas Eve, after closing and when security was light, seemed probable. By then, Lopez had also zeroed in on Rick during his investigation of the employees. And I'd been right in thinking that Elspeth and Rick had picked off too many Solsticeland actors. After I'd mentioned the high attrition rate to Lopez, he'd gotten curious and had looked into it. That had let him start connecting the dots, just as Freddie's arrest and the smooth, inside nature of the planning had done, too.

"Plus," Lopez said, watching his colleagues haul Rick away, "I always thought the perp had to be Santa Claus. *Always.*"

Well, yes. There was that.

"Vindicated at long last," I murmured dryly.

But once he recovered from thinking I might get my head blown off, Lopez started giving me some dark looks, and I realized he'd want some detailed explanations about what I was doing here in the middle of this *mess*, with Max, Nelli, and Lucky—none of whom he'd been pleased to find in Solsticeland tonight. Lopez also started muttering grimly about what the hell he was going to put in his report.

That was when Lucky decided that if the detective didn't object, then he'd be moving along now. Since Lopez apparently didn't want to have to explain to anyone what a Gambello hit man was doing at his crime scene, he agreed with this suggestion.

Then Lopez asked Max to see me safely home. Max agreed with alacrity. But I could tell from the parting look Lopez gave me that I would soon be facing a tense conversation about this night's work.

19

Max saw me home in a taxi whose driver was avidly curious about why I was dressed as a disheveled princess. I ignored him and didn't really hear what Max said.

After we arrived at my apartment building in the West Thirties, Max took the key from my cold hand, opened the front door, and came inside with me. He supported my elbow as I climbed the two flights of stairs in my homely old building. The ball gown I wore felt as heavy as a bag of bricks by now.

Inside my small, cheerfully shabby apartment, Max gently urged me to sit in the easy chair, purchased from a thrift shop, and then wrapped a blanket around me. He entered the kitchenette and puttered around, making me a hot cup of strong, sweet tea. When he handed it to me, I took a sip and, for a nasty moment of suspense, thought I might gag or throw up. Then I crossed some unseen threshold, started to calm down, and swallowed the tea.

Max sat watching me with concern while I drank the whole cup, bit by bit, feeling a little warmth start to creep through me.

Then I realized who was missing. "Nelli! Max, where's Nelli? We have to go back and get—"

"No, no, my dear, she's with Lucky. He's taking her back to the bookshop. He and I realized that getting you home and wrapped up was an urgent task that shouldn't be hampered by finding a cab driver willing to transport Nelli."

"Oh."

He offered to make me another cup of tea, but I declined. I was feeling better now, the shock and cold wearing off. I also noticed how gray with fatigue Max was looking, and I realized that tonight had been exhausting for him.

"You ought to go home and rest," I said, standing up to show him that I felt okay. "I'll call you a cab."

"I am rather fatigued," he admitted.

We chatted quietly, in soft, distracted voices for the next few minutes, while I looked out the window and watched for the taxi to pull up in front of my apartment building. I said I was so glad we had rescued the missing employees. He said he was relieved he and Nelli had succeeded in containing the demon.

We didn't talk about the police, or about whether Lopez had unwittingly caused the spectacular shower of fiery light which had distracted Rick enough for me to escape, or about whether we might have to pay for damaged Solsticeland costumes. It all seemed like too much to think about right now, when we were both stupid with fatigue and I was just glad that there wasn't a bullet in my brain.

The cab arrived, and Max rose to leave. He paused at the door to remind me about his Saturnalia feast tomorrow, which I assured him I would attend.

After I closed the door behind him, I stripped off the gown and stuffed it into a big garbage bag, planning to get rid of it the next time I went out. Then I threw my undergarments into the hamper and went into the bathroom, which was just off the living room, to have a shower. This was the coldest room in the apartment in winter, and I got goose bumps while running the water and waiting for it to heat up. Then I stepped under the hot spray, hoping to get warm all the way through.

After I got out of the shower, I patted myself dry with one of my threadbare towels. Then I slipped quickly into my heavy flannel bathrobe with a shiver—now the cold bathroom was *damp* and cold. I was so tired, but I hate going to bed with a wet head; so I picked up my blow-dryer and turned it on. My senses welcomed its soothing heat and prosaic noise, but I still felt a chill running all the way through me. After a few minutes, I realized I was clenching my jaw so tightly that it hurt. My jangled nerves were screaming for release. So, while I continued drying my hair, I half-heartedly did some exercises to relax my jaw and neck.

I almost became a homicide statistic tonight.

My face in the mirror was pale and tired, but otherwise normal. I didn't *look* like someone who'd nearly had her head blown off a little while ago . . . I wondered why almost being shot by a panicky criminal was still freaking me out, whereas I was already starting to recover from confronting a solstice demon tonight.

Preparation, I supposed. I had gone to Fenster's *expecting* to confront a solstice demon and its demented acolyte, so I'd been ready for that. Yes, it was terrifying; but I had braced myself for mystical Evil. However, it had never occurred to me that someone was going to pull out a *gun* and point it at my *head*.

Bastard.

I remembered the murderous intent on Rick's face as he threatened to kill me, remembered what it was like to be held hostage at gunpoint by someone I had liked and worked with . . .

My arm started shaking, making the dryer waver erratically. I tried to hold it steady, but the shaking just got worse. So I turned off the dryer, which suddenly felt very heavy, and set it down. My hair was still a little damp, but it would do for tonight.

I braced my hands against the bathroom sink and took slow, deep, rhythmic breaths, trying to calm down and steady my nerves.

The door buzzer rang. I jumped and gave a little shriek.

I pressed a shaking hand against my heart, which pounded in startled reaction to the jarring noise of the buzzer. I was panting a little.

Jesus, pull yourself together, Esther.

Then another chill swept through me as I realized it was after two o'clock in the morning. Who the hell would be at my door *now?*

This couldn't be good.

I stepped out of the bathroom and stood there uncertainly, staring at my front door, breathing hard with mounting anxiety as my heart continued pounding.

I reminded myself that everyone who had tried to kill me tonight was either in police custody or back in hell now—and solstice demons probably didn't use doorbells, anyhow.

So who was it? Who would come to my apartment in the middle of the night?

I flinched when the buzzer rang again.

Then I regained enough self-command to realize that the easiest way to find out who was downstairs would be to ask. I crossed the floor to the front door and pressed the intercom button, wondering if Max had decided to come back for some reason.

"Who is it?" I asked anxiously.

There was a moment of crackling static. Then: "It's me, Esther. Did I wake you?"

"Lopez?" I blurted in surprise. "Aren't you supposed to be—I don't know—locking people up?"

"I've done that. Now I have to figure out exactly what to say in my report." He sounded tired and cranky. "Let me in. We need to talk."

That sounded ominous.

"Now?" I considered insisting that I was too tired and we should do this some other time.

"Yes. And if you're thinking of putting me off, forget it. That's why I didn't call first," he said tersely. "Let me in."

"Um . . ."

"*Now*, Esther." Okay, *very* cranky.

I sighed and buzzed him into the building. After the jolt of adrenaline the buzzer had just delivered, I probably wouldn't be able to fall asleep for ages, anyhow. So if Lopez was determined to have it out, then I might as well get this over with now, rather than postpone the inevitable.

As I opened my front door and listened to him trudging up the stairs to this floor, I wearily ran lines in my head for the scene we were about to play. I would tell him that Lucky, Max, and I had gone to the store to prevent a solstice demon from entering this dimension. Lopez would urge me to seek psychiatric help and to submit to drug testing. He might also vow never to come anywhere near me again; this last bit would be subject to improvisation, depending on how combative he was feeling. Considering the late hour, though, I thought he might just wind up retreating quietly with a headache rather than trying to decide tonight what to do about our . . . let's call it friend-ship.

In any case, regardless of what note his visit might end on, I was so sure of how the central portion of this conversation would go that, by the time Lopez got to my threshold, I felt as if we had *already* talked.

Maybe he felt that way, too; instead of bursting into a torrent of questions and criticism the moment he saw me, he came to an abrupt halt when he reached my doorway and just stood there, staring at me in silence.

I stared back, not at all eager be the one to start the argument.

I realized it must still be snowing outside, since there was a faint white dusting of snowflakes on his wool coat. A few melting droplets sparkled in his black hair and clung to his dark lashes. He was breathing a little fast from the climb up the stairs. And now that he stood on my threshold, looking at me without speak-ing . . . his breathing quickened instead of slowing down.

Our gazes locked, and I stopped thinking about what we were going to say.

He could have died tonight, I thought, my heart thud-ding heavily inside my chest as I stared at him.

His dark expression faded, and he looked slightly dazed, almost surprised as he gazed at me—as if he were seeing me for the first time and hadn't expected what he found.

I suddenly thought of the first time he *had* seen me—

the night we had met, months ago. He had come to investigate a strange incident (which soon turned out to be stranger than my wildest dreams) at the West Village theater where I was in the cast of *Sorcerer!* An overworked precinct detective, he had been professional, polite, and amused rather than annoyed by the colorful strangeness of our complaint—our leading lady seemed to have vanished during the show's disappearing act. Despite my stunned confusion over the seemingly impossible disappearance, I had noticed Lopez that night. It wasn't really because of his exotic good looks, though I certainly liked those; I was used to good-looking men, after all, since I worked in show business. *He* was what I noticed. This man. The same one I was noticing right now, standing there in my doorway, his chest rising and falling rapidly as our gazes remained locked.

I could have died tonight.

I'd been one of a dozen nymphs in the chorus of that ill-fated Off-Broadway musical, all of us half-naked and painted green from head to toe. Lopez spoke to me that night, but it was strictly professional. It never occurred to me that he'd noticed me, too, anonymously covered in body paint and glitter, as I was. But he had. Fate ensured that we met again, and I found out that he had noticed me through the costume and makeup . . . The way he was noticing me now, despite the pale and fatigued face I'd seen in my mirror moments ago and the frumpy bathrobe I wore.

We had always noticed each other. Despite everything. Ever since that first night.

We both could have died . . .

And, having just survived the worst Christmas Eve of my life, I suddenly felt the biggest crime of this whole hellacious holiday would be for us to waste this moment the way we had wasted too many others.

He's alive. And so am I.

And he was here. Now. With me.

Suddenly all I could think about was how much I wanted to celebrate being alive and together right now. How much I wanted *him*. How much I had *always* wanted him, right from the start.

My lips parted and I drew breath to say something, but I couldn't think of any words. I could only think about the way he was looking at me now, the way this man could make me feel—even when I was bruised, exhausted, and wearing a drab flannel robe.

Lopez shook his head, as if to stop me from speaking. Then, in a burst of motion, he crossed the threshold, kicked the door shut behind him, and hauled me roughly into his arms.

His mouth was hot, his breath warm and sweet, his skin cold. I melted into his fierce kisses, clinging to him, suddenly so certain of what I wanted—what I needed.

I sank heavily against him, my arms embracing him possessively, my legs quivering and wobbly. He staggered backward and leaned against the door through which he had just come, his lips moist and hungry against my forehead, my cheek, my neck. He tangled his hands in my hair to hold my head still for his plundering kisses while I fumbled at the buttons of his coat, my hands clumsy and impatient. He wouldn't take his mouth from mine long enough to let me breathe. I felt dizzy from lack of air, and I didn't care. I went on drowning in his kisses, feasting on him . . . Until my fumbling and tugging made him laugh a little, and he pulled away enough to help me get his coat off, inefficiently shrugging out of it in fits and starts between warm nuzzling and hot kisses.

I whimpered in frustration upon discovering how heavily clothed he was beneath his coat—a sweater, a shirt, an undershirt, trousers, belt, holster, gun . . . I didn't think I could cope with all this in my fevered, trembling eagerness. Fortunately, though, he'd been undressing himself for years without my help, so we got most of it off pretty quickly. Shoes, belt, holstered gun, handcuffs, and other objects hit the floor around us, the thudding noises they made barely audible above our frantic breathing and the desperate little sounds we made.

He untied the belt of my heavy robe and slid it off my shoulders, letting it drop to the floor, too. When he ran his hands over me, I gasped and gave a startled laugh because they were still cold. I let him use me to warm them up as I pressed myself against him, flesh to flesh, sighing at how good his naked skin felt all along my body.

Lopez scooped me up into his arms and carried me into the bedroom, where we tumbled onto the bed together and lost ourselves in passion, in hunger finally unleashed. In each other.

The soft light from the bedside lamp caressed his golden-dark skin and gleamed against his midnight-black hair. The dusting of hair on his chest tickled my breasts as his weight pressed me into the mattress. I had a moment of tense anxiety as I remembered that the last time he had embraced me in this bed (albeit on a different mattress), it had suddenly burst into flames. He felt my tension and went still, lifting his head to meet my eyes. I thought I could drown in the blue depths of that gaze, which was now simultaneously passionate, quizzical, and tender.

I relaxed as I recalled that on that incendiary night in summer, he had been conflicted and angry. Whereas tonight, he seemed absolutely sure of what he wanted. And I was sure, too.

My enthusiastic kiss answered his unspoken question, and he relaxed, too. We rolled over and over together, limbs entwined, exploring each other with rich, uninhibited delight. I had dreamed of him like this, had thought so many times about what it would be like to have him in my bed. Now that he was here, his rough tenderness, his boldly exploring mouth, and his shameless hands were turning my fantasies into ashes, consuming me in flames more intense than anything I had ever conjured in my imagination. I surrendered uncon-

ditionally to his heat, his warmth, his fire. We melded
and melted into each other, our sighs and inarticulate
sounds of pleasure floating around us. We writhed ec-
statically together, clinging blindly to each other, consumed by this frantic inferno of desire until, at length,
the explosion left us weak, trembling, and gasping for
air.

After I got my breath back, which took a while, I was
too sleepily content to feel like talking. I turned off the
light and snuggled against Lopez in the cozy darkness,
my head on his shoulder, and enjoyed the contrast between his warm, smooth skin and the cool air on my
naked back. He stroked my hair, kissed my forehead,
and twined his fingers with mine, apparently also content not to talk. When I finally got a little chilly, he
helped me pull the covers up, and then we slept for a
bit.

When it was still dark, he woke me up to make love
again. It was slow and sultry this time—and so steamy
I was sure that, for the next few days, I'd succumb to
blushing every time I was in a public place and suddenly thought of tonight. He really *wasn't* the altar boy
he pretended to be.

When he was done with me, I fell asleep again almost immediately, limp with satisfied exhaustion. He
was snuggled up against my back, his arms around me,
his head nestled next to mine.

Dawn was creeping through the window blinds

when I felt him ease away from me. The mattress shifted, and I realized he was getting out of bed. I assumed he was just going down the hall for a minute and would come right back to bed. But when he returned to the bedroom, I heard the crisp zip of his fly and the metallic click of his belt buckle, and I realized he was getting dressed.

I made an inarticulate sound of protest, without lifting my head or opening my eyes.

A moment later, I felt the mattress dip beneath his weight as he sat beside me. "Are you awake?" he whispered.

I made a negative sound.

Lopez leaned over to brush my hair away from my face and kiss my cheek. "*Now* are you awake?"

"No," I grumbled.

I felt his puff of amusement against my skin before he kissed me again. "I have to go to work."

That made me open my eyes. I squinted at him in the dim, gray light creeping through the blinds. "Now?"

He nodded.

"Oh." I sighed in disappointment.

"Sorry." He stroked my arm. "I'd rather stay here."

"So stay," I mumbled.

"Can't," he said with regret. "It's Christmas."

"Huh? *Oh* . . . right." I'd forgotten. A lot had happened since yesterday, after all. I nodded. "Single guy, no kids. Your shift."

"Uh-huh. I'm already late." Lopez looked sleepy and sounded tired as he added, "And when your colleagues carry guns, you really don't want to be the reason they missed Christmas morning with their kids."

"But you were working all night!" When he laughed at that description of his nocturnal activities, I amended, "Well, until about two o'clock, anyhow. You deserve a break."

"I do," he agreed emphatically. "But that's a card I can't play on Christmas Day."

I reached for his hand, wishing he could stay for a few more hours. "You've hardly slept," I said with concern.

He grinned and squeezed my hand. "Believe me, last night was well worth the price I'm paying for it today."

I smiled, too, and our eyes held for a long moment before he spoke again.

"Luckily, we've got lots of coffee at work." He kissed me softly on the mouth, then rose from the bed. "Go back to sleep. I'll call you later."

"Hmmm." My lids felt heavy, but I kept my eyes open so I could watch him finish buttoning his shirt and then pull on his sweater. I liked seeing him getting dressed in my bedroom. I hoped I'd be seeing it often from now on. "What time do you get off work?"

"Six," he said. "But then I'm going straight out to Nyack. I'm sorry. If it were any other night . . . But I promised my parents, and I'll never hear the end of it if I don't go."

"Ah. That whole . . . *Christmas* thing again," I grumbled.

Oh, well, I'd see him when he got back.

In fact, I realized as I watched him straighten his sweater over his torso, I'd see *all* of him again. A little shiver of mingled pleasure and anticipation rippled through me as I remembered him frantically shedding his clothes last night and imagined him doing that again soon.

"Yeah, that Christmas thing." Lopez looked amused as he tugged his cuffs down. "Think you can adjust to my strange gentile customs?"

"Hmph. Well, at least you were circumcised."

He gave me a flirtatious look. "Oh, so you noticed?"

"Last night I was up close and personal with your . . . circumcisedness," I pointed out.

"So you were," he agreed with a grin.

"Though 'last night' was only a couple of hours ago," I added sleepily, glancing at the bedside clock. "You've really got to go?"

"I've really got to go." He glanced at the clock, too, and added with regret, "Right now."

I sighed again, wishing he were still beside me in bed.

Lopez stood looking at me for a long moment, curled up beneath the covers with my eyes barely open. Then he made an impatient sound, crossed the room, and pulled me into his arms for a long, deep kiss that made my head spin. I clung to him dizzily as he murmured, "I'll call you later."

I nodded in response as I nuzzled his neck. When I tasted the smooth, golden skin of his throat, he made an involuntary little sound and his hands tightened on me.

"No, don't," he said, breathing faster. "I have to go."

"Mmm?"

"Stop that," he whispered.

"I can't," I whispered back.

He kissed me once more, his hot, leisurely mouth and stroking hands turning me into a quivering mass of pulsing desire . . . And then, with a heartfelt groan and a pained expression that made me feel smug about my charms, he left for work.

20

I slept very late, then lay lazily in bed for a long time after I awoke, smiling and daydreaming as I remembered everything about last night.

I pressed my face against his pillow and inhaled. It didn't really smell like him; I supposed he hadn't been there long enough for that. But I pretended it did, and I inhaled again, then laughed with mingled pleasure, excitement, and embarrassment.

Things had happened in this bed in the dark that would make it hard to meet his eyes the next time I saw him . . . and, at the same time, I couldn't *wait* to see him again. To look into his eyes. To see the way he looked at me. And to . . . Well, yes, to do the same things all over again that were making me blush now as I got out of bed and contemplated going to Max's place for Saturnalia.

I glanced at the clock and discovered I was late for the feast.

I called Max to let him know I'd overslept and would be on my way soon. Then I checked my voicemail, in case I had slept through the phone ringing; but Lopez hadn't called yet. He probably didn't want to wake me. I checked for a text message, but he hadn't sent one.

With no more time for dawdling, I took a quick shower, then dressed in a festively bright sweater, wool trousers, and warm boots. I put on my coat, scooped up my purse, and left the apartment.

The streets were eerily quiet and somber, almost funereal. The sky was overcast, dull, and drab, and the city looked dreary and tired in this pale gray light. A cold wind whipped down the street, brutally sharp as it cut through my coat and stung my cheeks. I slipped on some ice and narrowly missed falling. I was shivering by the time I reached the subway; and as I descended the steps, this grimy underground world looked particularly bleak today.

But none of this could even *touch* the buoyant happiness that filled me. Only fear of breaking my neck on the ice had kept me from skipping and dancing down the street like the heroine of an old MGM musical. I restrained myself from bursting into song in the subway car, since I didn't want to frighten the handful of other people who were there; but I kept dissolving into giggles for no reason. It felt as if there was too much effervescence inside me to be contained, and so it kept bubbling out.

I wondered if he felt this giddy today, too.

Then I remembered that he'd gotten out of bed about five hours before I did. Bubbling happiness might have faded into bone-deep exhaustion and sleep-deprived irritability by now.

I should call and cheer him up.

As soon as I emerged from the subway near Max's place, I checked my phone for messages (none), then dialed Lopez's cell. After a few rings, to my disappointment, I got his voicemail.

"Hey, it's me," I said. "I'm awake. I'm on my way to . . . um, an ecumenical meal with friends." If Lopez was feeling irritable, or wrestling with his report about last night, I didn't want to wave Max's name in front of him like a red flag. "I hope you're not feeling too dead on your feet." I smiled in silence for a moment, thinking of him listening to this message later. Then I said, my voice a little breathy with emotion, "I've been thinking about you ever since I woke up." I wanted him to know that. I smiled again. "Well . . . call me when you can. I'll leave my cell on."

I put the phone in my pocket, where I'd be able to reach it easily when it rang. Then, stepping gingerly to avoid ice, I made my way to Max's.

The celebration was already underway in the bookstore. The big walnut table groaned beneath a buffet of carry-out Chinese food which Max was unpacking, Christmas carols were playing on the sound system, and Lucky and Nelli were playing tug-of-war with her new toy, a stuffed pink mastodon. I had a feeling the toy might not be long for this world.

Satsy was also there, having decided that a trip to Connecticut today to see his family was a little too much to pile on top of nearly being eaten by a solstice demon last night. Whoopsy Daisy had decided to join us, too. Whoopsy said he usually observed December 25th with a marathon DVD festival of his favorite movies (which included, to my surprise, *The Guns of Navarone* and *True Grit*, as well as more predictable fare); but he'd decided that a Saturnalia feast with friends sounded like a more alluring proposition. I was happy to see Whoopsy, and we enjoyed a good old chin-wagging reunion as we caught up on each other's news.

I left out that I had spent half the night having hot, passionate sex with a man of his acquaintance—one who had once arrested him, come to think of it; but that was before my time. Whoopsy kept commenting on how good I was looking, how my eyes were sparkling and my cheeks glowed. Feeling like I might dissolve into idiotic giggling, I got up to play with Nelli and her mastodon for a while, rather than keep chatting with a friend who was starting to eye me with speculative curiosity. This thing between me and Lopez was too new and too private to talk about yet—even to friends, even in a vague way.

At Max's urging, I picked up a plate and started piling Chinese food on it. That was when I realized I was famished. I ate a small mountain of food, then went back for seconds.

Some time after we finished eating, Whoopsy and Satsy invited us all to join them in going to a gathering of Pony Expressive employees and patrons at a Soho loft; but we declined, too tired for a big party. So we wished them happy holidays and waved them off.

"By the way," Satsy said to me, "I invited Lou to this party. I'll let you know if he shows up."

I wished Satsy lucky with his heartthrob from Fenster's receiving docks.

A little later, as I sat in one of the comfortable chairs by the gas fire, feeling full, warm, and content, a phone rang. My heart leaped with excitement for a moment, until I realized with disappointment that it was Lucky's phone, not mine.

He checked the screen and said, "It's the boss."

"The Don?" I asked.

Lucky nodded as he put the phone to his ear. "Yo, boss. *Buon Natale! Come va?*" They exchanged some family news, and then Lucky said to us, "The Don sends you both his best wishes. He says, 'May your Christmas be merry, and may the coming year be sweet and prosperous for you both!' He wants you to know how much he appreciates your help in clearing up this unfortunate matter and removing the suspicion that was so unfairly and unjustly placed on his family. The Gambellos are now twice indebted to you both, and the family doesn't forget who its friends are."

I felt a little ambivalent about being so warmly regarded by a notorious mob boss. But I smiled without reserve, so as not to offend Lucky.

"Please share our warmest solstice and Saturnalia greetings with Mr. Gambello, and our wishes for his good health and happiness in the year to come," said Max.

"Send him our Hanukkah greetings, too," I said. "*Shalom*."

Their conversation turned to business matters after that, and Max and I chatted casually as we started clearing up the food and plates. We packed away the leftovers in the little fridge, then sat down again with a glass of well-spiked holiday punch, the recipe for which, Max said, was older than he was. I took one sip and promptly started coughing as my eyes watered.

"They liked their punch *strong* back in the day, didn't they?" I said hoarsely.

Max smiled and admitted, "It's a bit of an acquired taste."

Lucky finished his call and came back to join us. "The boss talked to his lawyer today."

"Today?" I repeated. "It's Christmas Day."

"When you're Victor Gambello's lawyer," said Lucky, "you expect to work all kinds of hours."

"Ah. Yes, I guess so."

"Same for cops, though they don't get nearly the same paycheck," said Lucky. "Guess who Mr. Gambello's lawyer has talked to today?" When my eyes widened, Lucky said, "Yep, your boyfriend. And also an assistant district attorney who wasn't too crazy about being called in on Christmas Day."

"What did they talk about?" I asked.

"Mr. Gambello wants to make sure that justice will be done, the guilty punished, and the innocent left free to return to their perfectly legitimate business interests."

"I see."

"The Fensters had some lawyers working today, too," Lucky added.

So much for the quiet day Lopez had probably been hoping for.

Lucky continued, "And their lawyers agreed to an honest and open exchange of information with Mr. Gambello's lawyer."

"Why?" I asked.

"The Fenster lawyers became convinced that cooperating with Mr. Gambello's lawyer in this matter would be in their own best interest."

"Ah."

Max asked, "So do we have reliable news about the current disposition of the devious villains we assisted in apprehending last night?"

"We do," said Lucky. "Sad to say, things really *are* different for the rich."

"You mean they're going to get off?" I demanded in outrage.

"No, they ain't *that* different. But while the Powell

kid will get what he deserves, since his family's all outta dough, the Fenster girl will get off easier than she deserves. But that don't mean she's in for a picnic."

"What will happen to Rick?"

"Prison," Lucky said. "For a long time. He's being advised to skip a trial and plead guilty if he ever wants to see the outside again. They got him dead to rights on too many juicy charges. Conspiracy, assault with a deadly weapon, grand larceny, armed robbery, attempted murder . . . And they're just getting warmed up. Plus, the kid pointed a gun at *cops.* How dumb can you *get?*" Lucky shook his head in disgust. "And him such an educated boy, too."

"What about Elspeth?" I asked.

Max added with concern, "She is a dangerous person. A mystical talent coupled with an amoral and unstable mind."

"*Very* unstable," said Lucky. "They're saying the girl had a nervous breakdown overnight and is catalytic today."

"I think you mean catatonic," I said.

"The Fensters will negotiate to have the girl committed to some luxury funny farm for rich people who have an unfortunate tendency to commit felonies."

"Do you think that's sufficient, Max?"

"One can always hope for rehabilitation," he said kindly. "Treatment is more enlightened than punishment, and it may make her less of a danger to herself and others in the long run."

"Either way," Lucky said, "it's what's gonna happen. The Fensters may not stay rich for long, now that old Connie is dead . . . but they're rich now, while that girl's fate is being decided. And the rich usually get their way in these things."

"Elspeth may be a lot less dangerous with Rick out of her life, anyhow," I reflected. "Without his influence and manipulation, I think Elspeth probably would have remained inert and introverted, unlikely to experiment with the things she fantasized about doing. A lot of factors have contributed to her breakdown. But, above all, I suspect that she shattered upon confronting her own evil works; I think she was only cut out to *imagine* herself confronting them."

"I think you're right about that, my dear," Max mused. "Miss Fenster was a troubled person whose fate was inevitably decided not by herself, but by whether or not she met someone like Rick."

"That rotten family she came from didn't do her no good, either," said Lucky. "Some people just shouldn't be allowed to raise kids."

"Speaking of the family, what's going to happen to Freddie Junior?" I asked.

"Well, he's definitely gonna get off for shooting that driver. 'Not responsible for his own actions at the time,' blah blah blah."

"That has the merit of actually being true," I pointed out.

"He's being released, charges dropped." Lucky

added, "He might have bigger problems than this, though. It turns out Freddie's in debt to the Russian mob, and that's just never a good position to be in."

"Indeed not," said Max, his brows raised in alarm. "In general, one should always take care to avoid angering Russians. I speak from bitter experience on this subject—but that's another story entirely."

"So the big question now," Lucky said to me, "is what your boyfriend is going to put in his report."

"Mr. Gambello's lawyer doesn't have that information?" I asked dryly.

"An honest cop is such a nuisance to deal with," Lucky said. "Much trickier to frisk for information than expensive uptown shysters."

"I gather that means Lopez wouldn't discuss it with him?"

"Yep."

Seeing Lucky's inquisitive expression, I shrugged. "I don't know what he's going to do."

I knew that, to protect me, Lopez had fudged reports in the past to keep my name out of things. I also knew that he got angry at himself for doing it, felt it was wrong, and struggled hard with his conscience over it. So I couldn't ask him to do it. I *wouldn't* ask.

"Relax, Lucky," I said. "We just did a little breaking and entering . . . and, uh, maybe destruction of property—"

"You're not making me feel better," the old gangster said.

"But," I said, rallying, "we did it in a good cause, and the police know that. So even if we do wind up in Lopez's report, we have nothing to worry about."

"Hmph," he said, unconvinced. "You don't know cops like I do."

"Detective Lopez is an honorable young man," Max insisted. "He will do the right thing. And in complicated circumstances, he will struggle arduously with his options to determine what the right thing is. I feel confident in his integrity."

"Yeah," Lucky said sadly. "It would be so much easier if that wasn't the problem with him."

"Oh, cheer up, Lucky," I chided. "You have more to celebrate than to worry about. The Gambellos are off the hook for the hijackings."

"Yeah, we're off *that* hook," he said gloomily. "But thanks to those two wacky kids screwing around with armed robbery, instead of just being satisfied with raising a demon, OCCB has been all *up* in our thing lately, tearing our lives apart. I know it's business, not personal. With the media and the Commissioner breathing down their necks, they had to show juice. But it's not good for us to be raked over the coals like this. Not good at all."

In an effort to cheer him, Nelli picked up her pink mastodon and started nudging him with it, giving fiercely playful growls. He smiled and tugged on her ears.

Then, changing the subject, he said to me, "So I guess you're out of work now, huh?"

"Yeah, but I'll be back at Bella Stella after New Year's. And I'm going to light a fire under Thack then, too. I need some auditions!"

Meanwhile, it was easy to imagine how I could fill the time between now and then. I felt my cheeks burning as I thought of him again.

"You're looking very flushed, Esther," Max noted. "I'll turn down the fire."

"Uh-huh." I pulled my phone out of my pocket and checked it, wondering if the ringer was working.

"You expecting a call?" Lucky asked.

"Not really," I lied. "Just checking."

I glanced at the time. It was almost five o'clock. He was supposed to get off work within an hour. He'd probably call me then. Maybe when he was on his way to Nyack.

This being the darkest time of the year, when barriers between dimensions crumble, night fell soon after that. Nelli got restless after a while, so Max fastened her into her Christmas jacket and attached her jingling red leash to her collar.

"I believe the wind has died down," he said. "Why don't we all take Nelli for an evening stroll and observe the holiday lights of Greenwich Village? There are some lovely displays this year."

"I'm in," said Lucky. "Esther?"

"Um . . ." It was almost six o'clock now. I was thinking I might want a little privacy when he called.

"Aw, come on," Lucky urged. "Get in the Saturnalia spirit!"

That made me smile. "I'll get my coat."

The holiday lights of the Village were indeed lovely this year, and the air tonight was crisp and energizing despite the gray, unpromising start of the day. I linked arms with both of my escorts, walking between them, glad of their company. Nelli pranced cheerfully in her festive coat, evidently pleased to have confronted Evil and acquitted herself well. She greeted other dogs we met on our walk, and we greeted their people, all wishing each other Merry Christmas, Seasons Greetings, and Happy Saturnalia.

It was a magical night to be a New Yorker, strolling the streets of our city on a rare occasion when the pace was slow, traffic was light, and few people were crowding the sidewalks. It was a good night to commune with friends and loved ones. A good night, I thought, to be a Jewish elf in the Big Apple.

But in my coat pocket, I felt the weight of my silent phone, and wondered why he didn't call . . .

Author's Note

The question people always ask a writer is: "Where do you get your ideas?"

I'm very tempted to claim that I get mine by venturing boldly into the lawless underground world of black market story ideas, where a well-honed plot is worth more than a man's life and novelists will kill for a good concept.

But, alas, the mundane truth is that writers get ideas all of the time, from everywhere. We experience the world as a nonstop supply-chain of story ideas. That's just how our minds work—otherwise we probably wouldn't be writers.

Precisely *because* I see story ideas everywhere I look, I often don't even really know how I got the idea for a particular story. But in the case of *Polterheist*, I do remember the book's genesis—though it took many twists and turns after that.

Back around the time I was finishing *Disappearing Nightly*, the first Esther Diamond novel, I was on a long drive during the holidays, and National Public Radio saved my sanity on that lonely rural highway by playing David Sedaris narrating his *Santaland Diaries*, a darkly funny account of the author's experiences working as a department store elf one Christmas season.

While listening to Sedaris' essay as I drove on that icy, empty road under a darkening winter sky, I remember thinking that his workplace sounded like the anteroom to hell . . . And since I'm a fantasy writer, that started me wondering: What if struggling actress Esther Diamond discovered her humiliating seasonal job actually *was* the anteroom to hell? Or a gateway through which something *from* hell intended to enter this dimension? So then I did some research and soon discovered that various cultures over the millennia have worried about precisely this sort of thing happening right around that time of year, when night is longer than day and darkness is overwhelming . . .

And that's how I first got started on the idea for *Polterheist*, in which my Jewish heroine would get stuck participating in Christianity's most exhausting holiday while trying to prevent a dangerous mystical force from running amok in the Big Apple.

Please note, by the way, that Fenster's and Solsticeland are wholly fictional creations and are not based on any real store. Some of Esther's experiences there are loosely inspired by real life, though, since I've held many less-than-delightful jobs over the years, including seasonal ones (and I frankly think I'd rather go to prison than ever again deal with the public during the holidays).

Meanwhile, I'd like to thank the tremendous staff at DAW Books, the best publishing house I've ever worked with, for their support, patience, and enthusiasm. In particular, special thanks to editor/publisher Betsy Wollheim and to managing editor Joshua Starr. I also want to add a shout-out to Russell Davis, who edited a couple of my books years ago at another house; he gave me some excellent editorial advice back then which has been paying off ever since—something I recently had occasion to realize.

I hope you've enjoyed *Polterheist*—during whatever season of the year you happened to read it. This was the fifth Esther Diamond novel, and (in case you've missed any of them) the DAW Books editions of the previous four novels are all available to tide you over until Esther, her friends, and her nemeses return in their next mystical misadventure, *The Misfortune Cookie*, set in New York's Chinatown.

—Laura Resnick

Laura Resnick

The Esther Diamond Novels

DISAPPEARING NIGHTLY
978-0-7564-0766-7

DOPPELGANGSTER
978-0-7564-0595-3

UNSYMPATHETIC MAGIC
978-0-7564-0635-6

VAMPARAZZI
978-0-7564-0687-5

POLTERHEIST
978-0-7564-0733-9

To Order Call: 1-800-788-6262
www.dawbooks.com

DAW 145

Barbara Ashford

Spellcast
978-0-7564-0682-0

Spellcrossed
978-0-7564-0729-2

"[A] novel about the transformative power of the theater...a woman with an unsettled past...and the intersecting coincidences that move her toward the future. Maggie is relatable and her journey compelling. Four stars."

— *RT Book Reviews*

"[A] charming fantasy novel. Maggie Graham is enchanted and bemused by the Crossroads Theatre...but it takes Maggie a while to really grasp just how magical it is. Readers will figure it out much sooner, but there's enough mystery (not to mention romance) to keep readers interested.... A slightly bittersweet but appropriate conclusion left me wanting more, in fine theatrical tradition."

— *Locus*

To Order Call: 1-800-788-6262
www.dawbooks.com

DAW 206

Diana Rowland

"Rowland's delightful novel jumps genre lines with a little something for everyone—mystery, horror, humor, and even a smattering of romance. Not to be missed—all that's required is a high tolerance for gray matter. For true zombiephiles, of course, that's a no brainer."

—Library Journal

"An intriguing mystery and a hilarious mix of the horrific and mundane aspects of zombie life open a promising new series...Humor and gore are balanced by surprisingly touching moments as Angel tries to turn her (un)life around."

—Publishers Weekly

My Life as a White Trash Zombie
978-0-7564-0675-2

Even White Trash Zombies Get the Blues
978-0-7564-0750-6

To Order Call: 1-800-788-6262
www.dawbooks.com

D0207260

Also by Laura Resnick:

DISAPPEARING NIGHTLY
DOPPELGANGSTER
UNSYMPATHETIC MAGIC
VAMPARAZZI
POLTERHEIST
THE MISFORTUNE COOKIE*

Raves for the Esther Diamond series: